The Looking Glass Goddess

Amanda Hughes

ISBN: 1545479666
ISBN-13: 978-1545479667

ACKNOWLEDGMENTS

My thanks to Bill Brewer for his expertise on makeup and, as usual, to Madeline Hughes for lending an ear.

Chapter 1

Excerpt from an article in the *Minneapolis Sentinel*, August 19th, 1910:

Prominent Citizen Stabs Daughter

At 11:23 pm last evening, police were called to the residence of the late Arthur H. Durant, at 720 Grove Avenue, Minneapolis. Authorities searched the home and found his widow, Mrs. Lillian Durant in a third-story room clutching a pair of scissors. She offered no resistance when taken into custody. Moments later, her ten-year-old daughter, Elizabeth Durant was discovered hiding in the attic. The girl was taken to St. Mary's Catholic Hospital in Minneapolis, treated and released to the care of her grandmother. This is Mrs. Durant's second attack upon her daughter in the past year.

*   *   *

Minneapolis, MN.
1917

"Welcome back to the lie-factory," Libby muttered as she stepped out of the cab in front of her home at 720 Grove Avenue. Dressed in a suit from the House of Paquin with a pleated hobble skirt and hat cocked smartly on her head, Elizabeth Durant gave the impression of being much older than her seventeen years. Her light brown hair was bobbed, and she was holding a clutch of fine leather.

"Leave the grip by the back door," she said to the driver.

"Which one is yours?"

"The tag that says, *Elizabeth Durant*. The other belongs to my sister, Jennifer. Drop that at St. Mary's Hospital please."

"Yes, ma'am," he replied and took her valise to the service entrance, setting it outside the door.

"Thank you," she murmured, handing him the fare.

He drove off.

Libby turned and looked up at the house. She had been away at boarding school for seven years, and little had changed. She ran her eyes over the massive structure. "Ugly beast," she said.

Built in a style popular forty years earlier, the Durant residence resembled a small castle. Sandstone masonry, Romanesque arches, and turrets characterized the design, giving it a heavy, foreboding appearance. The green awnings were the only bit of color on the dreary façade.

The house seemed abandoned and silent as the grave. Even though it was near downtown, the expansive lawn and the park behind it muffled the sounds of the city.

Libby frowned. Where was Mrs. Zabek? Surely they had not dismissed all the staff after the death of her mother?

Ignoring the thick-pillared grand portico, she went

around to the service door. When she entered the kitchen, a recording of Enrico Caruso was playing on the Victrola, but the room was empty.

"Mrs. Zabek?" she called, pulling off her gloves. But there was no answer. Libby lifted the arm on the player silencing the music and called for Mrs. Zabek once more.

Someone had been chopping vegetables, and she picked up a piece of celery, taking a bite. A tiny chair in the corner by the dumb waiter caught her eye. It had been her chair when she was a child, and a little rocker was next to it. That had been Jennie's chair. The girls had spent hours there listening to stories from the housekeeper about Poland and Norwegian tales from the carriage driver and maid.

She turned away. She couldn't allow herself to reminisce. Memories were dangerous.

She opened a silver case and took out a cigarette. After lighting it, she tipped her head back and blew out the smoke. Although she was young, she already had a cynical, hard-edge to her character. Life as a Durant had not been easy. The money had provided a buffer, but eventually, the family illness could no longer be hidden. Fodder for yellow journalism, Libby had learned to survive the headlines by hiding behind a hard shell and a reputation as a party girl.

She stepped through the swinging doors into the dining room. "Hello?"

Again no answer.

Her heels clicked loudly on the highly polished, hardwood floor as she passed into the hall. The stained glass windows cast a ruby glow upon the room. Across from the front door was a large mosaic fireplace flanked on either side by carpeted stairs which led up to the second and third stories.

She stopped for a moment to listen. The only sound

was ticking from the grandfather clock.

Taking a puff of her cigarette again, Libby walked over and glanced briefly at the library and music room before going up to the bedrooms, the part of the house she hated. She stopped in front of a full-length mirror on the landing to check her hair. The last time she had looked in this mirror, she had been a little girl. Now she was a full grown woman, long and lean with smooth, caramel-colored hair and blue eyes under arched brows. She held her head high with the famous Durant confidence, but it was the Brennan insecurity that made her a fighter. Some thought her face was too angular and her lips too full, but if anyone agreed, they never dared comment. They would have been cut by her sharp tongue.

Staring at herself, Libby watched the smoke curl around her head and then continued up the stairs. The chubby iron cupid still sat on the banister holding a globe light, and she smirked when she saw it. His naked body used to make her and Jennie giggle, and they would cover him with doll clothes.

Taking a last puff, she stepped into the bathroom to flush her cigarette. It was a slick, white-tiled room with a square porcelain sink, a stool and claw footed tub. A long narrow chamber, it was lit by a floor-to-ceiling stained glass window at one end.

The moment Libby walked in, she regretted it. A memory returned.

"I'm sorry," she heard her mother say. "I said bad things to you. I said you couldn't be trusted."

"It doesn't matter, Mama."

"Yes, it does. Yes, it does. Yes, it does," Mrs. Durant repeated as she sat on the floor rocking back and forth. A woman in her middle years, she was thin to the point of emaciation, her eyes were glassy, and her dark hair was disheveled. "Yes, it does. Yes, it does."

"Let's go back to your room, Mama."

"No!" she barked. Suddenly Mrs. Durant jumped up and pulled open the medicine cabinet. "Must find something sharp. Need to cut my tongue out."

Libby dropped her cigarette into the toilet, pulled the chain and flushed. She walked down the hall to her room and opened the drapes, flooding the room with light. Although this was her bedroom, she was indifferent to it. She had never been allowed to decorate it herself, and she had no fond memories of time spent there.

She thought that the rich, heavy furnishings were suffocating. The walls were lined with dark walnut paneling, and a thick Turkish rug was on the floor. Her bed was a massive structure with a carved headboard of mahogany flowers. Although the room was large, it always felt close and smelled stuffy.

Libby opened her closet. Her trunk had arrived from Beardsley Hall. Her clothes were hanging up, and her hat boxes were on the shelves.

Something caught her eye in the hall. She had seen a woman sweep past the door in a white nightgown. When she looked, the hall was empty.

"Damn it," she said, rubbing her forehead. It had been memories of her mother again.

Libby splashed water on her face at the bedroom sink. She should have stayed in Italy. But who would have brought Jennie home from school? She had missed her mother's funeral, and for that, she wasn't sorry, but she couldn't plead distance as an excuse to abandon Jennie. They were best friends.

She sat down heavily on the bed and sighed. It was as if Jennie had stepped right into her mother's shoes. She too was having hallucinations now and had to leave boarding school after a violent outburst.

Libby wondered why she was not yet stricken with the illness. Was it oozing into her consciousness, like black ink staining paper, or would it strike suddenly like a bolt of lightning? Her mother had succumbed to the madness, an uncle and aunt, two cousins, and now Jennie was having spells. Perhaps Libby favored the Durant side and would escape the insanity. Her father had died from a different disease though. His affliction was of the bottle. Was there no escape?

Either way here she was immersed in it once more, dealing with lunatics, alive and dead.

Libby groaned and stood up. That settles it. She had to get out of this house. She would shop, stroll downtown or look up old friends, but she couldn't stay here.

Then she remembered. There *was* one place she would like to see again. Somewhere she always felt completely safe. It was the attic. Her mother never went there because she was afraid of it. So it had always been Libby's refuge and held good memories.

She started up the stairs giving the ballroom only a fleeting glance as she walked briskly across the dance floor. She passed down a hall and up the attic stairs. The ceilings were vaulted here, and the floors were littered with trunks, boxes, racks of old clothes and a menagerie of furniture and musty books. Everything was as she remembered it, a maze of nostalgia, familiar and comforting. It was hot, stuffy and smelled of mothballs, but she didn't care.

Sunlight streamed through the dirty windows, illuminating particles of dust drifting in the air. To Libby, they looked like fairies. She looked around. In that corner, she read *Anne of Green Gables*, *The Wind in the Willows* and *Kidnapped*, and there, under that window, she had cut out paper dolls with Jennie.

She walked around a dressmaker's mannequin to a large cedar closet and opened the door. It was still filled with furs and woolen overcoats as well as hats, gloves, and mittens. The smell of cedar immediately made her feel safe. When her mother had a spell, she had hidden here. Jennie always came with her, but it was unnecessary for her to hide. For some unexplained reason, Lillian Durant never attacked her younger daughter. Libby was always her target.

Closing the door, she wound through stacks of books, past an old bird cage, a wooden highchair and squatted down by an old trunk. This had been another hiding place. She opened it and looked inside. The brittle paper label on the inside of the lid said "Oshkosh Trunk Company." The old swimming costumes were still inside, all crushed and wrinkled as if she had just stepped out from hiding.

Libby sat back on her heels and looked around. Nothing had changed in seven years.

Suddenly she sneezed. "And the air hasn't changed either," she said out loud.

Dusting her hands off, she walked over to one of the windows. After several tries, she pulled it open. She could hear church bells ringing from the Basilica nearby, and leaning out, she took a deep breath of fresh air. The trees and flowers from the park made the air smell sweet and rich. For a moment it felt good to be home again, but the feeling vanished when she looked down and saw the pond on the terrace below. The marble basin had been drained, and the stone nymph in the center was broken. Libby remembered that the sculpture had been holding a shell that spouted water, but it was gone along with the arm.

Libby clutched her stomach and pulled back inside. She knew why it was broken. Her mother had landed on the statue when she had flung herself from the window a month earlier. Rendered senseless from the fall, she had drowned in the fishpond.

Libby pressed her eyes shut and took a deep breath, trying to hold the contents of her stomach down. Her knees felt weak, and she sat down heavily on the floor.

What had possessed her mother to do it? What sinister voice had seduced her to the edge? Was there an apparition before her eyes coaxing her to jump or was it just deadly impulse?

Libby's grandmother said her mother's attendant had fallen asleep, thinking Lillian was calm and coherent, but it had been a ruse. Lilly Durant was deep into hallucinations. No one was more loving and giving when she was well, but when she was sick, no one was more wily and dangerous.

I have to get out of here, Libby thought. She left the attic, crossed the ballroom and quickly descended the stairs to the second floor. As she passed her mother's room, she slowed her pace. A morbid curiosity suddenly flooded her. She simply had to see the window from which her mother had jumped, and she stepped inside the door.

It was a grand room. The walls were painted a rich gold, and the floors and trim were of dark mahogany. A delicate stencil of yellow flowers below the ornate cornices added femininity to the heavy masculine trim. There was a white marble fireplace, and the bed had a coverlet of gold and sage green. The room was fully decorated with oil paintings, figurines and a tortoise shell vanity set. These luxuries were possible because when Lillian Durant was in residence, she was deemed healthy. During a spell, she would smash things and become violent, so the moment her lucidity was tenuous, she had been whisked away to an asylum for treatment. The "lie factory," as Libby called it, had to be maintained. No one must know of the family illness.

Libby bit her lip and stepped forward. Was the window shattered? Had her mother crashed through the panes in a mad frenzy or had she opened the sash, teetered on the sill and then jumped?

Libby swallowed hard, pulled the drapes open and looked. The panes were not broken, the mullions were intact. Her mother must have opened the window before jumping.

She sighed. She was glad to know. It would have haunted her otherwise, and she felt her body relax. But when she turned around, the drapes on the other window were moving, as if someone was hiding there. Two bare feet were visible at the bottom, and she could hear someone giggling as they twisted themselves around and around in the fabric. Libby's heart jumped into her throat. It was another memory of her mother during one of her more violent fits.

Panting with fear, she backed up and ran from the room. Sobbing, she raced down the stairs only to confront another memory. Her mother was laying on the steps, her dark hair in tangles around her shoulders. She was on her back, her feet higher than her head. She propped herself up on her elbows and gasped, "Help me, Elizabeth! I can't remember how to climb the stairs!" She stretched her leg forward, trying to crawl upward. "Is this right?"

Libby froze. Just as her mother was about to grab her ankle, she heard, "Hello, little girl."

Standing at the bottom of the stairs was a large, red-headed woman wearing a dark dress, white cap, and apron. She continued in her Polish accent. "So glad you're home."

It was Mrs. Zabek, the housekeeper, and she pulled Libby back to the present.

Chapter 2

"Come to the kitchen now, little one," Mrs. Zabek coaxed. When Libby didn't move, the buxom housekeeper took her hand. "Come tell me about Italy."

After thirty years with this family, Mrs. Zabek knew the signs of trouble, and Libby had trouble written all over her face. She led her to the kitchen. There had been warmth, laughter, and good nature there, and she knew it would ground her again. The servants had hugged Libby and Jennie there, bandaged their scraped knees, kissed them and dried their tears there. This is where Libby and Jennie had found a loving family.

Mrs. Zabek guided her to a chair, brushed her hair back and said in her thick Polish accent, "Look at my girl. All grown up and pretty as picture postcard."

Libby blinked as if waking from a dream. She said at last, "Hello, Zabby. Golly, it's good to see you. You're the best part of home."

Reaching for her purse, Libby lit a cigarette. The act of doing something familiar grounded her, and she blew out the smoke as if she were sighing.

"Oh no, the smoking of the cigarettes. Not for lady,"

the housekeeper murmured. "I didn't know you at first. Your hair is short."

Libby smiled. "Yes, just like Irene Castle," and she walked over to the Victrola. "Nothing has changed here except this."

"I like the Victrola and this singer, Caruso. Did you meet this man in Italy?" Mrs. Zabek asked, starting to chop vegetables again.

Libby chuckled, "Yes, he asked me to dinner, but I was dining with Douglas Fairbanks."

"Who?"

"A bad joke," Libby muttered.

"How is our little Jennie?"

"She was good on the train. The nurse kept her asleep with injections most of the time."

"Your Grandmother Brennan arrived a few days ago. She come back to help you."

"Is she staying at the lake or on Summit?"

"The Summit house. She come see you tomorrow."

Libby nodded and looked out the window. Mrs. Zabek stole a look at her. To the housekeeper, the seventeen-year-old girl looked far too worldly. She had grown up too fast, and she was afraid the family troubles had made her hard. After Mrs. Durant's second attack on Libby, the sisters were sent away to Beardsley Hall, a boarding school in Massachusetts. The family thought it best that they did not come home for breaks or holidays; it was too dangerous. So they stayed at school permanently. It was a lonely existence, but they had each other.

During those years, Mrs. Durant made her endless rotation from home to asylum and back again. Even when she was deemed healthy, her lifestyle was risky and hedonistic. She would stay out late drinking, dancing and bringing home strangers. She had only one serious relationship after her husband died, and it had ended badly. She spiraled downward after that until she jumped to her death that summer.

"Where's the staff?" Libby asked.

"Your Aunt Bertie let everyone go. Cook is gone, the gardener and the two maids. She say no need after your mother passed."

"Not the Axelmans!" Libby gasped.

"No, no. The Axelmans stay. Your aunt is keeping them until family decides on what to do with the house."

Libby breathed a sigh of relief.

"Axel is doing upkeep on house now, but he move slower every day."

"Has he learned to drive the automobile yet?"

"No, he such old man, set in his ways," Mrs. Zabek said. "He say these machines are passing fancy."

Libby laughed. "He hasn't changed. I'm going to the carriage house to see them. How soon is dinner?"

"Not for hour. Shall I set dining room table?"

"No, that hasn't changed, Zabby. When the family is not here, I eat with you."

Libby crossed the driveway to the carriage house. The structure looked like the main house but smaller. It was built with the same bulky sandstone and had large wooden doors on the main level where the horses, tack, and carriages were kept as well as the automobile. There were stairs along the side of the building leading up to the living quarters where the Axelmans lived. For years Arnie Axelman had been the family's carriage driver and his wife, Marta, the head maid.

Libby picked up her skirts and walked up the stairs calling, "*Tante!* Axel!"

The door flew open, and a tiny woman in a long black dress leaned out. She was wearing a white starched cap and apron and had snow white hair tied up in a bun. *"Elskede!"* she exclaimed in Norwegian, hugging Libby. "Axel, look who comes!"

Arnie Axelman looked up from the kitchen table and held his arms up for a hug. He had rosy cheeks, a closely-cropped, white beard, and shiny bald head. He was impeccably dressed in the dark suit and tie of a domestic. Libby ran over and hugged him.

"Well, well!" he exclaimed. "I cannot believe my eyes, Mrs. A. Can this be our little girl?"

With the Axelmans and Mrs. Zabek, Libby felt safe and secure. They gave her a solid predictability she could depend upon. When she was a child, these were the people that grounded her, assuring her that not everyone was haunted by spiteful apparitions. Even though she was very young at the time, Libby could still remember the day she realized that Mrs. Zabek and the Axelmans saw the same things she did and heard the same voices she heard. It was a great relief to have a dependable point of reference in the vortex of madness.

"Come sit," Mrs. Axelman said. "We were just having coffee and ginger snaps."

"You still make those, Tante?"

"Of course, of course," she said putting a cup and saucer in front of Libby.

"You're a big girl now and drink coffee?" Axel asked.

"Yes, I drink all kinds of things," she replied.

They said nothing. They knew she was young and thought such talk was sophisticated.

Libby looked around. She had always loved it here. Mrs. Axelman had decorated their living quarters with a Norwegian flare. The colors were bright and happy, and it felt like a home. Instead of the heavy Victorian furnishings of the main house, their rooms were light and cheerful with furniture painted in different colors and decorated with floral designs. Tablecloths with Hardanger embroidery covered end tables, and white eyelet curtains were on the windows.

The feeling was the same in Mrs. Zabek's quarters off the kitchen. Although the woodwork was dark, the rooms had bright colors and the geometric patterns of her homeland in Poland. Libby and Jennie loved the nesting dolls on the cupboard and the hand-painted Easter eggs in a bowl on the table, gifts from Mr. Zabek to his wife before he died.

"Jennie is at St. Mary's Hospital safe and sound," Libby informed the Axelmans. "There was no problem on the way home from Beardsley Hall."

"Good, good. Will she come home soon?" Axel asked.

Libby shrugged. "I don't know, but the student she attacked has recovered."

"We are much relieved and have missed our girls," Mrs. Axelman said, touching her eyes with a towel. "Seven years is a long time."

"I've missed you too. Were there a lot of people at mother's funeral?"

"Yes and newspaper men outside with cameras," Axel replied. "They were around the house for days trying to photograph the--, " and he stopped, becoming flustered. He didn't want to upset Libby with talk of her mother's death.

"That's alright," Libby said, grabbing a cookie and standing up. "I already saw the fountain. You should know by now I'm used to all of this."

"Do not go yet! You haven't told us about Italy!" Mrs. Axelman declared.

"I was there only a few weeks. I saw The Forum, The Coliseum--" and when she saw their eager faces, she added, "And no, I did not meet Enrico Caruso."

*   *   *

Libby slept well that night which surprised her. She thought memories would haunt her, but she awoke refreshed and feeling energetic. Opening the drapes, she saw that the sun was just rising. She decided to dress and take an early morning walk in the park behind the house.

The Durant home was in an exclusive neighborhood not far from downtown in Loring Park. Lumber barons, bankers and mill owners had erected mansions there, testimony to hard work, diligence, and cut-throat business tactics. These palatial homes surrounded the manicured space that was filled with elms, oaks, and willows.

It was so early even Mrs. Zabek had not risen yet. Libby unlocked the kitchen door and slipped out, walking past the fountain without looking. She opened the tall, wrought-iron gate and in a few steps, she was in the park. Following the winding walkway, she passed rose gardens, a statue of a Norwegian violinist and headed toward the small lake where she paused on shore to watch the ducks gliding past. She remembered spending hours here as a child feeding the ducks with Jennie.

She sat down on a bench and looked around. It was peaceful here. Other than an old couple strolling by, no one was out yet. She looked at a park building and remembered jumping rope on the sidewalk there with her cousins one summer. She still could hear their voices singing the rhyme:

"My mother and your mother.
Live across the way,
Every night,
They have a fight,
And this is what they say.
Icky bicky soda cracker,
Icky bicky boo,
Icky bicky soda cracker,

Out goes you!"

Libby watched the ducks for a while and then stood up following the path toward The Plaza. It was a large, elegant residential hotel for wealthy tenants. A streetcar stopped in front of the main entrance, rang its bell and then rolled away.

She looked next door at "The Durant Center for the Arts," a public museum founded by her family. So they finally finished it, she thought. With white columns and two lions flanking the front steps, it was an imposing building. The Beaux-Arts design reminded Libby of ancient Roman structures she had seen in Italy but were now in ruins. The similarities to her own family were not lost on her. Here was a solid, sturdy structure built by people who were in their glory days, but some day it would all tumble down. In fact, her mother's side of the family was already crumbling.

In their day, the Brennans had been tough, hard-working, "St. Paul Irish". Libby's grandfather had worked in the steamboat business, and then invested heavily in J.J. Hill's up and coming Great Northern Railroad, amassing great wealth. He built a mansion on Summit Avenue, erected a summer home on White Bear Lake, and with his wife, raised a large family. Unfortunately, mental illness had always plagued them, and several of the children succumbed.

The Durants, on the other hand, were seduced by alcohol. They were tough, stubborn Minnesotans who not only worked hard but drank hard. In the early days of the state, they opened several sawmills on the Mississippi River, invested in hardware and became fabulously wealthy. Money may have been the family mistress, but alcohol was the master. All five of the Durant brothers and one daughter drank heavily. Early in life, it killed two of them and crippled one in a riding accident. Arthur Durant, Libby's father, started drinking to excess shortly after his marriage. By the time Jennie was born, both parents were completely immersed in their illnesses.

Libby strolled a bit farther and then stopped to look at her bodice watch. Mrs. Zabek would be making breakfast soon.

She returned home, swung open the service door and said, "Good morning, Zabby." The Victrola was playing again. "How is Enrico today?"

Mrs. Zabek was bending over the icebox, and when she straightened up tears were in her eyes. "His singing make me weep," she said dabbing at her cheeks with a hankie.

Libby smiled and sat down. "Is that the only recording you have?"

She nodded.

"You need more records," Libby said, cracking her soft boiled egg. "Who else do you like?"

"I don't know any others. Axel told me about Caruso."

"Well, there's a man named Cohan. You might like his music. Very patriotic. He became popular when we entered the war. And speaking of war," she said, leaning over and reading the headlines from the paper on the table. More battles and casualties were reported. "Ugh."

"Mass is at seven thirty," Mrs. Zabek announced. "You better hurry."

Libby stopped with her spoon in mid-air and looked at her. "Um--when I was at school, Zabby I stopped going to daily Mass. I just go on Sunday now."

Mrs. Zabek looked at her wide-eyed. "You don't go to church? What will Grandma Brennan say?"

Libby took one last bite and stood up. "*I* won't tell her," she said. "Will you?"

"You have become naughty girl," Mrs. Zabek grumbled.

"But I have *you* praying for me, so I'll be fine."

Libby went to her room, lit a cigarette and started pulling clothes from her closet. Grandma Brennan was a clothes horse, and she would certainly notice whatever she was wearing. She chose a pale green dress by a new designer named Coco Chanel. Libby knew her grandmother would recognize the design immediately.

Olivia Brennan continually amazed her granddaughters. She was their last remaining grandparent, and they adored her. Chic, distinguished and socially prominent, they could never imagine her at home raising nine children, and indeed she had little to do with caring for her children. She had staff for those dirty little details. Most of her time was spent doing fund-raising for the Archdiocese, sitting on the board of the Women's Club, and dabbling in the Suffrage Movement.

Yet when her children truly needed her, she was right there. She would sweep in like a hurricane, and take charge of their every need. If one of them was stricken with hallucinations or melancholia, she would roll up her sleeves and give them all her attention, calming and soothing them. She was fast moving, out-spoken, and incredibly kind. Advancing age had not diminished her Celtic good looks, and her sense of fashion added to this allure.

Late in the morning, Libby heard an automobile pull up under the *porte-cochère*. When she looked out, it was a brand new Franklin, and the chauffeur opened the door. Her Grandmother Brennan stepped out. Her dark hair was streaked with gray, and Libby noticed right away that she too had it cut short in the latest fashion. She was wearing a navy jacket dress complementing her tall, slim frame.

Libby took one last look in the mirror, adjusted a pin in her hat and left the room.

"Just look at our darling," Olivia Brennan said to Mrs. Zabek as Libby came down the stairs.

"Hello Grandmother," Libby said kissing her. She noticed fine lines on her grandmother's face, and she knew that not only time but the death of her daughter had aged her.

Mrs. Zabek went back upstairs to clean house.

"It has been too long," Mrs. Brennan said. "You are so grown up. Your mother would have been proud of you."

Libby smiled but was unsure if she believed the part about her mother.

"We can't see your sister today," Mrs. Brennan announced.

"Why not?"

"They transferred her to the asylum in Anoka."

"To Anoka? But mother was always in St. Peter. Is this a good place, Grandmother?"

"Very progressive. They just started taking women. Your sister will be in good hands."

"Does the train go up there?"

"Yes. When she is settled, we will visit."

Libby had hoped St. Mary's would send Jennie home, but there must have been another incident. Even though asylums used the latest techniques and treatments, they scared Libby, and she knew Jennie would be scared too.

Mrs. Brennan was holding a large blue hat and stepped over to the mirror, putting it back on her head. "Damn thing," she said. "I knock it off every time I get out of the automobile."

Libby smiled. Her grandmother was still the same. With all the money and social status, she had never been stuffy or pretentious. Always gossiping with the staff and saying things that were mildly shocking, she never forgot her humble beginnings in post-famine Limerick.

She put her arm around Libby and said in her Irish brogue, "I'm taking my girl shopping and out for lunch."

Libby grinned. "Where are we going first?"

"To Young Quinlan. I need some hosiery. Would you like a new hat?"

"Always," and then Libby lowered her voice. "Can we go to a music store too? I want to buy Zabby a new recording for the Victrola."

"Yes, indeed," Mrs. Brennan said.

They climbed into the Franklin and headed down Hennepin Avenue to the center of town. The chauffeur dropped them off in front of a small but elegant store in the Syndicate Building named, Young Quinlan, the first women's ready-to-wear apparel store in the country. The aisles were carpeted. There were chandeliers overhead, and it had the faint smell of expensive perfume. The fragrance department was the first thing shoppers encountered when they passed through the front doors of the store. There were face creams, atomizers and bottles of 4711, Chypre and *N'aimez Que Moi* in glass display cases. Beautifully decorated boxes of soap and powder lined the counters, all illuminated by shaded lamps. Libby stopped a moment to look at the latest trend for women, which was lip rouge.

Two middle-aged shoppers watched Libby and her grandmother. "That's Olivia Brennan," one of them murmured as if seeing royalty.

Even though she was from St. Paul, people in Minneapolis knew Olivia. Frequently pictured in the society columns, her face was instantly recognizable. But today they were more interested in the chic young woman walking beside her.

"Who's that?"

"It must be her granddaughter."

The first thing that caught their attention were the smooth, rolling waves of Libby's caramel-colored hair and her hazel eyes under arched brows. But how she moved is what kept people staring. It was sultry and fluid, alluring, but aloof.

If someone had told her that she was seductive, she would have laughed. Being unaware of it, made it all the more appealing. Combined with her poise and confidence, it was hypnotizing to both men and women.

Grandmother and granddaughter stopped in the hosiery department where the clerk obsequiously opened drawers and brought out thin boxes containing the finest stockings wrapped in folded tissue paper. Mrs. Brennan took her gloves off, scrutinized each article and bought several pairs.

She had come a long way since her early days in Ireland. Success had smiled on her and her husband when they immigrated to America, and when he died, he left her a very wealthy and respectable widow.

When she was done with her purchases, Mrs. Brennan noticed that Libby had wandered off. She looked around and spotted her walking up the main aisle, just closing her handbag. "I was browsing a bit," she explained.

"The hat bar is this way," Mrs. Brennan said, and they swept over to the millinery department. "Those old bats at the Women's Club turn up their noses at ready-to-wear, but I'm all for it. I don't want to wait for purchases if I don't have to."

Libby didn't hear her, she was trying on a large hat with a heavy, red plume.

"Too much for your face," she said.

Libby tried another.

"Too mature," and she directed Libby to a wide-brimmed, white hat trimmed with a wide, gold ribbon. She cocked it to the side of Libby's head and said, "The gold sets off the highlights in your hair."

Libby looked in the mirror and tilted her head from

side to side. "I have just the dress for it."

Mrs. Brennan gave all the information needed for purchase and delivery and then said, "Now, let's be on our way. I'm dying for a cigarette. I imagine you are too."

Libby looked at her, startled.

"I'm a lot of things, Elizabeth Durant but I'm no fool. I know you smoke."

The doorman signaled for the Brennan automobile, and they climbed inside. "Miss Durant needs to make a quick stop at Davidson Piano and Organ," she said to the driver. "And then to the West Hotel."

Mrs. Brennan held a cigarette case open for Libby. "Go ahead," she commanded.

After Libby had taken a cigarette, she did too.

"Did you purchase something while I was buying hosiery?" she asked Libby.

"No," she lied and looked out the window.

Mrs. Brennan raised an eyebrow and smiled. She knew that Libby was lying, but she wasn't going to press her.

They rode several blocks, and the driver pulled in front of a tiny music store. Libby ran inside and returned with several recordings of George M. Cohan's music.

Mrs. Brennan nodded. "Zabby will love it. Now, luncheon at The West."

The driver pulled up to the main entrance of The West Hotel, the finest hotel in Minneapolis. An opulent façade with gabled roofs, dormers and bay windows, The West was truly a grand hotel.

The doorman greeted Mrs. Brennan by name as they walked into the lobby. She asked, "How is Edith's gout?"

He inclined his head slightly and replied, "Much improved, madam. Thank you."

"Very good."

The lobby was a massive open area with huge pillars, a

sky-lighted ceiling and a marble and onyx staircase. Large enough to be the lobby of big city train depot, it was made cozy by four conversation areas with easy chairs, end tables, and plush rugs.

The hotel dining room was equally splendid with a high ceiling and Moorish décor. The maître d'hôtel seated them at a table by a window overlooking Hennepin Avenue. After ordering stuffed tomatoes and popovers, Mrs. Brennan said, "Now to business."

Libby didn't like the sound of it.

"I've enrolled you in Northrup Collegiate School for Girls."

Libby's jaw dropped. She didn't want to continue with school. She barely squeaked through Beardsley Hall. She snapped open her napkin and said, "Thanks anyway, Grandma but I don't think so."

Olivia Brennan's eyebrows shot up. "This is not open to discussion, Elizabeth."

Libby slumped back in her chair in a pout.

"Have you thought any more about what colleges interest you out East?"

"No," Libby replied sulkily.

"Well, then while you are at Northrup you can decide on a college and a major."

Libby knew the real story. Higher education for young women was not to explore or foster a career; it was to find a husband. Something in which she was not interested.

"Louise Robinson will be attending," Mrs. Brennan said. "Abigail O'Connor's girl, and your cousin, Penelope."

Libby's eyebrows shot up. "Pepper will be there?"

Mrs. Brennan narrowed her eyes. "Yes, and there will be no shenanigans, Elizabeth. I know you and Penelope have a history together."

Indeed they did. The two girls had been in many

scrapes, and Libby had loved every minute of it. Always taking chances, Pepper Brennan lived life on the edge, and so did Libby. When they were together anything could happen.

Smiling, Libby sat up straight again. She felt better now. As she reached for her teacup, her sleeve pulled up revealing purple scars on her arm.

Her grandmother noticed. "In a few more years those will fade, Elizabeth."

Libby pulled the cuff down quickly and dropped her hands into her lap. She hated the constant reminder of that night seven years ago. Her mother had been aiming for her face with a pair of scissors and just in time she blocked the attack with her arms. It was fortunate that she managed to escape to the attic to hide with Jennie. The incident had been the final straw for Grandpa Durant. He realized that he could no longer successfully circulate lies about the domestic harmony of the family and buying the press was no longer possible, so he sent the girls away to boarding school immediately.

Lunch came at last and eager to change the subject, Libby asked, "Have you been to the theater lately, Grandmother?"

"Yes, the Shubert, I saw Fanny Brice," she said, taking a bite.

"What! Was she hilarious?"

"Yes and Jimmy Durante too."

"The cat's pajamas!" Libby gasped.

"What are the cat's pajamas?"

"The same as wonderful, Grandma," Libby said.

Mrs. Brennan loved vaudeville. Although it was considered pedestrian by her peers, she didn't care. She went to shows constantly. When a performer came to town that she liked she would even go alone.

Libby had inherited that love of the theater too. She adored anything from legitimate stage to circuses. But photoplays were her favorite, more commonly called the movies. She loved the stories, the beauty of the actors and actresses and the sets, but what captivated her the most, were the illusions created by makeup. She found it miraculous that a performer could become younger, older, more beautiful, or more grotesque just with the application of makeup. One of her keenest desires was to go backstage and watch performers apply greasepaint and powder to transform themselves from mere mortals to stage legends. She could never pass by a toiletries counter without purchasing some cosmetics. Just that morning when her grandmother was looking at hosiery, she had slipped away to buy some lip rouge.

Libby sighed and looked out the window at the horses and automobiles on Hennepin Ave. It was so dull being back home. Her future sounded like absolute drudgery. She needed to have something to look forward to.

Mrs. Brennan was watching her. "So young lady, more news you won't like. The term has already started at Northrup, so you will begin on Monday."

"This Monday?"

I have only the weekend left. Then she remembered Pepper. I still have two more days of freedom. She'll know where to find some hooch and some boys.

Chapter 3

That afternoon after Mrs. Brennan dropped Libby off, she telephoned Pepper, who invited her over immediately.

After dressing and fussing with her hair, Libby asked Mr. Axelman to take her to her uncle's residence on Park Avenue. Axel was thrilled to be in the driver's seat once more. He sat tall and proud in the buggy with Libby in the back seat. Oscar Patterson, the horse, was equally pleased to be pulling the buggy, and he pranced down the street with his hooves clattering loudly on the bricks.

The only one not happy was Libby. She pressed herself back into the seat, trying to hide from view. In her mind, buggies were completely passé, and although she would never dream of hurting Axel by letting him know of her embarrassment, she was mortified.

When they turned onto Park Avenue, she noticed all of the new mansions lining the street. The rich and famous of Minneapolis were making an exodus from downtown and building farther out, away from the noise and hubbub of the big city.

Libby did not look twice at the Brennan home when

they pulled up. She was used to magnificent dwellings. It was a square, formal Renaissance Revival structure constructed of smooth cream-colored stone with a lacy, wrought iron *porte-cochère* and a fountain by the entrance.

Pepper Brennan, a perky, blonde girl with freckles was standing at the front door.

Libby ran up the steps to hug her. "You look so different, Pepper!"

"Jeepers, Libs, it's been seven years. I suppose I've changed. So have you. You're the first girl I've seen with bobbed hair."

Pepper waved to Mr. Axelman as he drove off. "I can't believe he's still not driving your automobile."

"I know. He's so old fashioned. I'm hoping no one saw me."

"No horse and buggy for us tonight. I'm driving the Willys Knight," Pepper said as they walked inside.

"No!" Libby gasped. "You can drive?"

"No, but how hard can it be?"

Libby, almost a head taller than Pepper, wrapped her arm around her petite cousin. "I've missed you."

"I've missed you too."

The girls walked up the wide, carpeted staircase to Pepper's bedroom.

"Are your parents gone?"

"They're in Brussels. They would have loved to have seen you."

"Grandma told me you're going to Northrup. So am I," Libby said.

"Hot dog!" she laughed. "You will make it so much better."

Libby had forgotten what an infectious laugh her cousin had. "Is it really that dreadful?"

"Yes, so boring and stuffy, but we'll shake things up."

When they walked into Pepper's room, Libby sat down at the vanity. "Do you have any cosmetics?"

Pepper unlocked a drawer and pulled out powder, eye liner and lip rouge along with cigarettes and an ashtray. "I'm not supposed to have any of this, you know."

"What shall we do tonight?" Libby asked, lighting a cigarette and leaning toward the mirror with the eyeliner.

"Shall we go to a show?" Pepper asked.

"Yes."

"The flickers or a live show?"

"Let's drive by and see who's appearing at The Gayety or The Orpheum," Libby suggested.

Pepper lit a cigarette and nudged her. "You still like those old geezers in vaudeville? Photoplays are better."

"I love any and all of it."

Pepper bent down to examine Libby's makeup. She had artfully applied liner, powder, and rouge to her face. From months of practice, she had a steady hand and keen sense of how to highlight and shadow the various angles of her face. With the right amount of lip rouge, she accentuated her full lips and darkened her arched brows with a pencil.

"You're good," Pepper said. "Who taught you?"

"I figured it out myself. Let me do you."

"Alright, but we will have to be quick and sneak out before Mrs. Carlson comes back."

"Who's she?"

"My guardian, my chaperone and my--"

"Jailer?" Libby added.

"Exactly."

"Will you get in trouble if we take the auto?"

"Yes, but it will be old news by the time my parents get home in a month."

Libby applied cosmetics to her cousin's face, and then they put on bandeaux. Libby's was a simple ring of gold leaves, and Pepper's was decorated with tiny blue beads. They both wore filmy ankle-length dresses, belted at the waist. Pepper's dress was aqua-colored, and Libby's was bronze.

"You look wonderful," Pepper said, taking Libby's hands and swinging her around. "Remind me again how to do the turkey trot."

"Have you been living in a cave?" Libby declared.

"Things take longer to get to the Midwest."

"What? Five years!" and she laughed.

"My parents insist I go to stuffy old cotillions where they only waltz."

"Jeepers, they have really tightened the reins on you, haven't they?"

With one hand on her cousin's waist and the other holding her hand with their arms straight out, Libby showed Pepper how to do the turkey trot, hopping, kicking and dipping around the room.

"I'm hopeless," Pepper said breathlessly when they were finished.

"I'll teach you later. Let's go."

Pepper opened the door a crack, looked both ways, and they snuck down the stairs out to the carriage house. "Isn't your driver around either?" Libby asked.

"His night off. I think he's out with my chaperone."

"Understood," Libby said with a wink. "That makes it easier."

They opened the doors, and Pepper climbed into a bright blue Willys-Knight touring car. Libby stood by the carriage house doors waiting to close them. When Pepper started the car, it lurched forward unexpectedly and almost hit Libby.

"God's nightgown, Pepper!" she cried.

"I'm sorry. I forgot to do something. Stand back!"

Pepper could barely see over the steering wheel. "Let's try again."

This time she pulled the choke, pushed in the clutch, and the automobile started. Three times she tried to ease it out onto the driveway, but it would always kill. The fourth time she was successful, and after closing the carriage house doors, Libby hopped in.

"I've got it now," Pepper announced as they jerked out onto Park Avenue.

"My neck is getting sore," Libby said, laughing.

They made their way slowly down Park Avenue and wound through downtown heading toward Washington Avenue and The Gayety Theater. By now Pepper's driving had improved. People stopped honking at her, and she had picked up speed. On two occasions she had to call out apologies to pedestrians, but by the time they reached the front door of the Gayety, no one was staring anymore.

They pulled over to the curb, parked and read the marquee. "Delores Joyce and Her Dancing Dogs." The girls wrinkled their noses and drove several blocks more down Hennepin Avenue to the Orpheum. They pulled over and looked at the headliners on the sign. The comic, Stub Kelly and the singer Josephine Campbell were appearing.

"I've heard Campbell's songs are pretty racy," Libby said with a raised eyebrow.

"Then that's the show for us," Pepper replied.

Suddenly a young man with curly blond hair and blue eyes thrust his head inside the auto and said with a grin, "Are you girls going to let us park this for you?"

His co-worker was leaning against a booth smoking a cigarette. He was tall and slim with dark hair. The corner of his mouth curled up when he saw Libby.

Pepper looked at Libby, wondering if she should let the boy park the car, and she nodded.

"Alright," Pepper said, sliding out.

"He'll give you the claim stub," he said, gesturing toward his co-worker. He jumped behind the steering wheel, delighted to be driving such a luxurious piece of machinery.

As the girls walked toward the booth, the attendant burned a look into Libby, and she returned his stare. He tore off the stub and handed it to her. "See you after the show," he said.

Libby did not reply, but she could feel him watching her as they walked away. She put a little extra sway into her hips to stimulate his interest.

"They were pretty fresh," Pepper said. "But cute."

"Yes, they were," Libby replied, her body humming with pleasure.

Pepper and Libby didn't notice the cherubs painted on the ceilings or the sparkling chandeliers overhead as they rushed through the lobby. The curtain was about to go up as they dropped into their seats. Lights flashed in the annunciator on the side of the stage, and Libby had just enough time to look at the name of the first act. It was a dance line named The Stardust Angels.

The house lights dimmed, and the orchestra began to play a lively tune. The curtain raised only part way showing only the feet of women as they danced. The sound of their taps hitting the floor in unison was deafening. After a few moments, the curtain went all the way up revealing a line of scantily dressed females in brightly colored, sequined costumes. They had bright red lips, shapely figures and wore helmet cloches decorated with large plumes. Libby and Pepper were mesmerized.

The next act was a cowboy doing rope tricks, then a black-face routine, acrobats, Stub Kelly the comedian and finally the singer Josephine Campbell.

"My sides hurt," Pepper said after the show. "Stub Kelly was hilarious."

"He was funny, but I liked all the costumes and makeup of the dancers. I would give anything to go backstage and see how it's done."

"Someday we will."

They left the theater and walked to the parking attendant's booth. The young men were busy retrieving automobiles.

When their turn came, Pepper nudged Libby and said, "Watch this." She murmured to the attendant who had parked their car, "You don't have any hooch, do ya?"

He smiled knowingly. "Wait 'til we get done. I've got whiskey for us all."

"Alright," she replied with a wink. "We'll go back inside and powder our noses."

The girls went back inside the Orpheum to the ladies lounge, smoked and freshened their faces. When they returned to the booth, the young men were standing beside the Willys-Knight.

"So you want to find some fun?" the blonde attendant asked.

"We do."

"I'm Wally, and this is Sam," he said nodding toward the attendant who had been staring at Libby earlier.

The girls introduced themselves.

"We need to go get the booze. How about a lift?" Wally asked.

"Sure," Pepper replied.

He ran to the driver's side of the car. "Let me drive?"

She made a face. "It's not far, is it?"

"Ten minutes."

"Alright, but this is my old man's auto so be careful," she said as she slid into the passenger seat.

Sam opened the rear door for Libby, and she climbed inside.

They drove off with Pepper and Wally in front and Libby and Sam in back. It was a relief for Libby to have Wally behind the wheel. He was actually a good driver. She lit a cigarette. "Where are we going?"

"Bryn Mawr," Sam said. "A neighborhood near here. We took rooms in a boarding house there. "We moonlight parking automobiles and work for the railroad during the day."

Wally chimed in, "Although our new employer is Uncle Sam. We enlisted yesterday."

"Going overseas?" Pepper asked.

"Probably."

"So you're looking for a good time before you go," Libby said as she blew out her smoke.

The boys started to laugh.

"We didn't need to enlist to have that be priority one," Sam replied. He held her eye a moment.

Libby found Sam extremely attractive. She liked his dark looks, and there was something about him that was dangerously exciting.

They turned into the Bryn Mawr neighborhood. It was a quiet little community not far from downtown which sprang up from the Minneapolis and St. Louis Railroad. The homes were not large but comfortable. The drove past a corner of brownstone buildings housing a grocer, hardware store, and druggist. Wally pulled the Willys Knight up in front of a two-story stucco home on Cedar Lake Road. Wally jumped out and disappeared inside, returning a moment later with a brown paper bag.

"Shall we go to The Meadows?" he asked putting the car in gear.

"Maybe," Pepper replied. "Have you got the goods?"

"Sure do," and he handed her the bag with the bottle.

She took a drink and then passed it back to Libby. "You think they'll outlaw the stuff?"

"It's getting close," Sam said from the back seat, taking a pull.

"So we'll drink as much as we can until then," Wally said, and they laughed.

They drove a few blocks to a park, stepped out and sat on the grass, talking and passing the bottle. Libby felt the glow of the liquor warm her veins. She couldn't see Sam's face in the shadows, but she knew he was warming up to her as he moved closer.

Wally took Pepper's hand and stood up. "Let's go for a walk, beautiful."

"No, I'm tired."

"We're not going to run. We're just going for a little stroll."

"We'll be right here," Sam said as he put his arm around Libby.

Libby started to feel uncomfortable. They had let things go too far. The boys were getting amorous, and everything could get out of hand very quickly. The hooch had clouded her judgment, and she wished that she had stopped Pepper from walking off.

Sam leaned close and whispered, "You smell good."

When he brushed her hair back and put his lips on her neck, Libby felt a thrill. Fighting desire, she moved away. "You don't lose any time, do you, bub?"

"It's just that you're so damned pretty and--"

"And I should send a boy off to war happy?" she said, trying to free herself.

"Yes, something like that," he said, kissing her neck. He took her chin, pulled her lips to his own and kissed her deeply.

Libby's desire heightened. She put her head back and returned his kisses, but when he eased her back onto the ground, she became uneasy again. She knew what would happen next. She remembered the weeks of anxiety waiting for her courses, the sleepless nights, and the prospect of being sent away to a "special" residence. Even though there had not been a pregnancy, she would *not* go through that again.

Her body went rigid. "We better not," she said, trying to sit up.

"I know you want me," he murmured, pulling up her dress.

"No," Libby said, trying to wiggle herself free.

Not listening, he crawled on top of her, spreading her legs with his knees.

"No!" she said again, trying to push him off.

"Come on. I can make you feel good," he mumbled, moving his hand between her legs.

Libby felt trapped. He was stronger than her and things were spiraling out of control. She had to do something fast, so she slid her hand down into his pants.

He moaned.

Clutching his testicles firmly, she said, "Get off me, or I'll crush your family jewels."

Sam froze. When he realized she wasn't joking, he jumped to his feet. "You filthy bitch!" he roared. He clenched his fists, and Libby thought he was going to hit her.

"Go to hell, you rich slut!" he snarled and strode off into the darkness.

Libby stood up, straightened her dress and ran her fingers through her hair. Her heart was pounding as she took a breath to calm herself. *That was close.*

Suddenly Pepper came running up out of the darkness. "Get in the auto quick," she yelled. "I just kicked that bonehead in the balls!"

"Oh jeepers!" Libby exclaimed and jumped into the Willys-Knight.

Pepper started the car, and they roared away. Moments later they were laughing.

*   *   *

Mrs. Zabek awakened Libby early the next morning informing her that her grandmother was picking her up for Mass in an hour.

Libby protested at first, but she got dressed and went to the Basilica with her. Even though the church was huge, when they brought out the incense, Libby almost retched.

After Mass, Mrs. Brennan invited her to the lake home on White Bear Lake, but Libby declined to remind her grandmother that she had school in the morning. In reality, she wanted to go back to bed.

Moments before she went up to her room, Mrs. Zabek said there was a phone call for her.

"Is this Miss Elizabeth Durant?" a voice said over the receiver.

"Yes."

"This is a nurse from the Anoka Asylum. We were unable to contact Mrs. Brennan this morning, and you were next on the list. There has been a problem."

Libby's heart skipped a beat.

"I'm sorry to tell you that your sister attempted suicide last night."

Libby was stunned. "What?"

"She is resting comfortably now though."

"So she is fine? She isn't--"

"Yes fine. After receiving some medical attention, she is sleeping."

"What--what happened?"

"She had a particularly disturbing episode. Seeing

things, hearing voices, and then—well—she tried to harm herself."

Libby swallowed hard. "Can I see her?"

"Visiting hours are from eleven to five."

"I'm on my way. Thank you." Libby put the receiver in the cradle, ran to the bathroom and threw up. Taking a deep breath, she squared her shoulders, picked up her hat and gloves and returned downstairs.

"Zabby, Jennie is ill."

"I'll tell Axel to get ready."

Moments later, Axel was driving Libby to the Milwaukee Road Depot.

"I can ride the streetcar up there, Axel," she protested, leaning forward in the buggy.

"No, no. The train is safer and faster. Fewer stops along the way, *elskede*."

The depot was alive with activity. Automobiles and buggies were everywhere. Axel lined up to drop Libby at the front door.

"I'll get out here," she announced suddenly. "I have to catch the next train out."

"But--"

Libby swung open the door and hopped out. "Thanks, Axel."

Before he could say anything, she was gone.

The large atrium of the depot echoed with noise as Libby walked inside. Passengers zig-zagged back and forth carrying grips, holding children and hat boxes. Porters pushed luggage carts as arrivals and departures came over the loud speaker.

Libby wound her way through the crowd to the ticket counter. "I would like a ticket for the next train to Anoka please."

"Track 8," the clerk said flatly. "Leaves in five minutes."

Libby paid him and rushed out into the train shed. It was a long narrow enclosure supported by steel beams and trusses. Putting her hand on her head to hold her hat, she walked briskly down the platform between trains. The engines were hissing and steaming waiting to be boarded. A conductor took her ticket and directed her to the correct car.

Moments later, the train jerked into motion. The coach was not full, and Libby was relieved she was sitting alone. She pulled off her gloves and stared out the window. The train chugged through the city slowly, building momentum as the route became rural. The terrain was flat here, open farmland with rows and rows of corn and cows grazing in green pastures. The farmhouses and barns were neat, tidy wooden structures, simple in design and functional. Any other day the pastoral scene would have been relaxing, but today, Libby was taut as a bow string.

What would happen to Jennie? Would they be able to help her, or would she sink into the nightmare permanently?

She pulled her hat off and rested her feet on the metal footrest. She closed her eyes and tried to rest.

"Care for a boxed lunch, ma'am?" a black porter asked. He was pushing a trolley filled with boxed lunches, milk, tea, and coffee. "There is no dining car on this train."

What Libby really wanted was a cigarette, but she said instead, "Just a cup of coffee please."

He handed her the beverage. She paid, him and he moved on to the next row of seats.

When she finished her coffee, she went to the women's restroom. It consisted of a vanity with a mirror in one room and a toilet in the other. Thankfully it was empty, so Libby lit a cigarette and sat down at the vanity. Opening her bag, she took out her lip rouge. It was in a small metal cylinder, and she slid a tiny lever to push the stick of rouge up to the top of the case. Leaning forward, she applied the color to her lips. Turning her head from side to side, she examined her face. There were dark rings under her eyes from last night's foray, and she looked ghostly white. She wished they would invent a cosmetic to lighten the black shadows under her eyes. But more than anything she wished there was something to cover the scars on her arms. She pushed back her sleeves to look. They were jagged, discolored lacerations and punctures running the length of both arms, particularly on the underside. She guessed that someone adept at makeup could hide them, but she was unsure how to do it herself. Until she found out how to conceal them, she would have to wear long sleeves and gloves.

She sighed, took a final puff of her cigarette and went to the toilet. Stepping on a lever, she opened the drain and tossed her cigarette directly onto the tracks below. She chuckled, remembering as a child being afraid of the rush of air, the clatter of the wheels and the sight of the ground below.

Libby could feel the train slowing, and she heard the conductor announce, "Anoka!"

Taking one last look in the mirror, she smoothed her hair and returned to her seat.

When she stood up, the conductor said politely, "Not yet ma'am your stop is the next one. This is downtown Anoka."

"Oh?"

"Yes, the train stops right out at the asylum."

"Oh, I see. Thank you," she said, sitting back down.

Moments later, Libby was standing at the depot of the Anoka Asylum. She followed other passengers up a walkway. It led to a large complex of brown, brick buildings arranged in a circle around a park with oak trees and a lawn. Above the entrance to each building, etched in stone was the word, "Cottage," and they were numbered, Cottage No. 1, Cottage No. 2 and so on. Libby noticed construction had begun on a tenth building which seemed to be identical to the rest.

There was a sign that directed visitors to the administration building. Libby swallowed hard. She had not been to one of these facilities since she was a child, and she felt her hands start to perspire. But Jennie was worth it. She took a deep breath and walked up the steps.

The floor was uncarpeted and scrubbed to a blinding white. There were heavy benches against the walls and straight ahead was a massive oak counter. A nurse in a white uniform with a cap stood up from a desk and walked over. She had a flat face with thin white lips. "May I help you?"

"My name is Elizabeth Durant, and I am here to see my sister, Jennifer Durant." When the nurse opened a large register, Libby added, "She is receiving medical treatment. There was an accident."

"Oh, in that case, the infirmary is in Cottage Five. Two doors down. You may inquire there."

"Thank you," Libby said.

She returned outside, and as she was walking to the infirmary, she suddenly heard a blood-curdling scream. Her heart jumped into her throat. It came from one of the cottages on the other side of the lawn. Libby sighed and started walking again. She had witnessed more madness than most people would ever see in a life lifetime, but she could never get used to it. It was the unpredictability of it that terrified her. Even a burglar or a thief operated in a somewhat logical fashion, but when madness struck, actions were impulsive, illogical and without warning.

From the outside, Cottage Five looked like all the other buildings, but when Libby opened the door the smell of iodine and rubbing alcohol hit her. Her nausea returned. A young nurse in a white apron greeted her with a smile. She was wearing a small cap that looked like a plump bun on top of her head, and it was tied in a bow under her chin. Keys dangled from her waist on a belt.

Escorting Libby down a down a hall, she explained, "This side of the building has fewer patients. We've only just started accepting females."

It was a long, narrow room with iron bedsteads painted an antiseptic white. Libby's shoes clattered loudly on the bare floor, and she tried to tiptoe. Most of the beds were empty, the white sheets and blankets tucked in neatly as if they were waiting for a guest. There were only four women on the ward, and they looked at Libby with lethargic, bloodshot eyes. One of the women mumbled incoherently, and Libby noticed they were strapped to the beds.

"Here is your sister, Miss Durant," the nurse said.

Jennie was asleep, her thick dark hair splayed out on the pillow. She had never realized until now how much she looked like her mother, but even more beautiful. Her skin was so pale, it was practically translucent. A sprinkling of freckles across her tiny nose made her resemble a sprite, yet her dark brows added depth and character to her face. Lips that were usually so pink today were white, and the skin over her hands looked thin and blue.

Libby saw leather straps on Jennie's wrists tying her to the bed frame. "Jennie?" she said.

There was no response.

Libby looked her up and down. "Where are her injuries?" she asked the young nurse. "She looks unharmed."

"In this case, there are no visible injuries."

"What? I thought she tried to--" and she stopped. "What did she do to herself?"

Taking Libby's elbow, the nurse moved her away from the bed and whispered, "You must understand, Miss Durant, we take every precaution here at Anoka Asylum. No sharp objects, no access to medicines, cleaning supplies, cords—but we simply cannot anticipate everything."

"I understand, but what did she do?"

The nurse sighed. "We give them Bibles to read for comfort."

"Yes?"

"Your sister tore off pages and stuffed them down her throat trying to choke herself."

Libby's jaw dropped. "What?" she gasped. She couldn't believe her ears.

"She tried to commit suicide in this fashion."

Libby was appalled. "I—I can't believe it."

"It was a surprise to us too. We have never seen anything like it. We caught her just in time and removed the paper from her throat. We aren't sure how long she was without oxygen though."

Libby put her hand to her forehead and exclaimed, "My sister wanted that to die that badly?"

"They don't always know what they want, Miss Durant, or what they are doing."

Libby pulled up a chair and sat down by Jennie.

"Only five more minutes please," the nurse said.

Libby nodded.

Another worker came into the ward, and the nurse left to attend to other patients.

Libby stroked Jennie's hair, murmuring endearments. At last Jennie opened her eyes. They were lifeless and vacant, like the eyes of a doll.

"Hello, darling," Libby said.

Jennie started at her, not blinking.

"How I've missed you," and Libby's eyes filled with tears. "I miss my best friend," she said thickly.

Jennie's eyes did not change.

Libby swallowed a sob and sat up straight. "Zabby wants you back home and Axel and Tante. It is too quiet in that big old house."

Libby took a deep breath. She must make small talk, or she would break down. "I went out with Pepper last night. She drove us downtown in an automobile." Libby chuckled. "No surprise, she was a terrible driver."

Jennie stared at her.

"We went to the Orpheum and saw a singer and a comedian. And then we snuck out with some boys. You should have been with us."

Libby continued, saying anything she could think of, trying to break through the wall of silence, but nothing worked.

At last, the nurse returned and said, "I'm sorry, but Jennifer needs to rest now."

Libby squeezed Jennie's hand and said, "I'll be back soon. I love you."

Libby staggered outside, and then suddenly like a damn bursting, she began to cry. She covered her mouth to stifle her sobs and ran under a tree, shaking with despair.

It is happening again. It is happening again, but this time to my darling Jennie.

When she, at last, took a deep breath of fresh air and dried her eyes, something caught her eye. A woman with large breasts and a bald head was staring down at her from the second story of one of the cottages. She was dressed in a loose gown made of fabric that looked like mattress ticking, and there were bars on the window. Although she was obviously an inmate, her look was not vacant or expressionless like the others. It was filled with sympathy and understanding.

She looked down at Libby with pity in her eyes.

Chapter 4

Like a sleepwalker, Libby boarded the train for home. All she could think about was Jennie. She was lifeless, beyond lethargic, dead. Had the illness progressed that quickly or was it brain damage from choking? Would she snap out of it and return to normal or remain that way?

The train rolled past small towns, farmhouses, and lakes, but Libby saw none of it. She could only see Jennie's eyes with their vacant expression.

Jennie's descent into madness seemed to happen overnight. Had she missed something over the past year? She sat back and closed her eyes returning to Beardsley Hall.

Both girls had been busy with school that semester, Jennie with academics, Libby with fun. Jennie was an excellent student, bright and motivated, always willing to help Libby with a difficult lesson or share her notes. And Libby helped Jennie make friends.

Jennie had been quieter than usual though and growing more withdrawn with every passing day. Libby thought Jennie was distancing herself because she disapproved of her pranks at school, but by spring she became quiet to the point of secretive. Libby wondered what she what was hiding. When she asked, Jennie would not tell her.

In hindsight, Libby wondered if she was guarding the voices. Had the demons started whispering to her like they had whispered to her mother? How could she have not seen the signs? How could she have been so thoughtless? Off she went to Italy with friends, leaving Jennie behind. She had invited her, but she declined. Jennie said that she had recently made new friends in a reading group, so she would rather stay at Beardsley over the summer.

Without a care, Libby left for Europe.

A month later, news came that her mother was dead. It was upsetting, but Libby made no plans to return. She resumed her tour of Rome, and then a telegram arrived saying that Jennie had attacked a student. It had been a random assault, completely unprovoked.

With knowledge of her mother's illness, Libby knew that the madness had now struck her sister. She returned home immediately. The hospital near Beardsley had locked her in an empty room, and when she saw Jennie, she was a different person. She was hearing voices and speaking incoherently. When Libby walked in, Jennie hit her and spit at her.

Sending wires back and forth, Libby and Grandma Brennan made arrangements to bring her home. If her rheumatism had not been bad, Grandma Brennan would have come herself, but she arranged for a nurse to accompany them back home instead. The nurse sedated Jennie heavily for the journey, and they returned home without incident.

And that was all Libby could make of it. Reviewing it had revealed nothing.

She rubbed her eyes. She was beyond tired. When the

train pulled into the station, she got off, dragged herself through the empty depot and hired the first cab she saw. Moments later she was home.

"How was she?" Zabby asked.

Libby told her.

"Go to bed, little one," Mrs. Zabek said. "I bring warm milk to help you sleep."

Libby went up and undressed. "Oh yes, and more to look forward to," she grumbled as she climbed into bed. She remembered that tomorrow she had to start a new school.

* * *

Northrup Collegiate School was within walking distance of Libby's house, only a few blocks on the other side of Loring Park. It was autumn and mornings were cool, so with her head down, and her hands buried in her coat pockets, Libby started for school. She followed the walkways around the pond, past the hotel and museum, and without looking, passed by the palatial homes of her peers.

Ten minutes later she was standing in front of Northrup. The grounds were like a postcard, the brown brick building with a tall grand entrance, surrounded by colorful oaks and maples. "A grand seat of learning, simply idyllic," she muttered to herself sarcastically.

Girls walked past her, arm in arm, talking and laughing, all of them dressed in uniforms. Libby had hers on too. It was a dark blue sleeveless pullover with a long sleeved white blouse.

She looked around one more time before climbing the steps. *Odd how it looks like the cottages at the asylum, only bigger.* Even the woman behind the desk in the office looked like the nurse that greeted her at the institution.

"Here is your schedule, your books and your physical education uniform," the clerk said. "Check in with your teacher. It's English in room 210."

Libby stepped into the hall, looking one way and then the other. A group of girls sitting in leather chairs by a fireplace in the entry started whispering when they saw her.

She heard one of them say, "Durant."

Libby climbed the stones stairs to the second floor, checked in with a sour faced, red-headed English teacher and sat down. After he had introduced her to the class, Libby slid down into her seat counting the minutes until she was done for the day. She didn't like school. She never had. She had hoped she wouldn't have to return now that she was back in Minnesota, but Grandmother Brennan wouldn't allow it.

Libby looked around at the other girls. She didn't fit in. She felt older, and she knew that she looked more mature. They were so rosy-faced and innocent. Girls that had been well tended like precious little flower gardens by their cultivated, well-heeled parents. She caught herself. She had come from money too, probably more money than any of them, and had been protected by it too. *But the lie factory doesn't hold on forever.*

"We will be starting *The Mill on the Floss*," the teacher said. "Read the first four chapters by tomorrow."

But Libby wasn't listening, she was feeling ashamed of herself. These girls had done nothing to her. Some of them had even smiled and said hello. *It just doesn't seem fair that Jennie is strapped to a bed in Cottage Number Five when she should be bright and healthy, sitting in class too.*

The bell rang, and Libby went to her next class. She rotated through classes until lunch. Stepping into the large, loud lunchroom, she got in line. It was crammed with chattering girls. As she wound her way around the chaos with her tray of food, she saw them staring at her. Relieved, she found Pepper at one of the tables.

When she sat down, Pepper introduced her.

One of the girls said, "There's a cotillion this weekend at Blake. That's the school for boys, Libby. It's homecoming, so it's a semi-formal."

"Really?" Libby replied, trying to sound interested. "We better work on our dance steps, Pepper."

Pepper laughed. "No, it's *me* who better work on *my* dance steps."

The girls included Libby in the conversation and were cordial, but whenever she looked away, she could feel their eyes on her.

Pepper walked with her to her next class. Both girls were holding books on their hips. "So what do you think of day one?"

"It's alright."

"Comments are simply flying around here about your looks."

Libby stopped and looked at Pepper. "What's wrong with my looks?"

"They're intimidated by you. You're, shall we say, too advanced for them."

"Well, they needn't be afraid of me. I don't give a rat's ass about *them*."

They went back to walking.

"You saw Jennie yesterday, didn't you?"

She nodded.

"How is she?"

"Distant. She's acting like mother."

"I was afraid you'd say that."

Libby sighed "I don't think she'll be home for a long time."

"Well, try to keep your mind off of it. Let's spice things up at the cotillion on Saturday. What do you say?"

"Alright. In the meantime," Libby said out of the side of her mouth. "You're going to have to show me where I can sneak off and have a smoke,"

Pepper winked. "It's tricky, but I know a spot."

"Good, show me after I finish my class on poise, etiquette and being a lady."

"Ha!" Pepper laughed and turned down the other hall.

Libby's last class of the day was physical education, and when she went into the locker room to change, she noticed her gym uniform was short sleeved. She stared at it in disbelief. At Beardsley, the gym clothes had always covered her arms.

She swallowed hard. Everyone would see her scars. She'd always known this day would come. *But why today with these venomous little princesses?*

Reluctantly she put on her uniform and went out into the gymnasium. Pretending to be cold, she hugged her chest and looked around. There were mats and thick ropes hanging from the ceiling, a pommel horse, and rows of wooden bars lining the walls. Libby slipped over and stood with the other girls. They were all wearing white blouses with black bloomers, tall black stockings, and gym shoes. Noise bounced off the high ceilings and hardwood floors, echoing loudly.

The teacher was a petite woman with a big voice. "Alright girls, let's warm up. To the center of the gym."

Libby followed the group. They faced forward, and Libby stood in the back so no one could see her. They ran through drills doing everything from jumping jacks to lunges. So far Libby had gone unnoticed.

The next set of exercises was running around the gym. Again no one saw her scars, but the final exercise involved climbing the bars on the walls. They were expected face outward and do leg thrusts.

Everything was executed in a neat, orderly fashion, and the girls lined up. Two of them climbed the bars, facing outward and waited. Next in line was Libby. She froze. She could feel the girls behind her urging her forward.

"Miss Durant, it's your turn," the teacher stated.

Libby didn't move.

"Miss Durant?"

Swallowing hard, Libby climbed up.

"Turn around, Miss Durant."

Slowly, Libby turned around and hung onto the bars with her arms over her head.

When the teacher stared, everyone looked up to see what had captured her attention. Libby's scars were visible to everyone.

"Yes, now let's carry on," the teacher continued, but it was too late. Everyone had seen.

When the exercise was over, Libby saw girls stealing looks and whispering. When she heard, "It was her mother," she walked out the door and straight into the locker room.

"That's it!" she exclaimed as she stripped off her clothes. "I won't do it," and threw her gym suit into the locker.

Libby dressed, slammed the door shut and walked out of the school.

*   *   *

That evening Grandmother Brennan received a call telling her that Libby had left gym class without an excuse and paid her a visit. The words ran hot between them, but at last Libby agreed to return to school.

Weeks passed, and Libby went through the motions of an education. Although Pepper encouraged her to attend extracurricular activities, Libby had little interest in socializing with the other students. She attended the Homecoming Dance but nothing else.

Her academic performance was growing worse. She

tried studying, but her attention would always wander.

Nevertheless, every weekend without fail, she took the train up to Anoka and visited Jennie. Jennie had at last awakened from her torpor, and the staff moved her from the infirmary to Cottage Seven.

Jennie recognized and spoke with her, but her expression was flat. She moved mechanically and often her words did not make sense.

"There is no question she is improving a little every day," the nurse said. "She is having good results from the hydrotherapy."

Libby was surprised the woman said she was improving. She didn't look better to her. "Will she be released soon?"

"We review her case next week, and at that time we will decide."

But months passed, and Jennie did not come home. Libby hated going there, especially being around the other inmates. Around thirty women were locked in the commons area of Cottage Seven. It was cold from lack of furniture and drafty from large mullioned windows. Although these windows were glass, there were bars across them. The floor was bare, and there was a drain in the center of the room in case someone was incontinent. The patients were scattered around the room, dressed in hospital gowns, some sitting on benches clutching their knees, others on the floor sitting cross-legged and rocking. Some of them babbled incoherently, others laughed inappropriately. Few noticed Libby at all; they were too busy with apparitions. One woman, in particular, unnerved her. Without warning, she would roar, "Get your finger out of me!"

Foul language paired with a complete disregard for modesty made the environment surreal.

"They say that every day you are a little better," Libby

said to Jennie as she combed her hair. It was always matted, and frequently she smelled of urine. "We simply have to get you home, darling."

Slowly Jennie turned her head, looked at Libby and said, "The apple took the high road."

"I know. I know," Libby responded. Snow was gathering on the window sill, and she said, "Look, Jen. It's snowing. Christmas is in a few weeks. Next time I'll bring cookies from Zabby and Tante."

"I like the poppy seed ones," Jennie said.

That was good! Encouraged, Libby continued, "What other kinds do you like?"

"Krumkakers, and ginger snaps."

"Me too. I like Zabby's almond cookies the best though. Remember those?"

Jennie cocked her head and replied, "But liberties have been taken with expeditionary forces."

Libby looked out again at the snow. "The nurse told me in the winter they get you around in tunnels underneath the building. That sounds fun. Have you been in them?"

Jennie nodded.

"Is that how you get to hydrotherapy?"

Again she nodded, but Libby wasn't sure she was listening. She sighed. It was time to go. They were approaching the shortest day of the year, and it was getting dark already. "Grandma Brennan's coming on Wednesday with Zabby. I have to go now. I love you."

She stood up, kissed Jennie and left.

*   *   *

It seemed to take forever, but at last, Christmas break came. Every day Libby went downtown with Pepper shopping, and in the evening they went to the movies. On one occasion they doubled dated with some boys from Blake who took them skating on Lake of the Isles. The boys hoped to loosen their morals with hot toddies, but Libby and Pepper stayed close, remembering the night several months back with the parking attendants.

Libby tried to stay as busy as possible. It felt odd being home for Christmas. She had been with Jennie over the holidays for the past seven years. They had either traveled with chaperones or spent Christmas with other students out East, but they were always together. Oddly enough, Libby would be home this year with her own family, and she was dreading it. At least she had Pepper. Her parents were still out of town so she would come with her to Christmas at the Durants.

Libby was not sure she liked the Durant side of the family. They were stuffy, narrow-minded and boring. *You'd think with all that drinking they'd be fun, but no. They even manage to spoil getting pigeon-eyed.*

She hadn't seen any of them since her grandfather had died three years earlier. Her Uncle Grayson and Aunt Lavinia were hosting Christmas Eve this year. Aunt Bertie, the only Durant who had not married would be there as well as Aunt Grace and Uncle Owen, the brother who was paralyzed in a riding accident.

Libby corrected herself. There was one Durant she liked. It was Uncle Owen. He was fun.

Stepping into her green silk gown with cream lace, Libby carefully arranged a matching bandeau on her head and left for the Durant house on Lake of the Isles, picking up Pepper on the way. They arrived a few minutes before eight, and everyone was gathered in the parlor by the fire, having drinks. The women were in evening gowns, and the men were in swallow-tail coats.

Lavinia Durant, a tall, pencil thin woman with perfectly coifed, brown hair, kissed Libby's cheek. "Merry Christmas, dear. Look at you, all grown up." She stole a peek at Libby's arms and then quickly looked away. "And here's Penelope. Welcome."

Grayson Durant, a large man with a bald head, shook Libby's hand, as well as Uncle Owen, who was seated in a wheelchair. Although in poor health, Owen was still a good looking man with dark wavy hair and kind eyes. His wife, Grace on the other had was short and squat with thin hair and a sour face.

Aunt Bertie Durant did not bother to rise. The big-boned family matriarch thought Libby should come to *her*. She was the oldest sibling in the Durant family and had an iron grip on them all. Unattractive with excessive chin hair, Libby detested her. She always thought if someone was homely, they should at least be pleasant, but this was not the case with Aunt Bertie. The old woman cocked her head for a kiss on the cheek, and Libby reluctantly complied.

Uncle Owen said, "It's a holiday, let these girls have a drink, Grayson."

Pepper and Libby smiled.

Uncle Grayson called to the servant standing behind the cocktail caddy, "Two old-fashioneds, Robert. Make them sweet."

Libby looked around the room. It was beautifully decorated for Christmas. A tree was in one corner covered in glass ornaments and candles. There were garlands draped on the mantle and hanging from the chandeliers. The decorations added color to the heavy, dark wood paneling of the room and plum-colored drapes on the windows.

The family resumed their talk of business. They preferred speaking of lumber, hardware, and money over anything else. In their single-mindedness, Libby found them utterly boring and one-dimensional, except for Uncle Owen. He could speak on a variety of topics and never be dull. He obviously found the rest of them ridiculous and would look over at the girls, roll his eyes or pretend to gag. Libby and Pepper turned away, trying not to laugh.

"Shall we adjourn to the dining room?" Aunt Lavinia said at last.

The staff lit a fire, and they sat down at a long table set with crystal goblets, Limoges china, and sterling silver. Everything glistened. Libby didn't notice the opulence, and neither did Pepper. They had lived amongst it their entire lives.

They dined on Oysters Rockefeller, turkey with cranberries and riced potatoes. After dessert, when everyone went to the library for after-dinner drinks, Pepper and Libby snuck outside for a cigarette. They stood on the terrace in back of the house with their coats on, smoking.

Pepper handed Libby a small wrapped gift. "Give this to Jennie when you see her tomorrow. It's the same thing I gave you--scented soaps, but hers is lavender."

"Thanks, Pepper. I'll wait until she comes home though. Someone will steal it at the asylum."

Pepper blew out her smoke. "Whatever you think is best, Libs. Is Grandmother picking us up for Midnight Mass?"

"Yes, she'll be here soon."

Suddenly the French doors flew open, and Uncle Owen wheeled himself out to join them. He was in a long camel hair coat, and there was a blanket over his knees. His blue eyes sparkled. "Caught you smoking!" he roared.

They laughed, and Libby ran and shut the doors.

He lit a cigarette too and said, "So what are we talking about?"

"Grandmother is picking us up for Mass any minute."

"Olivia Brennan," Owen said wistfully. "Now there's a woman."

"Oh stop it, Uncle Owen. She's old enough to be your mother," Libby said.

"I love that old gal's attitude. She's not only good looking, but she's saucy and lives life on her own terms."

He spied the gift Libby was holding and asked, "For me?"

"No!" and she pulled it away. "It's for Jennie. I'm going to see her tomorrow."

"How is she?"

Libby shrugged. "I don't know, Uncle Owen. I think she's having a hard time."

"It happened so fast."

"I know it."

They were quiet a moment. Owen looked up at the stars. It was a clear but cold night. "Things can change in an instant. I ought to know."

The girls said nothing.

"But you know, I don't regret any of it. My legs are the only things that are paralyzed on me. That group in there," and he jerked his head. "They suffer something much worse, paralysis of thought."

"Uncle Owen," Libby said cautiously. "I'm confused. Are you actually grateful for the accident?"

"You are the first person who has had the courage to ask me that question. Yes, I *am* grateful. It has made me appreciate life, and since that day, I have never taken it for granted. You didn't know me before the chair. I was like the rest of them in there, a one-dimensional, hard-driving businessman who never laughed or enjoyed a thing."

Pepper blinked. "It's hard to imagine."

He took a puff on his cigarette and shrugged. "I'm glad you didn't know me then."

Snow started to drift down lazily, blurring the lights shining out from the house.

"So girls, don't let them tell you how to live. And I don't just mean the family. I mean everyone. They'll try, and it will be difficult because you're females, but set your course and stay on it. Never give in."

Libby stared at him.

A smile flickered on his lips. "Yes, Elizabeth Durant, particularly you."

Chapter 5

School resumed shortly after the New Year. Libby would sit in class and stare out the window, thinking about anything but academics. By March she was cutting class regularly. Grandmother Brennan was the only family member who cared if she stayed in school, and she was in Asheville for the winter.

The weather was warming up, and on nice days, she would change clothes, sneak away from school, and take the streetcar downtown. For hours Libby would walk and think. Uncle Owen's words haunted her. He had challenged everything she had ever been taught and dared her to think for herself. It was deliciously exciting and terrifying at the same time.

One of the first things she noticed were people on the street. All her life she had been surrounded by the privileged few and never saw beyond the fashionable addresses and well-bred socialites. She saw shopkeepers, soldiers and greengrocers, seamstresses and cab drivers, garbage men, children at play, clerks, and police officers. And there were the poor; hobos walking up from the rail yards, women and children sleeping under bridges, and drunks laying in the gutter, an entire world beyond her previously narrow existence.

She also thought about the women in the asylum with Jennie. They had lives and families who loved them just as much as she loved Jennie. Maybe they had children. Were they suffering, like she and Jennie had suffered?

Libby was ashamed of herself. For almost eighteen years she had believed the Durants, and the Brennans were the center of the universe. She chuckled. Most of her family still did.

She went to motion pictures, and for the first time, watched and read the newsreels. She went to the public library and checked out books that interested *her*. In the evening, she attended shows at the Gayety and the Orpheum sitting in the front row to get a closer look at the makeup and costumes. She became so engrossed that she forgot to enjoy the productions; she was too busy evaluating the makeup, beards, and wigs.

During the day, Libby ate lunch at a variety of establishments, deliberately avoiding extravagant venues. She had experienced gilded opulence far too many times. Her favorite spot for people watching was the Columbia Restaurant. It was in the oldest part of the city near the train depots. A modest little eatery run by a Swede, the Columbia was patronized by blue collar workers, clerks, travelers and even the occasional hobo buying a cup of coffee.

It was a rough part of town called, "The Gateway," filled with saloons and flophouses, but Libby didn't care. She believed if she went during the middle of the day when the streets were filled with travelers, shoppers, and merchants, she was safe.

The first time Libby walked into the Columbia, heads turned. She thought it was because her clothing looked expensive and she made a mental note to dress much simpler next time. But what they noticed could not be altered with a change of clothes. It was her good looks.

She sat by the window and ate the blue plate special, which on Tuesday was lutefisk with cream sauce and green peas. So this is home cooking, she thought. No fancy canapes here, no Lobster Newburg or caviar, just good solid food that warmed the belly and the soul.

But she didn't always go downtown. When the dull gray of the Minnesota winter was too much, she would go the other direction, to the Uptown area of Minneapolis to eat at a cozy café with lots of windows. The bright, cheerful colors gave her a lift, and the bustling atmosphere woke her up.

At last, Libby came to a decision. If she was going to broaden her horizons and educate herself further, a formal education would only get in the way. She would not return to Northrup. Let Grandmother Brennan rebuke her; she was done.

One afternoon in April, after returning some books to the library, she stopped in Peter's Grill downtown. It was a small, unpretentious restaurant with tables, wooden booths, and excellent food. She sat down and ordered coffee and a piece of chocolate cake. Taking a bite, she sat back relishing the taste. This was so much better than English class or physical education, she thought with a smile.

She felt someone staring at her. It was a young man sitting at a table nearby. He nodded a greeting and returned to his turkey dinner. Libby ran her eyes over him. He appeared to be in his mid-twenties, had short dark hair and was dressed in working man's clothes.

He looked up at her again, wiped his mouth and asked, "May I join you?"

Libby considered it a moment and then nodded.

He grabbed the napkin out of his lap, picked up his plate and slid into her booth. Reaching over the table to shake hands, he said, "How do you do? I'm Rudy James."

"Libby Durant."

"Pleased to meet you. You live here?" and he looked down at her ring finger. "Miss Durant?"

"I do. And you?"

He took a bite of mashed potatoes and nodded. Swallowing quickly, he replied, "Yes, I'm just home from France."

"The war?"

"Yes, I was hit with mustard gas." He turned his head and ran his finger down his right cheek. "See the burns?"

Libby leaned in to look. "Barely."

"I cover them with stage makeup."

"Stage makeup?"

He nodded. "I work down at the Orpheum. I'm a carpenter. You know, sets, rigging, that sort of thing."

Libby took a sip of coffee and looked at him. This young man was suddenly very interesting to her. He was attractive *and* worked at the Orpheum.

"How about you?" he asked. "You work downtown?"

"No, I'm sort of in school right now."

"Seeing as it's one o'clock in the afternoon, I would say 'sort of' too," and he grinned.

Libby noticed his dimples.

"What school?"

"Northrup."

"Oh, hoity-toity. You a rich girl?"

"Are you poor boy?"

He laughed. "Alright, I deserved that."

He took another bite, and as he chewed he studied her face.

Libby lit a cigarette. "What's wrong?"

"Nothing," and he smiled. "In fact, nothing at all."

Libby felt herself blush and changing the subject asked, "How did you end up at the Orpheum?"

"My folks were in vaudeville. They had a song and dance routine, and we went from city to city. It's a hard life, and it killed them both. My uncle got me the job here at the theater a few years back, and I worked there until the war came."

"And now you're home again."

"Now I'm home."

He looked up at the clock. "Holy smokes, I'm late!" He threw his napkin onto the table and stood up. "You like photoplays, Miss Durant?"

"Who doesn't?"

"Have you seen, 'Society for Sale'?"

"The new Gloria Swanson? Not yet."

Reaching into his pocket, he tossed some money on the table and said, "You wanna go tonight?"

Libby stared at him a moment. She had met him only minutes go, but throwing caution to the wind, she said, "Yes, I live at 720 Grove Avenue."

"Down by Loring Park?"

"On Loring Park."

His eyebrows shot up. He opened his mouth to say something, reconsidered and stated. "See you at 7:30."

That evening much to Libby's relief, Mrs. Zabek retired early. She knew she would think it unsuitable that she was going out with a stranger so when Rudy James walked up the front steps, she darted outside.

"Well, hello," he said with surprise. "I didn't even have time to knock."

"I just happened to look out and see you," she replied.

Rudy was dressed in a clean but threadbare brown sack

suit, and tan vest. Under her spring coat, Libby wore a blue, pleated skirt with a sailor sweater.

They walked downtown. Hennepin Avenue was alive with activity. Automobiles chugged by, their engines sputtering. Streetcars rolled past, clanging their bells alongside wagons and buggies. Men lounged in doorways smoking, well-dressed couples stepped out of automobiles heading into restaurants as shop girls stepped off streetcars to see shows. Grocers and merchants finishing up for the day, rolled up their awnings and pulled their wares inside.

"I suppose you're used to being picked up in automobiles," Rudy said as they dodged pedestrians.

"I haven't had time to get used to anything," she replied. "I've only been home since summer. I was away at school for seven years."

"Why did you come back?"

Libby looked at him, caught off guard. Being from different backgrounds, he knew nothing about her family. It was an immense relief. "My mother died, and my sister has been sick, so I came back."

"There's been too much dying lately," he added.

Libby knew he was referring to the war.

"Did you have to take a streetcar to pick me up?"

"No, I am close enough to walk. I live with my Uncle Saul, just on the other side of the Basilica."

"On the Northside?"

Rudy nodded.

"Does he work at the Orpheum too?"

"Yes, he's the head carpenter there," he said, taking her elbow as they crossed the street. "The whole family is in show biz. My mother's side are Jews from Germany. They were all in the theater back in the old country. She came to America with her brother—the set carpenter, and she got on the vaudeville circuit singing and dancing."

"Were both parents in the theater?"

He nodded. "That's where they met. My father was a comedian. He was raised Christian, and his family wanted nothing to do with my Jewish mother or any of us kids."

Libby made no reply, knowing that is how her family would react.

At last, they arrived at the theater. Rudy purchased their tickets, and they walked inside. The Pantages was lavishly decorated with gold leaf, plaster swags, sculptured floral designs, and chandeliers. But Libby was more intrigued with what happened behind the scenes, not out front. When they sat down, she recognized the overweight woman playing the organ. She had been to the Pantages, Orpheum, and Gayety so many times, faces were becoming familiar to her. On impulse, she asked, "Would you get in trouble if you brought me backstage at the Orpheum?"

Rudy looked surprised. "Sure, but you'll be disappointed. All the magic is out front."

"Not for me."

He shrugged. "Alrighty then."

Moments later, the music from the organ swelled, the lights went down, and the movie started. In no time, Libby was lost in the story with the light flickering on her upturned face. At first, she didn't notice Rudy's shoulder pressing against her own. And then she saw him stealing looks at her in the darkness. A warm glow crept up on her cheeks. She liked him and found him attractive. His physique was robust and his muscles hard. Libby guessed it was from hard work, and when he smiled, he had deep dimples.

After the show, Rudy said, "The stagehands go to this late night place down by the Lumber Exchange called The New Palace. You feel like a cup of coffee?"

"I do," Libby replied, buttoning her coat. She liked that

he was not trying to ply her with liquor. Instead, he offered her coffee and conversation.

The cafe was nothing more than a long narrow room with a punched tin ceiling. A glass display case sat up front, filled with cigars and candy. White cloths covered round tables with wooden chairs. The restaurant was deserted, and they sat down by the window, ordering coffee.

Lighting Libby's cigarette, Rudy asked, "So you look like a girl who'll go to college."

She shook her head. "College is not in my future."

"Then let me guess," he said. "Marriage to a rich Minneapolis businessman?"

Again she shook her head. "Maybe for some girls but not for me."

The waitress walked up and poured them coffee.

"What about you?" Libby asked, tossing a spoonful of sugar into her cup. "Will you stay at the Orpheum?"

"Definitely. Someday when my uncle retires, I'm going to run that shop. I love what I do."

Libby searched his face. "I want that sort of passion. I want it so badly, I can taste it. Now I just have to figure out what it is."

"Well, it's a start. You have a passion for a passion," and he laughed. "You are an unusual girl. You think for yourself."

Libby liked the sound of that.

They sat for over an hour talking until Rudy looked outside and said, "Welcome to spring in Minnesota. It's snowing. We better get you home before the streetcars quit for the night."

They jumped on a deserted streetcar and minutes later they were on Libby's doorstep. Rudy put his arm around her and pulled her close. "I've been wanting to do this since I met you this afternoon," and he kissed her.

Libby leaned in, pressing herself against his coat. She had wanted to kiss him too. When he pulled back, his hot breath turned to vapor in the cold night air. "People from our worlds don't mix, Libby Durant. You're dangerous for me."

She smiled.

"But I know that I won't be able to stay away."

"Then don't," she replied and went inside.

*   *   *

"What are you going to tell Grandmother?" Pepper asked Libby as she was cleaning out her locker at Northrup.

"I don't know yet."

"Don't forget to add that you are dating a Jewish carpenter from the Northside whose family are theater people. Geez, Libs, can you get any more rebellious?"

"I know, but he sure is good at kissing," Libby replied.

"Knowing *your* history, he's better at more than that."

Libby smiled and slammed her locker shut.

They were indeed doing more than kissing. Libby and Rudy had been seeing each other for weeks. Rudy had not pressed Libby into intimacy, but her attraction to him was so strong that, she not only allowed his caresses, she encouraged them.

Three nights a week, they met at his home when his uncle was at work. He was the first lover to satisfy her. Until now, she had always been with boys who were in a rush to gratify themselves; Rudy always made sure Libby was having fun too.

But once again she was worried about pregnancy. Her measures of prevention were far from reliable. A girl at Beardsley Hall had been to an underground clinic and given Libby some birth control, and although the device helped, it was certainly not foolproof.

Nevertheless, she was happy for the first time in a long

time. Rudy was the first young man to capture her attention. She thought about him constantly. He was fun, attentive and a good listener. Not only did they share a bed, but they shared each other's hopes and dreams. Not often, but sometimes they spoke of their fears and pain.

It took several dates, but at last Libby told Rudy about the family illnesses, and he spoke of his experience in France. He was self-conscious about his burns; Libby was embarrassed about her scars. When she told him her mother had inflicted the wounds, he was stunned, and she was equally horrified when he explained the circumstances under which he had been gassed. She realized that Rudy's lungs had been compromised. When they lay quietly together, she could hear a slight wheeze in his breathing.

They saw each other almost every day, even if only for coffee late at night. Rudy's hours were unpredictable. Sometimes he worked during the day and sometimes well after midnight, tearing down and building sets for traveling acts, skits and musical numbers. Spring was a particularly busy time of year, but at last, he was able to take her backstage.

"Mornings are the best time," he said. "No one will be around before eight."

Libby was beyond excited. He took her down an alley through the stage door and into the theater. Backstage was indeed different from out front. It was like opening a beautiful music box and examining the intricate mechanism buried inside.

After coming in from the sunshine to darkness, she was blinded. "I can't see!" she said, laughing.

Rudy took her hand. "No windows backstage Libby and much of it is painted black."

At last her eyes adjusted. They walked out on stage, and she was able to look out at the front of the house.

Her jaw dropped. "So this is what *they* see."

"Maybe someday it will be you out here performing," Rudy said.

"No, I love watching but not acting. Too much like school—all that memorizing."

Rudy continued to show her backstage. There were ropes on pulleys attached to sandbags, lights hanging everywhere and walkways crisscrossing the ceilings which he called "catwalks."

And when they went downstairs, Libby was amazed. There was an entire world a floor below, dark and with low ceilings. It looked like a medieval dungeon. There were pipes running overhead, boilers, stacks of boxes and crates.

Libby tried to commit to memory everything she saw, grilling Rudy with questions.

"Here's my area," he said, at last, opening a door to a workroom. It looked like an ordinary carpenter's shop with tools, benches and saw horses, smelling of sawdust and paint, but these projects were far more fanciful than building houses. There was a half completed façade of a ship, a gazebo and the face of a large dragon.

At one end were two huge doors. "Those doors are for getting the sets out. Much of our time is spent on stage putting it all together," he explained.

"What are you working on now?"

"A plantation backdrop for Jolson's blackface routine."

"Al Jolson?"

"The very one."

"You want to see costumes now?"

"Yes!"

"It's limited though, Libby. We don't have our own company here. Most of the acts bring their own costumes and props."

He unlocked the door to a room that had racks of

clothing, hats, fans and boxes of costume jewelry.

Libby gasped. She dashed over and combed through everything, running her hands over the fabric, trying on wigs and pushing bracelets up her arms.

Rudy watched her and then looking over his shoulder, he grabbed her. "We'll come here late some night and dress you up like Cleopatra. Then we'll have some fun."

"Is that what you like? Not someone demure like Juliet?"

"No, I want a vixen," he declared, slapping her backside. "It's getting late. Ready to see the dressing rooms?"

"I certainly am!" This is what Libby had been waiting for, and her stomach jumped.

They walked down the hall, but when Rudy opened the door and turned on the lights, she was disappointed. They were just empty rooms with dressing tables. Large bulbs lined the mirrors flooding the tables with light, but the counters were clean.

"Where's the makeup?"

Rudy looked at her with surprise. "The theater doesn't supply makeup. Each actor brings their own. Didn't you know that?"

She shook her head.

Rudy could see she was disappointed. "You really need to be here to watch them apply it. I'm sorry."

She shrugged. "It's nothing. Either way, I loved the tour. Thank you," and she squeezed his hand.

As they walked to the stage door, Rudy said, "I wish I knew some way to get you into see them."

"You don't know any of them?"

"No, they are here only one or two nights and then on to the next city."

"That's alright. I could never put the makeup to use.

It's not like I want to be an actor or anything. Who showed you how to cover the burn on your cheek?"

"A dancer who was here for a few nights. She's long gone," Rudy replied. "Hey, why don't you get a job here? Then you could sneak in and watch them."

"Me? That's a laugh. I've never worked anywhere."

"You have to start sometime. You could try out for some bit parts."

"Acting?" Libby frowned. "No thanks."

"Can you dance?"

"No."

"Work in the ticket booth?"

"Terrible at making change."

"Sew?"

"Ha!"

Rudy scratched his head. "Clean?"

Libby raised her eyebrows. "I could learn that."

"Done," he said. "I'll ask Mr. Daniels what he has available."

"I don't want to use my real name."

"Alright, who do you want to be?"

"Um, Libby--"

Suddenly a short, squat, balding man in a derby came through the stage door.

"Mr. Daniels!" Rudy said.

"Hello, James," he grumbled, passing them.

"This young lady is a friend of mine," Rudy called after him. "And she's looking for a job cleaning."

Mr. Daniels turned around, came back, looking her up and down. Pulling the cigar from his mouth, he asked in his gravelly voice, "What's your name?"

Libby murmured it.

"Libby what?" he barked.

When she didn't reply, Rudy jumped in with the first

name he could think of. "Dworsky. Libby Dworsky."

"What the hell? Let her speak for herself, James. Where do you live?"

Libby drew a blank. She couldn't say Loring Park. He would recognize the neighborhood and wonder why a rich girl would want a job cleaning a theater. Then she remembered the neighborhood where she drank with the parking attendants and blurted. "Bryn Mawr."

Mr. Daniels puffed on his cigar and stared at her. The smoke was so thick, Libby had to stifle a cough.

"I know of it," he said. "A good solid, little neighborhood. We've got a girl sick—so there's a temporary opening. Be here Monday at 8 a.m., Dworsky."

"Yes, sir," she replied.

Libby had her first job.

Chapter 6

Libby followed Mrs. Zabek around all weekend watching her clean. She pretended to be visiting, but she was actually taking notes of how she dusted, scrubbed floors, how she used the carpet sweeper and even followed her into the bathroom to watch her clean the tub, sink, and toilet.

These were all things she had taken for granted. She had never appreciated the back-breaking labor involved in making things sparkle until now. Mrs. Zabek kept stealing looks at her wondering why she was following her, but she said nothing, enjoying the company.

The next day was Sunday, and like every other Sunday, Libby visited Jennie at the asylum.

"It's a beautiful day," Jennie's attendant said. "Would the two Miss Durants like to have their visit outside?"

"Is it--is it alright?"

"It most certainly is. Your sister has had no incidents now in almost a month. I think it's time. Her treatments are going so well."

Libby looked at Jennie. "It is a beautiful spring day. Shall we sit outside?"

Jennie smiled. "I'd like that."

Libby's heart jumped. Although her reactions were slow, Jennie seemed grounded and not plagued by voices. Every week she seemed a little better. *Could she be coming out of the fog? Is it possible to even hope for recovery? Oh to have her home again!*

The attendant said, "I'll just get my paperwork and come out with you."

Jennie put a sweater on over her gown and walked outside with Libby. It had been months since she had been out of the locked ward, and she squinted in the bright sunshine. They sat down in wooden lawn chairs placed on the grass. There were trees, walkways, and two flower gardens. Several of the patients were out already, some in wheelchairs, others on the arms of attendants. Libby noticed brick boxes about knee high scattered around the park area. They had little mesh windows in them. "What are those?" she asked the attendant.

"They're ventilation and light for the tunnels that run from cottage to cottage," she replied.

"Very ingenious," Libby observed.

The attendant pulled her chair away to give them privacy and placed it under a tree. Sitting down, she opened a file and began doing paperwork.

Libby turned back to Jennie. "Shall I read to you?"

"No," Jennie replied slowly. "How about I read to you?"

Libby's jaw dropped. "Really?"

"Really."

Libby handed her the book. "Do you remember where we left off?"

"I do."

For over a half hour, Jennie read to Libby from *Ethan Frome*. Although her speech was slow, her inflection was correct, and she seemed to understand the story. Libby was thrilled. She studied her sister while she read. She was thin, and the bones of her face protruded but there was color in her cheeks once more, and her lips were pink again. The skin on her hands no longer looked like tissue paper, and the blue veins were no longer as defined. There was no question; she was getting better.

At last, Jennie dropped the book onto her lap and sighed. "I'm getting tired, Libby."

"Yes, you read for a long time."

"When am I going to meet your new beau?" she asked.

Libby's jaw dropped, and she laughed. All the times she had spoken of Rudy, she didn't think Jennie had heard her. "Well, I hope soon. Keep getting better, and you can come home and meet him."

On the train that night, Libby felt like singing. She hummed a tune knowing the noise of the train would cover the sound. Maybe life would get back to normal. She knew that normal was having Jennie nearby. She had never had anyone else. They had been companions all through childhood and been best friends all through school.

Libby had supper that evening in the carriage house with the Axelmans and Mrs. Zabek. Excitedly she shared the good news about Jennie. They were overjoyed.

"She actually read to you?" Mrs. Axelman asked.

"Yes," Libby replied, taking a bite.

"Was she seeing anything strange?"

"Only the words on the page."

They sat back and sighed with relief, looking at one another.

"*Tak*, this is good news," Mrs. Zabek said.

There was an air of celebration at supper, and they spoke of many things, talking, laughing and teasing each other.

"And how about you, *Elskede*?" Axel asked. "How is school?"

Libby had not told them about Northrup. "Fine," she said, dropping her eyes. She hated lying to them.

Mrs. Axelman looked up from cutting pie and said, "Have you made friends there?"

"Just Pepper."

"Has there been--" and Mrs. Zabek hesitated, knowing about the incident in the gymnasium. "Teasing about your mother?"

"No, nothing like that," Libby replied, shifting in her chair. "Let's talk about something else."

Mrs. Zabek exchanged looks with Mrs. Axelman. She announced, "Margot, the housekeeper at the Summit house, says your grandmother is returning at the end of May. That's good news."

"Oh, that is good news," Libby said with a half-smile.

That obviously wasn't a good subject either.

Suddenly Mrs. Axelman thought of something that Libby would like, "Axel, put a record on the Victrola."

"Good idea," he replied, rising from the table. He put on "The Maple Leaf Rag," and started dancing around stiffly, snapping his fingers.

Libby started laughing.

"Oh sit down, you old Norwegian fool." Mrs. Axelman said.

The music changed the tenor of the conversation, and Libby was back to feeling light-hearted again. They listened to several more recordings, and then she kissed them all goodnight.

For the first time since she had returned home, Libby did not dread climbing the stairs to her room. Even though it was lonely up there and every move she made seemed to echo, Jennie would be home soon to fill the void.

She dropped into a chair, lit a cigarette and looked around. There were no phantoms, no fleeting glimpses of her mother passing in the hall, no eerie sounds. The painful memories which had haunted her for months had at last ceased. She was moving on with her life, and when Jennie returned, they would create new memories. They would bring youth and vitality to the house again and sweep away the cobwebs of melancholy.

Remembering that tomorrow was her first day on the job, she put her cigarette out, undressed and dropped into bed. How would she do? Would she make a mess of things? Would she get confused with all the duties?

All in all, she didn't really care. She was getting backstage. She fell asleep dreaming about dressing rooms filled with performers stepping into costumes, strapping on shoes and transforming their faces from the mundane to the extraordinary with makeup.

*   *   *

Libby arrived at the Orpheum fifteen minutes early. For the first time, she felt like she was a part of the world. Day in and day out most people rose from bed, had coffee, dressed and went to work. Now she would do that too. There would be no more school, and no more staying away from the house pretending to be in school.

Housekeeping was in the basement and when Libby walked in an elderly woman sitting behind a desk looked up. She had gray hair and was smoking a cigarette.

"Dworsky?"

Libby nodded.

"I'm Mrs. Hitchcock, head of housekeeping. The locker room's through that door. Put on a uniform."

Libby changed into the gray, baggy uniform and returned to Mrs. Hitchcock. The room smelled of stale smoke and cleaning supplies. The ceiling was open with plumbing pipes overhead, and there was a loud rumbling noise. Libby assumed it was the boiler.

Mrs. Hitchcock squashed out her cigarette and rose stiffly from her chair. "We'll keep you on only until the regular girl returns. Understood?" she said gruffly.

"Understood," Libby replied. She only wanted to be here long enough to observe the performers a few times anyway.

"Grab a bucket of supplies. We'll get started."

The housekeeper seemed bored as she walked Libby through training. Everything she said seemed like rote, and she droned it out mechanically. Nevertheless, Libby was thrilled to be backstage and seeing every detail up close.

All morning long Libby used the carpet sweeper cleaning the lobby and then swept the floors between the seats.

In the afternoon, Mrs. Hitchcock sent her backstage. "Start in the men's dressing room. But hurry up. They'll be getting here soon, and they won't want to wait for you to finish."

Although she was getting tired, Libby was glad to be backstage at last. She pushed her cleaning cart into the dressing room, wiped the counters, and swept the floors. As she was emptying the trash, she noticed several empty containers of makeup. She picked them up and turned them over, examining them and memorizing the name of the manufacturer.

Suddenly she heard someone say, "Pretty good lookin' in that uniform."

"Oh! You scared me, Rudy."

He was leaning in the door wearing overalls and a tool belt. "I can't stay. Uncle Saul is crabby today. But I just had to see you."

He dashed over, kissed her and ran out, his tool belt jangling.

"See you tonight," she called after him.

Libby pushed her cart to the women's dressing room next. When she opened the door, five little dogs rushed forward to greet her.

"Oh hello!" she exclaimed, dropping down to pet them.

"I wish everyone was like you," a middle-aged woman said. She had masses of dyed blonde hair and was wearing a robe with an Oriental pattern. "Most of these killjoys around here don't like 'em. That's why I have to come early."

"You have a dog act?"

"Yes, we do. They walk the tightrope *and* do arithmetic for the audience."

"Smart dogs," Libby said, running her hands over them. She stood up and asked, "Do you mind if I clean?"

"Have at it, doll."

Libby started wiping down the tables, wanting to ask the woman a thousand questions, but she was unsure whether she should speak with the performers. She saw the woman open a battered leather case and take out several sticks of greasepaint. She had dark circles under her eyes, heavy wrinkles in her forehead and laugh lines on her cheeks. Wondering if she could conceal these imperfections, she stood back and watched her.

First, she applied a base of skin-colored makeup, set it with powder and with an expert hand dabbed on another color to lighten the bluish circles under her eyes. Next, she highlighted and shaded her eyelids, concealed her wrinkles, set it with more powder, contoured her face under her cheekbones and applied a bright red lipstick.

It was a miracle. Although the makeup was extremely thick, the woman looked ten years younger.

"All done," she announced. "Now I need to get dressed and get out before those little bastards arrive."

She stepped into a brightly colored, tight-fitting

costume and asked, "Can you hook me, honey? Damn, it gets harder every year. I guess I'm getting old."

Libby stepped over and hooked the back of her costume. "Thanks, sweetie. Come on, kids," she said to the dogs. "Let's get outta here."

The dogs scurried out, and she shut the door.

Libby finished sweeping and just in time. The other performers began arriving, and there was a flurry of activity everywhere. On weekends when there were non-stop performances she would have to work around them, and that is exactly what she wanted. She could watch and learn.

At the end of the day, her back ached, and her feet hurt, but she was satisfied. Libby was starting to understand the magic of the theater.

*   *   *

That Saturday, the dressing rooms were filled with performers doing several shows a day. There were jugglers dressed like clowns, children who tap-danced, comedians and singers. They were all crammed in the dressing rooms, vying for the mirrors. There were costumes, props, and chaos.

"I need this table," a young woman barked, pushing a singer aside. "I'm on next."

"Make way for true talent," the slighted singer announced, "She dances holding a chair in her teeth."

Everyone laughed.

"Very funny," the dancer said in her Bronx accent. "It takes skill."

Libby walked around them, picking up trash, emptying waste paper baskets, watching and listening.

Most of the makeup they did was routine, women enhancing their looks, but occasionally one would do a clown face, dress as an exotic from the East, or even an animal. Those were challenging and sometimes involved facial hair, spirit gum, and putty. It fascinated Libby to watch the techniques, and she was amazed at the diversity of talent among the performers. Many of them could sing, dance, sew their own costumes *and* apply their own makeup. Others were not so clever. Their looks were amateur with makeup applied improperly and ill-fitting wigs.

She also noticed many of the performers seemed old, tired and their costumes were faded. Life on the circuit was apparently hard.

Nevertheless, Libby was young and just getting started. She loved the world of illusion, and she was determined to be a part of it one way or the other.

After work one afternoon she stopped at Harvey's Theatrical Supply and bought several boxes of Leichner's stick makeup, French's powder, some cheesecloth, spirit gum and artificial hair. She was going to try theatrical makeup at home.

She experimented for hours, starting out with enhancement on herself, looking in Vogue Magazine trying to duplicate some of the looks. Throughout the week, she had Pepper come over, and she made up her face up several times. Some of the looks were for every day, others were glamorous evening applications. Pepper loved trying on the various wigs Libby had purchased too. Libby would stand over her and style them different ways from conservative to flamboyant.

Rudy even allowed her to put makeup on him several nights a week at the theater after the performers had left. The first night she made him up as a Shakespeare character and another night she experimented with facial hair, making him look like an old man.

"You're good at this and getting better, Libby." Rudy said, peeling off a mustache she had applied. "When are you going to try something really difficult, like turning me into an animal or a monster?"

"I'm not ready for that yet," she said, handing him some cold cream. "But did I tell you that I've started a portrait painting class?"

Rudy smeared cream on his face. "You've decided to paint?"

"Not really. It will help me to study the lines and angles on faces and the shadows too."

"Good idea. How did you ever think of that?"

Libby shrugged. "I think up this stuff when I'm not thinking of you," and she dropped down onto his lap.

Laughing, she started kissing his face full of cold cream, smearing it all over her own.

Libby also spent hours learning to conceal her scars. Rudy shared some of his techniques, and she developed some of her own. She shadowed the bulges, so they weren't as prominent and highlighted the undamaged skin nearby. She lightened the discolored areas blending the pigment into surrounding skin, so the jagged lines disappeared.

"I think I'm ready," she told Rudy one afternoon. "Before we go out today, I'm going to put makeup on my arms and roll up the sleeves on my shirtwaist."

"Good, I think it's time. If I can do it, you can do it."

They spent all morning at Rudy's house. He rented the upstairs from his uncle which consisted of a sitting area with a bedroom and sink. It was a modest two-story stucco home in a neighborhood on the Northside of Minneapolis settled by Jewish Americans. It was the first working class home Libby had ever experienced. To her, it was small but cozy. On the first floor, there was a small parlor with a fireplace, a dining room with a buffet built into the wall and leaded glass windows. The house always smelled good, like someone had just cooked a hearty meal there. Libby wondered why the people she knew needed such big houses. There was more than enough room here to live comfortably.

Libby's presence was a secret from Uncle Saul. She had seen him only a few times at work, and he never seemed to have noticed her. Not only would he disapprove of Rudy having a young woman in his rooms, but he wanted him to date only Jewish girls. The divide that crossover marriages created was distressing to him.

"Are you hungry?" Rudy asked, buttoning his shirt after they spent the morning in bed. There were clothes thrown everywhere and dirty dishes on the floor. "Or should we do it again?" he said, grabbing her breast.

"Stop it," she said, pushing him away and laughing. "Yes, I'm hungry but not for that. Let's go back to Brochin's Grocery. But I want to cover my arm with makeup first."

She sat down at Rudy's desk, opened her kit and applied the makeup.

It was a bright sunny day in May, and Libby knew the glaring light would be the true test of her skills. They walked down Lyndale Ave, and several shoppers passed them on the sidewalk. No one took notice of her scars.

At Brochin's Deli, the reaction was the same. Three elderly men with long beards sat at a table in the corner, reading Yiddish newspapers and looked up for only a moment when Rudy and Libby walked inside, paying no attention to Libby. The owner, a slim, balding man in a white apron, took their order and Libby deliberately reached up over the glass meat case to take their corned beef sandwiches. With instructions to watch his reaction, Rudy reported that the man took no particular notice of her scars.

Feeling satisfied, Libby said, "Let's eat outside. It's such a nice day."

They found a park bench and settled in for lunch. Just as she reached up to take a bite of her sandwich, a woman walked by with a little boy. The child slowed his pace staring at Libby's scars.

She sighed and dropped her arms into her lap. "Back to the drawing board."

Rudy nudged her. "You're almost there, kid."

Libby continued with the trial and error, and at last, she found a technique that blended away most of the noticeable disfigurement. She tested it several times in public, and it seemed to disguise the scars well. She was overjoyed. This was a major accomplishment.

With each passing day, her skills in makeup and wigs increased. With the help of a book she found called, *The Art of Theater Makeup*, the painting class and her experimentation on Pepper and Rudy, she was improving.

The housekeeping department kept Libby at The Orpheum for over a month. Gradually she gained confidence approaching the performers for makeup tips, and every free moment, she asked them questions about technique. Sometimes they would demonstrate application for her, and sometimes they allowed her to work on them. She worried she would get caught and fired, but after a while, she didn't care. She was not there to clean but to learn.

One Saturday afternoon while she was wiping down dressing tables, a family came in. Since men were not allowed in the women's dressing room, the man stood in the doorway watching his teenage daughter helping her mother into the bathroom. The mother was leaning heavily on her daughter's shoulders.

Libby could hear the woman retching in the bathroom, and she looked at the man.

"She eat something bad," he said in a thick Italian

accent. "We have a show in an hour."

"What do you do?" Libby asked.

"Comedy skit."

Eventually, other female performers came into the dressing room, and the door had to be shut. Libby had other areas to clean, but when she returned, the woman was on a cot in a corner behind a Chinese screen. She was still sick.

"Damn it," Libby heard one of the chorus girls bark. She pitched down a stick of makeup and said, "It looks like hell. I'm sorry, honey." She had been trying to apply makeup to the daughter of the sick woman. The girl was dressed like an elderly lady, and there was a gray wig on the dressing table.

The girl started to rub off the makeup and said quietly, "That's alright. I can try to do it myself."

"It's getting late. You better hurry," one of the acrobats said. Then she noticed Libby. "Say, was that you working on makeup with Adelaide the other day? As I recall you were pretty good."

"That was me," Libby answered.

"This kid is taking her mother's place in the show and has to play an eighty-year-old lady. Do you think you could do her up?"

Libby's heart began to pound.

"The guy on stage has one more song, and then they're up."

Libby could hear someone onstage singing, 'I'm Forever Blowing Bubbles.'"

Swallowing hard, she nodded. "I can do it."

"You've got ten minutes until curtain."

"Alright."

Not giving a second thought to the scars on her arms, Libby rolled up her sleeves, washed her hands and stepped up to the dressing table. Opening jars, arranging sticks and powders, she got started.

The female performers gathered around to see if she could do it in time.

After applying a base coat of makeup, Libby told the girl, "Frown for me."

The girl scowled, and Libby quickly filled in the wrinkles between her eyebrows and in her forehead. Next, she highlighted the same wrinkles to give them a three-dimensional look.

"Now smile," she said.

When the girl smiled, she drew in laugh lines, and with a brush of dark powder, she contoured in sunken cheeks. Next, she added dark circles under the eyes, made the brows gray and set it all with powder.

"Less than five minutes left," one of the performers said.

Libby took a gray wig off the stand and anchored it with spirit gum. Next, she brushed powder quickly around the wig line to make it look natural.

There was a knock on the door. "One minute, Sally!" the girl's father shouted.

With a comb and a few quick adjustments, Libby arranged the girl's hair and pushed her out the door.

The women applauded.

"Where the hell did you learn that and that fast?" one asked. "You have talent, honey."

A heavy set, aging singer, declared, "Eureka! At last, someone to make me look twenty years younger and forty pounds lighter!"

They all laughed.

It was the best day of Libby's life. She didn't know what she was going to do with her newfound talent, but at last, she had found her passion.

*   *   *

After that day, Libby's reputation was set. As new acts

hit Minneapolis, they passed the word about her talent and performers asked for her help and advice. It was tricky keeping it a secret from housekeeping, but in the end, it didn't matter; the girl she replaced was returning soon anyway.

"Are you sad about it?" Jennie asked when Libby visited her the following Sunday. They were sitting in the courtyard.

"No," Libby replied, taking her hand. "Because I can be with you now that you are coming home."

That afternoon when had Libby arrived, the nurse told her that they would be releasing Jennie in two days. No more locked doors, she had been moved to an unsecured cottage.

"I would much rather be with you," Libby said.

Jennie smiled. Her reactions were no longer slow. She had put on weight, and she seemed grounded in reality. Libby noticed that she had regained her beauty again.

"Is Grandmother back from North Carolina?" Jennie asked.

"No, she's in Chicago. Aunt Mary is sick again."

"Is it her spells?"

Libby nodded.

"I don't know how she does it," Jennie said. "Grandmother is always taking care of one of her sick children."

Libby liked what she was hearing. Jennie was aware of other people's feelings again.

"I had a dream about mother last night."

"Jennie, let's not talk about her."

"It was a good dream though. Mother told me that she is at last released from the demons. She looked so beautiful, Libby. Remember the happy times when she was healthy?"

"Yes, I try to remember, but it's hard."

"I loved it when she would dress up and go out. Now that I'm an adult I can appreciate her beauty."

Libby smiled. "I remember her gowns and her perfume."

"I bet that's how Grandma Brennan looked when she was young."

"Speaking of Grandmother, I have to see if her driver can bring me here to pick you up on Tuesday."

"I can't wait," Jennie said.

Libby hugged her and left.

*　　　　*　　　　*

With news of Jennie's return, Mrs. Zabek and the Axelmans burst into action, shopping, cooking and cleaning. Libby contacted Grandmother Brennan sharing the good news and arranged to have the driver from the Summit Avenue house take her to Anoka.

Tuesday morning, the chauffeur picked Libby up, and they set out for Anoka. Libby was beside herself with excitement. She hadn't realized until now how lonely she had been for her sister.

Earlier that day she had called the asylum and confirmed that they would be picking up Jennie at noon. All the way up, Libby fidgeted. She thought about the late night talks she would have with Jennie, suppers with Zabby and the Axelmans, and having her sister sleeping again in the next room.

But the closer she got to the asylum, the more uncomfortable Libby became. She rubbed her forehead. Why was this happy time being ruined with this ominous feeling? Something didn't feel right.

Suddenly she remembered last Sunday. Jennie had dreamt about her mother. "Mother told me that she is at last released from the demons."

Libby gasped.

She leaned forward and said to the driver, "Please hurry," and they picked up speed. When they pulled up to the asylum, a large iron bell was clanging on top of the administration building, and attendants were running back and forth across the courtyard.

Libby jumped out and stopped one of them. "What's happening?"

The nurse ignored her and kept running.

Panicked, Libby grabbed the arm of an attendant and asked, "Is my sister, Jennifer Durant alright?"

The young man blinked and said, "Of course she is. Come with me."

Taking her elbow, he whisked her up the stairs and into an office. "Please sit down. Doctor Iverson will be with you shortly," and he dashed off.

Libby dropped down into the chair, her chest heaving. The bell stopped ringing, but the pandemonium on the grounds had agitated the patients. Some were shouting nonsense, others were laughing hysterically while others wailed. The atmosphere was surreal.

She jumped up and started to pace. When she looked outside, all activity had ceased in the courtyard. No staff was around.

Suddenly the door opened, and Dr. Iverson came into the room. He was wearing a white coat and a serious expression.

Libby stared at him.

"Miss Durant, I have some distressing news."

Chapter 7

Libby clutched her chest and stared at Dr. Iverson.

"I'll get you some water," he said, stepping out the door.

This cannot be happening. I'm having a nightmare. Jennie is still alive. Only two days ago, she was fine.

A hundred feelings swirled around Libby like malevolent phantoms. She sat on the edge of the chair staring straight ahead, trying to make sense of it.

Hospitals make mistakes all the time. Yes, that's it. They've confused her with someone else.

"I think there's been a mistake," she stated when the doctor returned. "My sister's name is Jennifer Durant. She is going home today."

The doctor shook his head. "I'm sorry."

Libby continued, "She is in your unsecured cottage."

Young Dr. Iverson looked down and shook his head again. At last, he said, "I was not her attending physician, but I worked with Jennifer several times. There is no question. It was your sister, Miss Durant. But, of course, if you want to identify--"

"How?" Libby blurted. She said it so loudly, she almost

shouted. "How did she do it?"

The blood drained from Dr. Iverson's face, and he dropped his eyes, burying his hands in the pockets of his lab coat. Looking up again, he said, "We aren't sure the exact time she left the cottage. But a few moments before noon, knowing you were on your way, one of the nurses went to get her. When she couldn't find Jennifer, she notified us and we put the facility into a lockdown while we searched." He took a breath and said, "We found her hanging from the overhead pipes in one of the tunnels."

"Oh, my God!" Libby screamed, and she jumped up, covering her face. "Oh dear God!" and she started to sob.

*   *   *

Libby hated her mother. Jennie's words haunted her. "Mother told me that she is at last released from the demons."

She had been the cause of Jennie's death. Her words had caused her death as sure as driving a knife into her heart. She had killed her with the promise of serenity in the beyond. Would that woman's violence never cease?

Mrs. Zabek went upstairs to check on Libby in the middle of the night and found her sitting in her mother's room in the dark. The drapes were open as if she had been looking out the window at the pond below.

"My little girl, what are you doing?"

Libby did not respond. She didn't even know Mrs. Zabek was there. "Come to kitchen. I will make warm milk."

She took Libby by the shoulders and guided her out of the room and down to the kitchen. She moved like a sleepwalker.

Mrs. Zabek muttered to herself, "This house is wicked," as she opened the icebox.

Taking the night train from Chicago, Olivia Brennan arrived the next morning and took Libby to her home on

Summit Avenue in St. Paul. She announced that the house on Grove Avenue was not good for her. It had too many memories.

Libby remembered nothing from the funeral. The family tried to keep the service as quiet as possible, but the reporters were relentless. Libby did not come out of the fog until a few days later. When she was cognizant enough to write Rudy a note, she told him what had happened. All of the papers carried the story, but she knew he seldom read the dailies.

Libby was glad to be at the house in St. Paul. It was a grand, sprawling Tudor Revival home with twelve bedrooms and seven baths, more than enough room for her to have privacy, but not be alone. It had lots of light, and the design was not as heavy and foreboding as the home on Loring Park.

The bedroom was a decidedly feminine room with pink floral wallpaper, a white coverlet on the bed and fringed lampshades. Although the woodwork was dark, the windows were large, and there was no stained glass. Natural sunlight flooded the rooms making everything cheerful.

And there was also more activity. Libby's Uncle Roger, his wife, and three children lived there too. Libby could hear the children in the morning getting ready for school and their laughter in the afternoon when they played in the yard.

Nevertheless, she spent a great deal of time sleeping, and she was listless, showing little interest in anything. Grandmother Brennan wanted her to return to school, but Libby refused.

She would sit and look out the window for hours, agonizing over Jennie. Her life had been so short, and she had experienced so little. She had never been to a dance or even been on a date. Libby doubted if she had ever been kissed. And she would never experience motherhood, but maybe that was just as well. Libby wondered what happened to the children of the patients at Anoka. Who took care of them? When her mother got sick, Zabby was there or the Axelmans. Who took care of the children of the poor? She rubbed her forehead. She couldn't worry about that now. She pulled the drapes and went back to bed.

One morning when she was drinking coffee in the breakfast room, the housekeeper handed her a telegram. It was from Rudy. He was worried about her. He wanted her to meet him somewhere—anywhere.

Libby didn't want to go. She replied, telling him that she needed more time. The next day there was another telegram saying that he would be calling on her within the week. She guessed it was an idle threat, but she could not take a chance. She agreed to meet him after work the next day outside the Orpheum.

Forcing herself to bathe and dress, she looked in the mirror for the first time in weeks. She had lost weight, and her complexion was gray. Before Jennie's death, she would have pulled out her makeup and transformed herself, but today she didn't care. She actually hoped Rudy would find her unattractive and leave her alone. She was far too tired to try to entertain him anymore.

Libby no longer wanted challenges. Before Jennie's death, she would have relished her independence and taken a streetcar over to Minneapolis, but now she just wanted what was easiest, and had the driver drop her off at the Orpheum's stage door.

Rudy was waiting anxiously for her with his hat in his hand. When Libby stepped out of the automobile, his smile faded. She was thin, ghostly white, and sallow. He took her hand and kissed it, searching her face. Any other time, he would have hugged her, but she seemed cold and aloof.

"Hello, Libby."

She mustered a smile. "Hello, Rudy."

"I—I'm sorry about Jennie," he said haltingly. "I'm tongue-tied. I don't know what to say."

"Don't say anything. I don't want to talk about it anyway."

"Alright," he said quietly. "Shall we walk down to The Palace?"

She nodded.

The Palace was busy, but they found a table in the back. Rudy ordered a sandwich, but Libby had no appetite. She just ordered coffee. Rudy shared news about work and the latest shows at The Orpheum. He also told her how much he missed her.

"The performers coming through still ask for you. Their world is smaller than you think. You've established quite a reputation for being talented at makeup."

Libby nodded and looked down at her coffee.

When she raised her eyes again, she noticed that Rudy was beginning to look frazzled trying to keep the conversation going. She felt sorry for him and asked, "How is Uncle Saul?"

"Fine, fine. He's in his glory. He has us working on a Moulin Rouge set for an Eddie Cantor number. Uncle Saul knows Cantor."

"Really?" Libby replied, trying to sound interested. She just wanted to go home and go back to bed.

When Rudy finished his sandwich, he said, "I have a surprise for you."

"What?"

"I bought a Chevrolet."

Libby's eyebrows shot up. "You own an automobile?"

"I do. Wanna go for a ride?"

For the first time, Libby's eyes brightened, and she smiled. "Yes!"

Encouraged, Rudy paid the bill, and they walked back to where he had it parked behind the Orpheum. It was a shiny, black Royal Mail Roadster.

"It's only a 1914, but it's what I could afford."

"It looks new to me," Libby said, running her gloved hand over the fender. "It looks fine, just fine."

"Get in," he said, opening the door.

Libby stepped onto the running board and slid into the car. Rudy walked to the front and turned a lever a few times. He came back adjusted some controls by the steering wheel, cranked the car again, and it started. Hopping behind the wheel, he said, "The top's down. Hold onto your hat. Here we go!"

Away they went down Hennepin Avenue rolling past shops, saloons, and The Basilica of St. Mary. "Where are we going?" Libby shouted over the roar of the wind and the chugging of the motor.

"How about around the lakes?"

"Alright!"

They wheeled around Lake of the Isles, past the homes of some of Libby's friends, rode over a little bridge and careened around Cedar Lake until at last Rudy pulled over. "We're getting into the country now. You want to drive?"

"Oh no, I don't know how."

"Time to learn," he said gaily and jumped out.

"Not today, Rudy. I'm--"

He opened her door. "Get out."

She slid out and got behind the wheel.

"Now, there are three pedals on the floor," he said, and he explained their functions. "And here's the throttle." He pointed to a lever on the steering wheel.

"What's a throttle?"

"That makes the car go."

"Show me where the brake is again," he stated in review.

She showed him.

"Alright, let's go. Push in the clutch."

Libby swallowed hard. She was nervous but thrilled to be trying.

"Now slowly move the throttle—that's right--the one on the steering wheel. Move it down, to go forward and let the clutch out slowly."

Libby got flustered. The car lurched and killed.

"Try it again," Rudy said.

Libby tried again, and it killed again. After the third try, she started to laugh.

Rudy laughed too. "Let's do it again. You'll get it."

This time, they took off, and Libby was driving. She gripped the steering wheel rigidly and stared straight ahead, biting her lip. They drove past the lake, by open fields and along railroad tracks gradually picking up speed.

"How do you like it?" Rudy shouted.

"I love it!" she replied.

After a while, he said, "We need to go back now. Your driver comes at six. Pull over here."

Libby pulled over. When she stopped the car, he took her face in his hands and gave her a big kiss. "You did it!"

"Yes, I did."

Libby was elated. It was the first time in weeks she had forgotten her sorrow and had fun. They traded places again, and Rudy drove back to the Orpheum.

Moments before the driver arrived, she kissed him. "I had a wonderful time today. Thank you."

"You realize I'll be hounding you now to come out again."

"I hope you do."

*   *   *

Libby continued to have good days and bad days. There were times she could not rise from bed and stayed under the covers all day, but other days, she went for walks, spent time with Pepper or went out with her grandmother. Gradually she emerged from the despair and became active again. She knew her grief would never vanish, only lessen.

Rudy hounded her to take up makeup again, but she seemed to have lost interest. Nevertheless, he was determined. He knew it was her passion, and that kind of talent should not be ignored.

"I'm going to keep on asking you until you come back," Rudy said one afternoon in his room after a tryst. They had reignited their affair, and Libby visited his house several days a week.

She stopped putting on her stockings and looked at him. "Rudy, give up. It's been over six weeks since I've been down there. It's almost August. They've forgotten all about me."

"No, they haven't. Granted, everyone is busy telling horror stories about this flu, but we can remind them again. I've seen them. So many are awful at makeup. The women end up looking like clowns, and they aren't even in comedy. They need you."

"Even if I wanted to go back, how would I let them know? I don't work there anymore."

Rudy put his hands behind his head and laid back onto his pillow, his bare chest uncovered. "Let me think."

Libby went back to dressing.

"I still work there so--" he said, considering all the options. "Hey, I could give them flyers—even better cards! Have some cards made up."

"I don't know if that's enough," she replied, slipping on

her shoes.

"How about a booklet of sketches or even snapshots showing your work?"

"Grandmother does have a Brownie camera," she admitted.

"A portfolio!" Rudy said, sitting up. "That's it. I can show them your portfolio."

"How will they get in touch with me?"

"Just show up. Every day as they're arriving, stop in to see if they need you."

"This sounds like a lot of work."

"Anything worth doing involves hard work and ingenuity. How do you suppose your grandparents made all that money?"

Libby finished combing her hair and said, "Come on. Let's go. We'll talk more later."

*   *   *

Rudy did not let up. He hounded her constantly, and several times, they ended up in a fight. But gradually Libby regained her interest in makeup and wigs. She had Pepper over to the house on Summit, made her up and took snapshots. But she noticed the makeup changed drastically with the camera, so she began mixing her own makeup, adjusting the colors.

She had supplies strewn all over her dressing table one afternoon when Pepper arrived. "Gosh, Libs. What's all this?"

"Carmine, lard, gelatin, rosewater, fuller's earth--"

"You sound like a chemist."

Libby laughed. "If I'd taken chemistry in school, I would have hated it, but in this setting I like it. I'm trying to create my own colors that work for the camera."

"Gelatin? Cotton? And yuk, this looks like fish skin," Pepper said.

"It is. I'm experimenting with putting weight on an actor's face when they're playing someone larger than themselves. I'm going to turn Rudy into Falstaff tonight."

"Speaking of Rudy, I like him," Pepper said. The three of them had lunched together Saturday. "When are you going to introduce him to the rest of the family?"

"This family? When hell freezes over. We're having fun now. I'm not going to ruin it."

"He *is* your biggest fan," Pepper said picking up a small tub of lard and grimacing.

Libby laughed. "Poor misguided fool."

"Libs," she said, suddenly turning serious. "Are you two in love?"

Libby stared at her a moment. "No, we know it can never last."

"But if it could?"

Sitting down on the edge of a chair, Libby reflected a moment. "Rudy may be the nicest person I've ever met but-_"

"But?"

"But I don't think he is the great love of my life."

Pepper nodded. "Nevertheless, he has faith in your talent."

"Yes, and he thinks I should charge the performers when I do their makeup."

"Well, of course, you should charge them."

"You can't be serious! I'm just learning."

"Poppycock. You're a pro now."

"You really think so? Rudy says they won't take me seriously if I don't make them pay."

"He's right. You don't have to make them pay an arm and a leg but charge them something."

"Well," Libby said, frowning. "Alright."

All week long with the help of Rudy she worked on her

portfolio. She had pages showing standard enhancement makeup for men and women, clown makeup, Shakespearian, 18th Century aristocrats, exotics, elderly and even a few animals. When photographs weren't suitable examples, she did sketches.

She had business cards made and purchased a makeup case with several tiers and drawers. At last, she was ready.

"Today is the changing of the guard," Rudy said one morning after a tryst at his house. "New acts will be coming in this afternoon. Are you ready?"

She took a final puff on her cigarette and said, "I'm ready."

Dressed in a white shirtwaist and plain blue skirt, Libby carried her makeup kit and a white apron under her arm.

The theater was filled with performers. Rudy unlocked one of the single dressing rooms reserved for the headliners. "Use these rooms to make up the men. They're usually vacant. Now, go get 'em, kid," he said and left.

Libby took a deep breath and walked into the women's dressing room. It was loud and chaotic and filled with smoke. Women were chattering and laughing, sitting at the mirrors, stepping into costumes and fussing with props.

Her palms were perspiring, and her knees were shaking. She cleared her throat and announced, "Ladies, may I have your attention!"

Everyone kept talking. No one noticed her.

Libby swallowed hard. This was going to be difficult. She had to get their attention somehow. She spotted a gong in the corner. She picked up the mallet, hit it and jumped onto a chair. The sound reverberated around the room.

Everyone stopped talking and looked at her.

"Who wants to look ten years younger?" she shouted. "I'm Elizabeth Durant, and for a nominal fee, I'll make you beautiful for your performance."

The women stared at her.

Libby held up a piece of paper. "Sign up here. But do it quickly, I have appointments at the Pantages today too."

The moment she stepped down from the chair several women came up and started asking questions. While she was answering them, others were signing up for appointments. After she had passed out cards, she grabbed a table, put on her apron and opened her box. Her first appointment, a singer, sat down, and Libby got started.

Libby was busy all afternoon and barely had time to do makeup for the men. As suspected, they were more difficult to convince. Too embarrassed to admit that they wanted to look younger or more attractive, standard stage makeup was good enough for them. Nevertheless, one performer hired her to make him look Chinese for a comedy skit, and a young magician asked for a more mature look. Everyone seemed satisfied with their results.

Libby did not really have appointments at the Pantages, but it she thought it made her sound as if she was in demand. But by the next week, performers at that theater and the Shubert and Orpheum in St. Paul actually started requesting her, and on two occasions she worked at the opera as well.

Every day of the week she had appointments, and for the first time in her life, Libby felt as if she had purpose. The demand for her increased every day, and it consumed her life. She was either doing makeup or traveling on a streetcar going somewhere to do makeup.

Since most of her work was in Minneapolis, she moved back to her home in Loring Park. But this time the gruesome memories and nightmares did not plague her. She fell into bed every night too exhausted to even think.

"I know you are on the go all time. What is it you are doing, Elizabeth?" Grandmother Brennan asked one afternoon at the Kaiserhof, an elegant restaurant in downtown Minneapolis.

"I'm still involved with my painting and art," Libby replied, putting her guard up. She didn't want to lie, so she chose her words carefully. "I have a sort of studio where I work. That's where I spend most of my time."

"I would like to see your work sometime."

Knowing her grandmother frequented the theater, Libby smiled and said, "Oh, you will."

Their food came, and Grandmother Brennan changed the subject. "I met with the family attorney yesterday. "Now that you are eighteen and in light of what just happened--" and she paused, not wanting to mention Jennie's death. "You are now the sole owner of your parent's estate. This includes not only money but the house on Grove Avenue."

Libby nodded, feeling uncomfortable.

"It is a great deal of responsibility, Elizabeth. And I must warn you. Be wary. There are many predators out there looking to make a profitable marriage."

"I'm not interested in marriage."

Olivia Brennan's eyebrows shot up. "Well, you should be. It is your duty to the family."

Libby made a face. "Why?"

"You need to carry on the line."

Libby took a sip of her tea and chuckled. "Honestly, Grandmother, you act like we're royalty."

"Successful merchants *are* America's royalty."

"Theater is where the royalty is now," and she took a bite of her salad.

Olivia's eyes flashed. "You *would* say that!"

"What?"

"I know you're hobnobbing with theater people, doing their makeup and God knows what else. And I also know that you are dating a Jewish carpenter."

Libby's jaw dropped.

"Our world is smaller than you think, Elizabeth Durant. I have known for some time. You will stop this frivolity immediately. Theater people are *not* the sort of people we frequent. They are low and common."

Libby was thunderstruck. For this first time, her grandmother sounded like a pompous hypocrite. She blurted, "How soon you forget, Grandmother. Low and common is just how they described the Irish." Libby picked up her purse and left.

Chapter 8

Libby's success only lasted a few months. An epidemic called The Spanish Flu gripped the country, and everyone was advised to avoid large crowds, the theater included. Ticket sales dwindled, the front of the house was empty, and acts were canceled. Everyone was terrified, the pandemic had reached epic proportions and was spreading. Everyone was at risk, not just children and the elderly.

Libby and Rudy strolled around Lake of the Isles one fall afternoon, both of them too preoccupied to notice the brilliantly colored leaves at their feet. Libby tried not to look at the crepes hanging on the front doors signifying a death in the family, gray for the elderly, black for someone middle-aged, and white for the young.

"Things can change so quickly," Rudy said. "When they closed all the theaters in New York and Chicago we had every big name performing here. It was wonderful."

"I know it. Never in my wildest dreams did I think I would be doing makeup for Elfie Fay or Trixie Friganza," Libby added.

"But it has dwindled to almost nothing."

"I haven't bothered to go down there in a week."

"And tonight is the Orpheum's last performance."

Libby stopped and looked at him. "Rudy!"

He nodded. "They're closing all public places. Uncle Saul is housing performers. They have nowhere to go.

"Are they closing theaters out West too?"

"They are. We have magicians, dancers, and actors scattered all over the living room floor. They can't pay for rooms if they can't work."

He put his arm around her shoulders, and they walked again.

"Are you sharing your room too?" she asked.

"Yes with two brothers who do a comedy routine."

Libby thought of the sprawling houses her family owned, and guilt twisted her stomach. People were homeless, but life went on as usual in the Durant and Brennan gilded mansions.

"Same time day after tomorrow?" Rudy said, at her doorstep.

"You have time?"

Rudy shrugged. "Unfortunately I have lots of free time, and it's good to get out of that house."

Libby shut the door and sighed. The world was suddenly a very different place. She took off her hat and gloves and went into the kitchen. Zabby looked up and said, "It will just be you and me for supper tonight. Axel is feeling poorly."

Libby's eyes widened. "Oh, Zabby. It's not--do you think?"

The plump housekeeper looked down. "We will pray, little girl."

Libby didn't ask any more questions. After supper that night, she looked out the window at the carriage house. A light was burning in the Axelman's bedroom. She slept a few hours, rose and looked out again. The light was still on.

Worried, she went downstairs to wake Zabby, but she was gone. Pulling her wrap closely around herself, she walked up to the carriage house. She knocked, but there was no answer. When she walked in, she could see a light coming from the bedroom and voices. Someone was crying.

Her chest tightened, and she looked in the room. Axel was on his back, ghostly white with his mouth open. He was not moving.

Libby froze.

Zabby had her back to the door, and Marta Axelman was sitting on the bed with a hankie to her nose. She looked up and exclaimed, "Oh, *elskede*, our Axel is gone!"

"No!" Libby cried, dropping to her knees and hugging Marta. With tears streaming down her face, she repeated, "Tante, oh, Tante."

*　　　　　*　　　　　*

That morning the undertaker took Axel's body away. Caskets were in short supply, but Libby and Zabby finally found one in Northeast Minneapolis for Axel's remains. Funeral directors were far too busy to locate one.

"It happened so fast," Libby said to Zabby in her sitting room that evening. It was a small cozy parlor with a fireplace and two easy chairs. Tante had gone to stay with her sister in St. Paul until there was word of the funeral.

"Yes, he was fine in morning and suddenly the fever. Next thing, he couldn't breathe, and he was gone. I can't understand it," Zabby said, shaking her head. "And now we wait until they can find time to bury him."

"I called Aunt Bertie," Libby said. "She said she would make some phone calls to help move things along."

"Good, good."

Libby was stunned. Her family was gradually slipping away from her, and it was chilling.

She looked at Zabby. There were rings under her eyes too, and for the first time, Libby saw gray hair mixed with the red. Zabby is losing her family too, Libby thought, first my mother, then Jennie and now Axel.

When she kissed her good night, she said, "Don't go out if you don't have, Zabby. I'm starting to think it is a good idea they are closing everything down."

The next morning as Libby was coming down to breakfast, Mrs. Zabek was hanging up the phone. "That was your Grandmother Brennan calling from Chicago. She said not to go near the house on Summit, your Uncle Roger and the children have the grippe now."

"No! How bad are they?"

She shook her head. "We won't know for a while."

All morning Libby helped Zabby clean the carriage house so Mrs. Axelman could return to a clean home. Days passed, and there was still no word on Axel's funeral.

Time seemed to stand still. Libby read, experimented with wigs or visited with Zabby, but she was growing anxious. Libby had gone from working day and night on her new business to almost complete inactivity and isolation. She would talk on the phone to Pepper and occasionally to Rudy, but several of the performer's had contracted the flu, and he was busy.

One afternoon the phone rang while she was upstairs reading. When she came down Mrs. Zabek's face was pale, and she seemed flustered.

"What is it, Zabby?"

"My brother is sick."

Libby searched her face. "The flu?"

Zabby nodded. "Will you be alright if I go, little girl?"

"Of course, I will be alright. I am not your little girl anymore."

Zabby patted her cheek. "You always will be my little

girl."

At noon the next day, Zabby was on the train to Mora, and for the first time in her life, Libby was all alone in the house. It was an odd sensation. She was glad she was seeing Rudy in the afternoon. "I own this damned house, and it still gives me the creeps," she muttered.

Libby thought it felt close and stuffy, so she opened some windows. She wanted the house smelling fresh since she would be bringing Rudy back to see it after their ride. She rubbed the back of her neck as she walked up to her room. The muscles had been bothering her all morning, and she wondered if she had slept on it wrong.

Lighting a cigarette, she started pulling clothes out of the closet. Rudy was picking her up in an hour, and she wondered what to wear. Everything she put on felt too heavy and warm but a last she decided on her indigo blue tailored jacket and skirt.

She looked in the mirror to adjust her makeup, and the first thing she realized was that she needed no rouge; her face was flushed. She brushed on some powder, wrapped a scarf around her head and was out the door.

Rudy looked sharp in his cable knit sweater when he pulled up in the automobile. Libby hopped in, kissed him, and they drove off. Ordinarily, she loved riding, but today she couldn't get comfortable.

When they arrived at Minnehaha Falls, she went over and sat down on a bench right away. Rudy sat next to her, putting his arm around her. "I've missed being with you. Uncle Saul's house guests are putting a damper on our love life."

"I know, but I have good news. I have the house to myself."

"What?"

"You can come to *my* house for a change."

"No one's home?" Rudy said with a gleam in his eye.

"Not for days," Libby said, easing the cigarette from his fingers and taking a puff.

"Well, I'll be damned. This is the best news I've heard in a long time," and he and pinched her backside.

"Some things are going to change now that I have come of age, and if I want to have you as a house guest, I will."

"Not up to your room though," Rudy said with hesitation.

"No, I wouldn't do that to Zabby, but you can call on me."

"Well, since she's not there, let's get back now and test drive your bedroom," Rudy said.

When they returned to the house, Libby had him park under the *porte-cochère*. "I'll give you the grand tour," she said with a smile as she unlocked the front door.

Rudy was in awe. "I've never been in a mansion before."

"Oh, don't talk like that. It's just a house. Are you hungry?" she asked as she pulled off her scarf.

"I could eat something."

As Rudy followed her to the kitchen, he looked around at the plush furnishings, paintings, and stained glass, but what he truly appreciated was the artistry of the woodwork. "What company did the finishing work here?"

"Golly, I don't know. Is it alright?"

"Alright!" Rudy said laughing, "It's--" but he stopped. "Don't you feel well? Your face is flushed."

"I'm alright."

When they stepped into the kitchen though, Libby slid onto a stool and leaned heavily onto the counter. "Just help yourself to anything in the icebox. I am starting to feel pretty rough."

Rudy stared at her. "Maybe I should just help you up to bed."

"I'm not *that* bad," she said, but she put her head down.

"Yes, we are going up," he said taking her arm. As they approached the stairs, Libby's legs buckled, and he had to carry her the rest of the way.

Rudy was scared. He had no idea who to call or how to even find the phone numbers. The housekeeper was gone attending to her sick brother, and Libby said her grandmother was in Chicago with her aunt who was in an asylum. He knew the grippe could take a life in a matter of hours so, with no time to lose, he rolled up his sleeves and made ready to take care of her.

He started to undress her. "Where do you keep your nightgown?"

"Rudy, go home. I'm just tired." But she was as limp as a rag doll.

"Are you going to deny me the chance to be your hero? Is there someone I should call?"

"Why would you need to call anyone?" she asked.

"Libby, this might be the Spanish Flu. I want you to know the truth, so you can get ready to fight."

"No, it's not. I'm fine," she murmured as he eased her back onto the pillow.

He brushed her hair back. She was burning up with fever. "You are a little trouper," he said with a half-smile.

"Did I ever tell you, I love your dimples," she slurred.

"You sound like a drunk. Now be quiet and rest while I get some cloths to cool you off."

Libby watched him walk out of the room. He had said she should get ready to fight, but she was so tired, so very tired. She decided to sleep, but something caught her eye, and she looked around the room. Her lips parted. *Oh no! I have to tell him there's been a mistake.* She tried to call for him, but the words would not come.

When Rudy returned, Libby had lost consciousness. She had been trying to tell him that he had placed her in her mother's bedroom.

*　　　*　　　*

Libby slid in and out of consciousness for two days. At last, when she woke up, a woman in a white uniform was standing over her. Libby looked around. She was in her own bedroom, but who was this person?

"Drink this," the stranger said and helped Libby sip some water. "I'm Miss Ingram, your nurse. You look so much better. You have survived the flu."

She eased Libby back down. "Where's Rudy?"

"Rudy? I don't know any Rudy."

"Your Grandmother has been calling several times a day though. She has been very worried. I was hired by one of the other Brennans in town here."

"Who?"

"I believe they live on Park Avenue," the woman replied.

"Pepper's parents," Libby murmured.

"Now you rest. You need to get your strength back."

It took several days, but Libby recovered. The Durants and Brennans paid a steady stream of nurses to attend to her, and at last, she was able to go downstairs to make some phone calls.

"Eat something first, Miss Durant," the nurse suggested. "And then make your calls."

"Alright." She wasn't going to argue. She was hungry.

Libby was sitting in the library eating lunch when the nurse told her she had a phone call.

"Libs?" the voice on the other end said. "It's Pepper. Jeepers, it's good to hear your voice."

"Hello, cousin. Thanks for sending someone to take care of me and tell your parents thanks too."

"You sound weak, but the nurse says you'll be fine."

"I am fine. How did you find out I was sick?"

"Rudy called us."

"He did?"

"Yes, he called us the day after you got sick. I don't know how he found our number. He took care of you all through the night and well into the next day. He's a good guy, Libby."

"He is. I'm going to call him right now."

"See you soon?"

"See you soon."

Libby hung up and dialed Rudy's number. She had never called Uncle Saul's house before, and a man with a foreign accent answered the phone. Libby didn't know if it was Uncle Saul or not.

"May I speak with Rudy please?"

There was a long pause.

"Hello?" Libby said, thinking the call had been disconnected.

"Rudy can't come to the phone. He died last night—the flu. Who is this?"

Libby didn't answer.

Chapter 9

Upon hearing the news, Libby had a relapse. Her appetite diminished, and her strength waned. When she was at last strong enough to come downstairs again, she didn't know who to call about Rudy's funeral. All of her contacts were through the Orpheum, and it was still closed. At last, she decided to dial the theater hoping that someone might be there who could give her information. A building maintenance man answered and told her they had buried Rudy a few days ago. Tears filled her eyes, and she stammered a thank you, hanging up.

Libby felt lost. She had been with Rudy for less than a year, but in that short time, he had become her best friend. His death left a hole inside her almost as large as the void left by Jennie. A knot formed in her stomach that she knew was not illness. It was loneliness and a nagging feeling of abandonment. Where was everyone? Even during her illness and recuperation she only had strangers around her.

She missed Axel too. He had been like a father to her. They had buried him while she was sick. But at least Zabby's brother had survived, and the Brennan children had recovered as well as their father.

"You are very lucky. The papers say young people are hit the hardest by the grippe," Zabby said one afternoon as she brought lunch in on a tray for Libby. She was sitting in the library with a blanket over her knees.

"Yes, so lucky," she said, blowing out her smoke. She didn't care how Mrs. Zabek interpreted her remark. Her grief was now turning to cynicism.

Mrs. Zabek put the newspaper down and returned to the kitchen. Libby took a bite of her sandwich and opened it. The front page was still covered with articles about the armistice, and there were more photographs of people celebrating all over the world.

She read a few articles, closed the paper, and lit another cigarette. The world was celebrating; she could not. The war ending only reminded her of the bitterness she felt about Rudy's death. Somehow he, and thousands of other young men managed to survive the battlefield only to return home and succumb to the flu. Life was so cruel.

Libby threw the blanket off her knees and walked to the window. It was a cold November day. The sky was slate gray, and the trees bare. The wind was strong, and it looked like it may snow. The thought crossed her mind to light a fire, but she dismissed it. That would be too much work. Everything seemed like too much work.

She turned and looked around the room. It was the coziest room in the house yet it still felt cold and empty. Her whole world felt cold and empty. Jennie and Rudy were gone, Grandmother Brennan was in Chicago nursing family members, and Pepper was busy with a new beau. Zabby and Mrs. Axelman were still here, but she needed more. She had to have her own life and her own direction.

Libby sighed and sat back down rubbing her head. *What now? What now?*

*　　　*　　　*

It was well into December before Libby could put her grief aside and think about her future. She paced in her room struggling to find a way to fill her world again.

The flu had at last subsided, and public places began opening up once more. Schools were back in session and theaters reopened, so Libby started going out. She was glad to leave the house. There was a heaviness here that was pervasive. She knew if she remained it would eventually kill her, so she walked. She walked through Loring Park and around Lake of the Isles. She walked uptown and downtown. She revisited her favorite haunts, The Columbia, Miller's Cafeteria, and even Peter's Grill where she first met Rudy. And gradually she started looking outside of herself once more. She looked into people's faces and saw happiness and joy but sometimes grief and despair, the same despair and loneliness she felt. She noticed sick and poor people huddled in doorways, under bridges and in gutters, people stricken with disease like her mother and Jennie. Many of them babbled to themselves or talked to phantoms. Some had children with them. And again she wondered what happened to those children if the parents were put in asylums, became violent, or took their own lives.

One afternoon after having coffee at one of the cafes, Libby wrapped her muffler around her face and walked down to the Gateway District. Sitting down on a park bench she watched the hobos walking up and down, stomping their feet to stay warm. She saw a woman waving her arms and shouting at someone who was not there, her little girl cowering nearby on a bench.

Libby squeezed her eyes shut, trying to think. Her thoughts returned to her own life. What was nagging her? Should she take Grandmother Brennan's advice and marry? It was the safe route and one that was expected. But then she remembered Uncle Owen telling her to never give in and set her own course.

She had to think, but the wind off the Mississippi River was too cold. It numbed her fingers and burned her skin, so she started walking again on Hennepin Avenue.

A Mabel Normand comedy was playing at The Apollo Theater, so she bought a ticket and went inside, happy to be in where it was warm. The movie was a good escape for Libby, but the moment it ended and the lights came up, the ennui returned.

Everyone gathered their coats and started shuffling out of the theater. Libby was walking behind two men, and she heard them talking. "Moving pictures is what everyone wants nowadays," one of them said.

"Ya, vaudeville's all washed up. The movies is where things is fresh and new. They ain't afraid to try new stuff."

"I'd like to try new stuff like Mabel Normand."

"Aw, she's nuthin'. Give me Theda Bara any day."

The men stepped out onto the street and were gone, but their words stayed with Libby. "They ain't afraid to try new stuff," kept going through her head.

It was dark, the street lights were on, and the avenue was slushy from melted snow. She barely noticed the streetcar when it pulled up in front of her. She stepped onboard, paid her fare and sat down. Staring out the window, she saw nothing, but she could still hear the words, "They ain't afraid to try new stuff."

Moving pictures were indeed the grand experiment. Everything was fresh and new, expanding and evolving. Ideas and techniques were still in their infancy and movies *were* the next new American phenomenon.

At last Libby knew where life had been leading her. She was going to take her box of illusions, go out to California and make her mark in the motion picture industry.

*   *   *

She didn't know where to start, but she was determined to make it happen. One thing she knew for sure was that she had to achieve her success without the help of the Durant fortune or reputation. Minneapolis and St. Paul were still considered small Midwestern towns, so she didn't have to worry about name recognition, but there was the money. It would be easy to use it to open doors, and she refused to fall into that trap. She did not want to spend the rest of her life wondering if her success was earned or bought. She would do it herself or not at all.

A week later, Olivia Brennan returned to town and, as usual, came to take Libby out to lunch. Enough time and trouble had passed since their last meeting, and they had called a truce.

"Thank God you're well, Elizabeth," Grandmother Brennan said, kissing her. She looked chic in a gray silk day dress with a wide ruched waistband. "You're a bit thinner, but your color is good."

"At last, I have my strength back," Libby replied, pulling on her gloves. "So the Brennans fared well, Grandmother. Everyone survived."

"Thank the dear Lord. I wore a hole in my rosary," Olivia replied, stepping into the automobile. "Donaldson's Glass Block, please," she said to the driver.

They shopped at the large department store, nicknamed The Glass Block because of its multitude of windows, dining afterward in the Japanese Room. It had colorful lanterns with tassels overhead and carved Oriental paneling.

"I received a call from your Aunt Bertie Durant," Grandmother Brennan said, taking a sip of tea. "A prominent businessman is interested in buying your home."

Libby looked up with surprise. "Really? Someone wants

the old monster?"

"Yes, a funeral home director wants to turn it into a mortuary."

Libby started to laugh. "How appropriate!" She stopped a waiter and asked, "May I have an ashtray please?"

Grandmother Brennan straightened up. "Elizabeth, ladies do not smoke in public."

"This lady does," Libby said, as she opened her cigarette case.

Olivia pursed her lips and continued. "Bertie and I believe it is too much house for you, so we have decided to accept the offer."

"Oh, you have, have you? Well, thanks for consulting me," she said sarcastically. "But I don't care to sell."

"I beg your pardon?"

"I have other plans for the house."

"What sort of plans?"

"I have been speaking with the family attorney about turning the old relic into a home for children. Mr. Gustafson is drawing up the necessary paperwork and putting me in touch with people who know how to establish a foundation."

"Have you lost your mind!" Olivia gasped.

Libby took a puff of her cigarette and smiled. "That's what my family does best."

"I find your humor offensive."

"The foundation will house children who are homeless because their parents are in asylums. I will be donating the house and the bulk of my estate to this endeavor. The house will be turned into a sort of orphanage."

Olivia started to laugh. "Oh and I suppose you'll roll up your sleeves and minister to these children?"

"No, I will have no part in it. I am moving to California

to work in motion pictures."

"What?" she gasped. "This is madness. I forbid it!"

Libby did not respond. She ashed her cigarette and continued to smoke in an unconcerned manner.

"Now you listen to me, young lady. I am tired of you and your rebellious attitude."

Just then the waiter stepped up and served their lunch. Libby started her soup.

"This will stop, and you will find a young man to marry, and settle down."

Libby put her spoon down carefully, looked up and said, "Things may have been different if you had just been around more, Grandmother. I may have listened to you. But I have learned to be independent. The family gave me no choice. I will no longer allow you to sweep in here three times a year and tell me how to live my life. I will be moving to California before the month is out."

Olivia Brennan was stunned, and she stared at Libby. At last, she raised an eyebrow and started buttering her popover. They sat rigidly, saying nothing the rest of lunch. When the meal was over, Grandmother Brennan opened her handbag, took out a cigarette and lit it.

Surprised, Libby looked up at her.

Olivia said, "I think Zabby and Mrs. Axelman would make excellent employees at this new home."

Libby smiled. "I agree."

"You're a Brennan to the core, Elizabeth. You're a fighter, and you think for yourself."

"It was actually a Durant who told me to think for myself," Libby replied.

"*And* you're a contrarian. Who told you that?"

"Uncle Owen."

"That doesn't surprise me. He was always trouble."

"He thinks you're fascinating," Libby said.

Olivia arranged her cuff. "He's trouble, but the man has impeccable taste."

*   *   *

Libby may have given the bulk of the estate away, but she was no fool. She kept just enough money so she could live comfortably for a year while she built her business. Well aware that this padding was more than some people had in a lifetime, she gave it little thought; she had earned every penny the hard way, being a member of the Durant and Brennan families.

It took well over a month to organize things for the foundation, settle on a mission statement and set long term goals but, with the help Gustafson and Sons, her attorneys, she found the right people to establish the home. Realizing it could take over a year to put things in order, she decided not to stay in Minnesota any longer, spring was approaching. Correspondence could be done via the phone, the post, and Western Union.

There were tearful goodbyes with Zabby, Mrs. Axelman, Pepper, and Grandmother but, at last, Libby was on the train for Los Angeles. She purchased a private compartment with a sofa which converted into a bed, and she had her own private toilet as well.

The moment the train pulled out of the station a sense of elation overwhelmed her. For the first time in her life, Libby felt completely free. She had broken the bonds of the family, shed the nagging worry of madness and was starting a new life. Indeed, she was alone, but she could now surround herself with new people, people who knew nothing of her past, people who had no expectations of her. Libby had not known it, but she had been waiting her entire life for this moment. She felt as light as a feather, as giddy as a drunk and she slapped her thighs and laughed. *So it begins!*

For several hours, she watched the Midwestern landscape fly past until at last, she decided it was time to begin her studies. She flipped down a little table, kicked off her shoes and got started. Before she left, she had sent away to Los Angeles for a phone book, maps, and copies of *Variety*. She ordered publications specific to the film industry and trade papers about the business. She also purchased lighter magazines called *Photoplay* and *Moving Picture World* both of which had articles on how to break into the film industry. She took all her meals in the compartment, but by dinner on the second day, she was ready to go to the dining car.

The train was, at last, snaking its way through the Rocky Mountains. As the light faded, Libby decided to dress for dinner and apply her makeup. She knew that from now on, she had to make herself look at least twenty-three or twenty-four years old. She wanted to look believable as an established artisan. So after carefully highlighting and shading her face, she made up her eyes. Satisfied with her work, she opened the narrow closet, put on her purple georgette dress embroidered with black beads and slipped on a matching headband. She applied some lip rouge, grabbed her black evening bag and was out the door.

Tonight she would test her new persona. To break into motion pictures, she knew she had to be bold, or they would never notice her. She had done her homework and was ready to try her new identity out on some passengers. She smiled. She too would have to be a bit of an actress.

"It's very busy tonight, ma'am," the steward said when she stepped into the dining car. "My apologies. The only seat available is at the end of the car with two gentlemen."

Libby was familiar with the practice of seating passengers together in the dining car and said, "That will be fine, thank you."

Heads turned as she walked down the aisle. There were rows of tables covered with white linen and formal place settings, each seating four with tiny lamps illuminating each table.

When the steward pulled out a chair for Libby, the two men sitting at the table stood up. One was a distinguished gentleman with gray hair wearing an expensive double-breasted sack suit, the other was short and red-faced, wearing a loud jacket. Libby noticed him slip off his wedding ring when she sat down.

The older gentleman was the first to speak. "Allow me to introduce myself, my name in Ernst Baumann."

His name sounded familiar.

"I'm Georgie Sargent," the other man said in a loud voice. "Nice to meet ya."

"My name is Elizabeth Durant. It's nice to meet both of you," Libby replied, picking up her menu.

"Would you care for a beverage, miss?" the waiter asked. Like the majority of the dining attendants, he was black and wore a white jacket with a black bow tie.

"Yes, I'll have a manhattan please," she said, and he left.

She ran her eyes quickly over the menu and picked up a pencil on the table. Passengers always wrote orders themselves in the dining cars. Libby marked the pheasant in aspic jelly. The waiter returned with her drink and took the card.

Libby could feel the men watching her as she opened her cigarette case. Mr. Sargent lunged forward with a lighter. "You going to Los Angeles?" he asked as he lit her cigarette.

"Yes."

"That's where I'm headed too," he said, handing her his business card. "I am in sales, toilet paper."

Libby raised her eyebrows and said, "Oh, I see."

She noticed Mr. Baumann smother a smile.

Mr. Sargent continued, "Where'd ya get on?"

"Minneapolis," Libby said and turned to the other gentleman. "Where are you from, Mr. Baumann?"

"Chicago, but I have a home in Los Angeles as well," he replied in a thick German accent. "Are you visiting relatives, Miss Durant?"

"No, I am going out on business."

The waiter served the gentlemen their entrees. Mr. Baumann continued, "So you are a business woman. What sort of business?"

"I am a makeup and wig specialist."

"Oh, you're in the flickers!" Mr. Sargent exclaimed. "Pardon me saying so, Miss Durant but with a swell face like that, you should be in front of the camera."

"Thank you, but I prefer to remain behind the scenes."

"Are you just getting started?" Mr. Baumann asked, cutting his roast beef.

Libby took another sip of her Manhattan and said, "No, I have been in the field for some time now. I have just accepted a commission to be Gloria Swanson's private makeup specialist."

Mr. Baumann looked up with surprise. "What a coincidence. Miss Swanson is starring in my next motion picture."

Libby's stared at him, dumbfounded. *My God, that's where I've heard his name! He's a producer!* As her heart started to pound, she said to herself, Libby, remain cool. Swallowing hard, she ashed her cigarette and replied casually, "Well then we will be meeting again, Mr. Baumann. I'm certain."

"Yes, how very fortunate," he said with a smile.

Libby drained her glass, hoping the liquor would calm

her nerves. The next moment her food came, and Georgie Sargent took over the conversation, telling them about his favorite screen stars and favorite movies. He kept on until they had finished eating, and it was time to go.

As they were leaving, Mr. Baumann handed Libby a business card and said graciously, "If you need anything at all, Miss Durant, I am staying at The Beverly Hills Hotel."

"Thank you," she replied. "Good night."

"Good night."

She escaped back to her private compartment and slammed the door behind her. Collapsing against it, she started to laugh. "You need to work on your act, kid."

*   *   *

It was a long journey but at last Libby arrived in Los Angeles. She had never been to the West Coast and didn't know what to expect. The first thing she noticed was the difference in temperature. It was warm here, and she shed her coat the minute she stepped out of the depot.

She had reservations at The Hotel Hollywood which was on the outskirts of the city, so she hailed a cab. All the way there, she leaned forward looking out the window. The Santa Monica Mountains were to the north and citrus groves, vineyards and bean fields lined the road. Oil wells rose up in the distance.

The hotel looked new, like the handful of other buildings in the area. It was a grand, sweeping Mission Revival structure set in the hills with verandas and colorful awnings. The lobby was also large and cool with potted ferns and a fountain.

The front desk clerk was a tiny man with a black pencil mustache and a Spanish accent. "Before you go to your room," he said to Libby. "You must see the stars in the dining room."

"Stars?"

"Yes, on the ceiling. Movie stars dine here regularly and have their own seats. Above their seat, we place a star on the ceiling with their name on it."

He took Libby into the dining room, and she looked up. There on the ceiling, she saw the names of Rudolf Valentino, Louise Brooks, Harold Lloyd, Douglas Fairbanks, and Lillian Gish.

"Many people working in moving pictures live here permanently," he explained with pride. "Every Thursday evening we have a ball here for guests and residents."

Libby smiled. This is just where she wanted to be. "May I see my room now?"

"Of course, of course."

Libby's suite was large with a sitting room, bedroom, and bath. There were plush carpets on the floors, sconces on the walls and heavy Mission Revival furnishings. It was on the second floor and looked out over the gardens, lemon groves, and mountains.

The moment the bellhop left, Libby threw her hat and gloves onto a chair and collapsed onto the bed. She liked it here. The country was beautiful; the weather was warm, and there was opportunity.

She had the entire day to finalize her plans for Monday morning. She bathed, changed into a cooler dress and took a walk past the kidney-shaped swimming pool and through the gardens. After eating a light supper in her room, she retired early. She wanted to be well rested for her first day in Hollywood.

Chapter 10

Libby's first stop was Famous Players Studios. She would have preferred United Artists where the big four were at the helm; Pickford, Fairbanks, Chaplin, and Griffith, but the new studio was still getting organized.

Famous Players consisted of four large buildings set in the middle of a hot, dry, lot. It would have been unremarkable except that all the buildings were open to the sky. To capture sunlight for filming, the studios had no roofs. Libby looked up. Instead of ceilings, there was white canvas draped overhead.

Workers were scurrying around, carrying props, ladders, and cameras. Men were shouting instructions, and somewhere in the distance, she could hear a crew sawing and driving nails. It made her lonely for Rudy.

Even at this early hour, the sun felt hot, and it smelled dry and dusty. Carrying her makeup case and dressed in a light-weight suit, Libby wound her way across the studio lot until she found an active stage. Three men were standing near a camera that was on a tripod, talking. Two of them wore suits, and one of them was in shirt sleeves. The set was a street scene that resembled New York City. An actress dressed in rags and holding a shabby umbrella stood on the set staring at them. She had her arms crossed and was tapping her foot. A little boy was sitting on a barrel next to her. He had his cap on backward and was concentrating on a lollipop.

Suddenly, the actress threw down the umbrella and walked over to the men. They argued for a while but at last their voices dropped, and Libby saw her opportunity. She squared her shoulders and stepped up. "I beg your pardon. Do you know where I might find Miss Francelia Billington?"

The men stared at her, and the woman ran her eyes over Libby. One of the men said, "Wrong studio. She's at Universal."

Libby's jaw dropped, and she acted flustered. "Oh, how stupid of me. I thought they said in the wire she was at Famous Players."

The same man looked down at her makeup case and asked, "You work for her?"

"Yes, I do. I apologize," she said, handing them her business cards with Hotel Hollywood handwritten on the back. "I've been commissioned to do her makeup."

"She has her own makeup person?" the actress asked. She had a whiny, coarse Bronx accent.

"Yes, I personalize it for her."

"Really? How so?"

"Not now, Blanche," one of the men barked.

Libby smiled. "I'm sorry to interrupt. Thank you."

She could feel their eyes on her as she walked away. With any luck, there would be a call from one of them in the next few days.

Libby played the same game at every studio all week long. She went to Universal and dropped Mary Miles Minter's name feigning surprise when they told her she worked at Famous Players. Then she handed them cards.

She went to Max Sennett Studios, Mayflower, Photoplay, and Artcraft, every studio big and small that she could find and did the same thing. She went into downtown Los Angeles to the restaurants that theater people frequented and put on the same act, this time in the lounge or the lobby. She went anywhere and everywhere distributing cards. She was always sure to approach actresses or actors, knowing they would be eager to learn the trade secrets of other stars. In their competition for the limelight, she hoped to profit from their rivalry.

The Thursday night ball at the Hotel Hollywood was on Libby's list too. It was the perfect place to make connections, but unfortunately, they shut down the ballroom for expansion.

Every day when she returned to the hotel, tired and footsore, she would ask eagerly if there were any calls or notes for her. Almost three weeks passed, and there was nothing, except a letter from Grandmother, one from Uncle Owen and telegrams from her attorney.

Libby was trying hard not to get discouraged. *I must keep trying to find work.* But she felt as if she was running out of ideas.

She looked back and realized she had been extremely lucky breaking into the vaudeville circuit so quickly back in Minnesota. The work seemed to just fall into her lap. That time in her life seemed like a dream, yet some seemed like a nightmare as well. She missed Rudy and Jennie terribly and tried to stay busy to not dwell on the loss, but at night, when she was falling asleep, memories haunted her.

Late one afternoon, after a long day of walking around Los Angeles distributing cards, she decided to sit by the pool and relax. She vowed never to stay in her room knowing she would accomplish nothing there. She had met a handful of movie people in the hotel, but so far it had produced few leads. Nevertheless, she would continue to try.

She was paging through "Vanity Fair" when the front desk clerk told her there was a call for her.

"Miss Durant?" a man said on the other end of the line. "This is Ernst Baumann. We met in the dining car on the train."

"Yes, hello again," she said.

"I happened to remember you are staying at the Hotel Hollywood. I am just finishing up at the studio. Would you have a moment for a drink?"

Libby hesitated and then said, "Of course."

"I'll meet you in the hotel lounge in a half hour."

"That would be fine," she said, hanging up.

She did not like the sound of it. She knew about the exchange of sexual favors for opportunity in theater, and she prepared herself for a proposition. She went up to her room and changed into something conservative.

The lounge was off the dining room and similar in style to the rest of the hotel. The chairs were upholstered and comfortable. There were ferns in every corner and a highly polished bar with wood carvings.

The room was almost empty when Libby walked in. Ernst Baumann was at a table in the corner. He jumped up, kissing her hand. "Forgive me for being old-fashioned," he said. "From the time I was a young man in Germany we kissed the hands of ladies. I am very old."

Libby smiled. "I think it's nice."

"Please sit down," he said, holding her chair.

The waiter walked up, and Mr. Baumann asked, "What would you like?"

"A gin fizz, please."

"The lady would like a gin fizz, and I'll have a glass of sherry. Thank you."

Mr. Baumann was dressed in a beige, double-breasted

suit and gold tie. "The weather is certainly warmer here than in the Midwest. Is it not, Miss Durant?"

"It is certainly is, but for now I like it."

Libby kept her replies short, maintaining a polite but aloof demeanor. "Do you mind if I smoke?" she asked when her drink came.

"Of course not," he replied and lit her cigarette.

Mr. Baumann cleared his throat and leaned forward. "Miss Durant, I'm sure you are extremely busy, so I will come to the point. I am wondering if you would consider taking on a new customer."

Libby kept her cool facade. She refused to get excited until she heard the whole story. She blew out her smoke and asked, "What are you proposing?"

He started twisting the wedding band on his finger, and she raised an eyebrow.

"It would require a good deal of discretion. I am, of course, a married man."

Here it comes, Libby thought.

"I have had a lady friend for many years. She is a lovely German woman, a stage actress, but she needs help transitioning into motion pictures. The camera is not flattering to her."

Libby's brows shot up. She liked the sound of this after all. The flicker of a smile returned to her lips.

He continued. "She can be difficult, but after many outbursts, she realizes I am right."

"I am very busy, Mr. Baumann. Everyone wants their makeup personalized," she bluffed.

"I understand, but I will make it worth your while, and my favorite cameraman will be at your disposal. I would be ever so grateful if we could get started as early as tomorrow and I will gladly pay extra. We have a motion picture to shoot."

Libby flicked the ashes on her cigarette and said, "Very well. I'll see if I can move some things around."

*   *   *

The next day she met Mr. Baumann on one of the sets of Famous Players. It was designed to be the parlor of a fine home. Standing next to him was tall, big boned woman with frizzy brown hair and large eyes. Her brows were heavy, and her skin was mottled. She lifted her chin and looked away when Libby approached.

"Thank you for coming, Miss Durant," Mr. Baumann said. "This is Gerta Linden."

Gerta gave Libby a cool look.

"How do you do?" Libby said.

There was no response. *Baumann had been right. She did seem difficult.*

"Until now her experience has been in legitimate theater in Berlin, nothing in front of the camera."

"I see. How do you like the United States, Miss Linden?" Libby asked, trying to break the ice.

Miss Linden shrugged and took a puff from her cigarette holder.

Something caught Mr. Baumann's eye, and he exclaimed, "Oh splendid! Here's Mr. Aberdeen."

A tall, thin man walked up, carrying a Bell and Howell camera and tripod. He had a gaunt face, was in shirt sleeves and was wearing a vest and cowboy hat.

"Miss Durant, this is Clay Aberdeen."

"How do?" he said. He had a Texas accent, and when he smiled, she noticed he had buckteeth.

Libby was taken aback. He did not look like a cameraman at all. He looked much more like a stunt man in a Western photoplay.

"Mr. Aberdeen is one of the best," Ernst Hauptman said. "He apprenticed with Griffin Gardner."

Libby didn't know who that was, but she acted impressed.

"The three of you will be working together," Baumann said. "I leave you, Gerta, darling, but I'll see you at lunch," he added and left.

Libby looked from one to the other. "Let's begin."

Even though her experience with camera makeup was limited, she took the lead, not letting on that she was, in reality, still learning. Looking around the set, she moved a chair center stage and said, "Miss Linden, would you take a seat here please?" Turning to Clay Aberdeen, she asked, "Would you run a bit of film on her now?"

"Sure thing, Miss Durant," he replied, snapping his gum and setting up a tripod.

As he was getting his camera ready, she stepped up to Miss Linden, gently took her chin and moved her face from side to side. She examined her bone structure, the brows, the lips and the hairline.

To use the camera, Clay Aberdeen had to take off his cowboy hat. Libby noticed his mass of kinky, red hair.

He drawled, "Ready when you ladies are."

"Roll the camera please."

Aberdeen leaned down looked through the side lens and started cranking the camera, humming.

"Turn your head to the right, please, Miss Linden," Libby said.

The actress turned her head.

"Now to the left, please. Yes, thank you."

Libby filmed Miss Linden sitting, standing, looking up and looking down, in close-ups and long shots. The entire time Mr. Aberdeen continued to hum as he cranked the camera.

"What *is* that you are humming, Mr. Aberdeen?" Libby asked at last.

"Why it's 'Turkey in the Straw.'"

"They all do it," Miss Linden replied in a thick German accent, rolling her eyes. It was the first thing she had said all day.

"It helps us keep the correct rhythm while cranking," Aberdeen said. "That way we don't go too fast or too slow. But I'm sure you already know that."

"Of course. I just couldn't think of the name of the tune," Libby said, trying to cover her ignorance. "Now, let's alter the lighting, Mr. Aberdeen."

"I thought you'd never ask," he replied excitedly. He put an unlit cigar in his mouth and started chewing as he dashed around pulling ropes to adjust the curtains overhead. "By the way, call me, Clay."

"Very well, Clay," Libby called back to him. "I'm Eliz--" and she stopped. "Call me Libby."

"Alrighty, Libby."

"Let's film her first in different angles of natural light, and then let's try some arc too."

"Lighting *is* everything," Clay replied.

"Yes, just about," Libby agreed.

After they had taken footage in natural light, Libby suggested, "Let's do the Klieg light now."

"Yes, ma'am."

Libby liked Clay Aberdeen. He was not only good-natured and personable, but he also seemed exceptionally talented. He had a multitude of suggestions and was open to all new ideas. "Experimentation is the name of the game in moving pictures," he said. "It's all so new. No one knows what works."

All morning long they took footage of Miss Linden, with and without makeup, and after lunch developed the film. Libby looked at the footage and saw firsthand what she had read about in the trade journals. The camera changed the color of everything, especially the complexions of actors and actresses. Without makeup, skin tones blackened. She knew actors tried to counter this effect with the application of heavy white makeup, but the result was a corpse-like effect especially on close-ups. Rouge could no longer be used because it too would show up as black on camera. Everything changed on film, and Libby was learning the nuances very quickly here.

"I need to make up a substance that is more subtle. This makeup is unsuitable," Libby said as she looked at the footage.

The three worked together the rest of the day experimenting with makeup and lighting. Libby would apply makeup, they would film Miss Linden, scrutinize the outcome and try again. Miss Linden's stamina surprised and impressed Libby. Although she was aloof and arrogant, she sat for hours under the hot lights and endured numerous applications of makeup without complaint.

One of the first things Libby did was pluck Gerta's eyebrows and experiment with wigs. She also arranged for her to see a stylist to soften and settle down her wiry hair.

For days, the three of them worked together, and each night Libby would stay late mixing and creating substances which would be the perfect combination for Gerta's face. During the day, Clay adjusted and perfected the lighting for her particular bone structure and complexion, sometimes putting gauze over the camera.

By the end of the week, their creation was complete. Under the critical eye of the camera *and* Ernst Baumann, Gerta Linden was breathtaking.

"She is simply stunning," Ernst said as he watched the footage in the editing room. Gerta stood next to him holding his hand. "At last, we are ready to start shooting. Everyone be here tomorrow at seven."

As Libby was putting her makeup away, Clay said, "Buy you a drink, little lady?"

"I'd like that. I think we need to celebrate."

"Actually, I'm not buying the drinks. We're going to a studio party for the opening of *The Miracle Man.*"

"Really?" Libby said, pulling on her gloves. "I haven't been to a studio party."

"Well, sometimes they're on the set. This one has a friend of mine starring in it. He is not only a talented actor but a master of makeup like you."

"What's his name?"

"Lon Chaney," Clay said, falling into step beside her. "Heard of him?"

She shook her head.

"Oh, you will."

*　　　*　　　*

It was Libby's first studio party, and Clay told her to dress for it. She put on a filmy cream-colored chiffon gown with a wide belt that laced in the front and a bandeau decorated with delicate seed pearls.

When Clay picked her up in the lobby, he was dressed formally as well, in a tuxedo with tails, but he was still wearing his cowboy hat.

Libby smiled.

"What?" he exclaimed and looked up. "The hat? I'm a Texan. This is what we do." He laughed and opened the door of the cab. "Shall we skedaddle?"

The party was on the backlot of Famous Players Studios. When they pulled up, a crowd of fans surged forward hoping to see stars, but they were disappointed. It was only Libby and Clay.

A banner that said, '*The Miracle Man*' was strung over the entrance and when an attendant stepped up, Clay showed him his pass.

The party was jammed with guests laughing and talking, drinking and dancing. Just beyond the crowd, Libby could make out the set of the movie. It was the façade of a cottage covered with vines placed among some trees. The street lights were merely cardboard, so the party was lit with Chinese lanterns.

"Did you work on this picture too?" Libby asked Clay.

He nodded.

"What's it about?"

He had to shout his reply because of the noise. "Con artists doing phony faith healing. Right here on this sidewalk, I filmed Lon giving just a jim-dandy performance. The man is going to be a big goddamn star. You got my word on that."

"Is he here?"

"I don't see him, but I know he's here somewhere."

A band was playing, "The Walper House Rag," and several couples sailed past, dipping and hopping as they danced. One of them narrowly missed sloshing a drink all over Libby, and the woman called, "Sorry!"

Libby watched the guests. Everyone was young, attractive and dressed in the latest fashion. If they weren't dancing, they were drinking, laughing or kissing. A photographer wound his way through the crowd taking pictures of all of them.

"Is everyone here involved in the movie?"

"Yes, it's mostly cast, crew, and their friends."

A waiter came by with champagne and Clay took two glasses, handing one to Libby. "Knock that drink back, Miss Libby and get yourself ready to meet some of my friends."

Libby put her head back and drained her glass.

"Well, damn! I didn't mean you *really* had to knock it back," Clay exclaimed. "Alrighty then. Bottoms up," and he drained his glass too.

Clay introduced her to other cameramen, set carpenters, costume designers, editors, actors, and actresses. Almost everyone was involved in the motion picture in some capacity, and they all were having a good time.

Libby too was having a good time. She danced almost as much as she drank, stopping momentarily to devour some caviar and once more when they brought out the six-tiered red velvet cake. She met a host of new people and spent very little time with Clay. But he wasn't lonely. Every time she looked at him he had a different woman on his arm, all of them extremely attractive.

Hours flew by until at last he grabbed her hand and said, "Come on, beautiful. Time to go home. We gotta work in the morning."

"Just one more?" Libby said. She was talking to a handsome, blond actor and had no intention of leaving.

"You're in your cups already, darlin'. I have to get you home, but first I want you to meet a friend of mine."

Libby turned around, lost her balance and stumbled into the man standing next to Clay. He had dark hair, a weathered face, and sad eyes.

"Oh, I'm sorry," she blurted, stepping back and straightening her bandeau.

"Libby, this is my friend, Lon Chaney," Clay drawled.

"Hello," Libby replied with a smile. "Clay says you are soon to be a big star."

"I wish I had a nickel for every time he said that," Mr. Chaney replied.

Libby noticed that when he smiled, deep wrinkles creased his face.

"I hear your specialty is makeup, Miss Durant."

"It is. I got my start in vaudeville."

"Haven't we all? It's entirely different here, isn't it?

Especially with makeup."

"It is!" Libby gasped. She was delighted to be talking with someone who understood. "I was shocked when I saw my makeup on film. So now I'm experimenting with some new formulas."

"What sort of formulas?"

They talked back and forth, exchanging ideas for several minutes.

"Mr. Chaney! Over here for a photo," someone called suddenly.

"Not now," he replied and turned back to Libby. "What do you use for close ups?"

"Well, I have found if you mix--"

"Mr. Chaney, please!"

He groaned and said, "Please wait, Miss Durant. I'll be back."

But he never came back. The guests demanded too much of his time. At last, Clay convinced Libby that it was time to go, but she was not disappointed. At last, she had met someone who understood her passion, and she did not feel quite so isolated.

She liked this Mr. Chaney, whoever he was, and she wished him well.

*   *   *

"Don't you dare touch me!" Libby heard someone scream as she dodged crew members and cast on the set of *The Dewey Affair*. Running in high heels was not easy, and her makeup case was heavy. She thought her ankles would break.

As suspected, Gerta Linden was throwing a fit.

"Darling Gerta," Ernst Baumann pleaded. "Mr. Russell will do your makeup exactly the same way."

"I want Miss Durant!" she screeched.

"Here I am," Libby announced breathlessly as she ran

up.

"There's my Goddess of the Looking Glass," Gerta gasped. She was sitting in a chair with a towel over her chest.

"Thank you, Mr. Russell," Libby said to the makeup specialist. "I'll take it from here."

"Gladly," he said, slamming his case shut. When Gerta wasn't looking, he stuck his tongue out at her and marched off.

The past few weeks, Libby had been overwhelmed with work. After Miss Linden's makeover, the phone started to ring with job offers from all the studios. She tried to be on the set every day for Gerta, but sometimes it was impossible. Ernst hired other makeup artists to substitute for Libby, but Gerta would not have them. Filming had to wait until she had her Miss Durant.

"I am sorry I told anyone about you, Elizabeth," Gerta said, pushing her lips out in a pout. "Now you have no time for me."

Libby smiled as she pulled on her white work coat. "Every free moment I have, I'm yours. Gerta."

"Because of you and that cowboy, I will be a great star someday."

"I *know* you will be a great star," Libby said, opening her case.

And Gerta Linden did become a great star. Her talent as an actress was unsurpassed in the film industry. In no time, she was being cast in best motion pictures with box office receipts rivaling Gloria Swanson's. But it was Clay's genius at lighting and Libby's ingenuity with makeup that made her legendary. They became the most sought after team in all of Hollywood. Every actor and actress clamored for a chance at their customized lighting and makeup.

Nevertheless, Libby was not satisfied. She had to

continually challenge herself, so she expanded into character makeup too. She studied historical documents for accurate wigs and hairstyles for period pieces. When a movie demanded an Oriental character, she made Caucasians look Asian. She aged actors for elderly parts or made them appear younger. If the director wanted sinister, she delivered sinister. If he wanted grotesque, she delivered grotesque. Libby did it all and loved every minute of it.

She couldn't believe what was happening. Uncle Owen had been right. She was setting her own course and making her own dreams come true.

Chapter 11
Hollywood 1925

Griffin Gardner wiggled to make sure the strap holding him to the outside of the plane was secure. "No smart ass crap today, Dash!" he called to the pilot as he lowered his goggles. "We can't lose this camera." The Mitchell was bolted to the fuselage in front of Griffin as he lay on the spine of the bi-plane.

Jack Jakes, a portly, slightly wheezy movie director was standing nearby getting ready to send the Curtiss JN 4 plane, commonly called a "Jenny," up for stunts. He knew it would go well today because Griffin Gardner was behind the camera. The man could film anything, anywhere. He could step into a lion's den and film the big cats with a steady hand. He could crawl onto a skyscraper and flawlessly shoot a tightrope walker, or stand on a boat careening down the rapids and capture clear clean footage. Multiple times he had strapped himself to the front of automobiles for chase scenes or sat on top of moving trains and presented wonderful film. He could hang from the sides of tall buildings or stand on a race track as horses thundered past and still deliver impeccable work. The man was a phenomenon.

A small crowd had gathered to watch the show; journalists, fans and some of the local farmers. "Who is that crazy bastard doing the filming?" a reporter asked one of the crew.

"His name's Gardner."

"Oh, so that's who it is," he replied, snapping his gum. "I've heard of him. He's supposed to be the best in the business."

"Gardner's the best, but he's also the most stupid. It's dangerous, and there's no goddamn glory in it. The actors get noticed but never the cameraman."

The crewmember walked over, cranked the propeller on the Jenny, and the motor burst into a roar. Upon hearing the engine, a short, muscular man dressed in a blonde wig and long tutu jumped into the plane.

"Now, who's that?" the reporter asked as the crewmember walked back.

"Rodney Bell, he's the stuntman. He doubles for the actress who supposed to be dancing on the wings."

"Wing walking too?"

"Oh, boy," the crewmember said, sarcastically clapping his hands. "Sometimes they even get killed. Put that in your little notebook, bub."

The plane moved off with Gardner on the back cranking the camera. It rattled down the open field and then sailed up into the air. After clearing some trees, the pilot banked her and came back to the crew.

John Dashby, the pilot, looked down. He was satisfied with the altitude and ready to level off. He signaled to the stunt man that it was time to start. Rodney, a small, fine-boned athlete who frequently doubled for women and children in dangerous movie shots, climbed onto the wing, the wind blowing his wig and pink tutu.

Griffin chuckled and shook his head. Bell would do anything for a buck. He climbed onto the top wing and stood up, leaning onto a wire invisible to the camera as Griff continued to crank, peering through his goggles, not missing a shot.

With a wide smile, Rodney performed a plié. Next, he

then extended one leg and then the other ballet style and finally he twirled, the wind blowing his tutu. Before finishing, for Griff's benefit, he broke into a Charleston.

Griff started to laugh.

Suddenly, the plane dipped, and Rodney's knees buckled. Losing his balance, he stumbled toward the edge of the wing. Catching a wire, he steadied himself. Looking back, he grinned.

The dumb bastard. That was close. The last thing Griff wanted to do was capture the death of his friend on film. They had come close too often during the war.

Griffin, Rodney, and Dash had all been together in The Great War. They had narrowly escaped death many times and as a result developed a false sense of security. Thinking they were invincible, they tempted fate, constantly taking risks. To make matters worse, they made money at it in the movie business.

There was one more stunt to do, and Dash adjusted the altitude holding the plane steady. Per the director's request, Rodney was to do a "breakaway," simulating an accident. He dropped to the lower wing and started to dance again but this time near the edge. Suddenly, pretending to fall, he dropped off the wing and dangled in midair, holding onto a wire with his teeth. Soaring hundreds of feet in the air, over trees and open fields, Rodney clutched this lifeline with a special mouthpiece. He waved his arms and legs around frantically as if he was terrified spinning around and around. Griff captured every bit of it on film. When the scene was complete, Rodney drew his legs up, caught a loop on the wing and climbed back to his seat.

Griff stopped cranking and relaxed. *The stunts were perfect.* He couldn't wait to get back to the lab to edit. Jakes will love it, he thought.

He sighed and ran his eyes over the landscape. Now he could enjoy the rest of the ride. He loved going up in a Jenny. He thought flying was nothing short of a miracle. It was a whole new way to see the world, never experienced by man until now. The only thing he loved more was capturing it on film. He looked at the rows and rows of orchards, oil wells, the rolling hills and the mountains. He saw it from the perspective of an eagle, and it was thrilling.

Then, without warning, Dash whooped and took the plane into a loop. Griff was suddenly hanging upside down, praying the straps wrapped around him would hold. He lunged for the camera trying to steady it. "You son of a bitch!" he shouted, but Dash couldn't hear him.

Next, they went into a nosedive toward a dirt road. Just before plunging to the earth, Dash pulled the Jenny up and squeezed her between two telephone poles. Soaring up again, he leveled the plane off and did a barrel roll.

When they landed, everyone cheered. Dash jumped out, whipped off his goggles and did a deep bow. Two women rushed up and kissed him. He put his arm around each one and posed for still shots by the reporters. With black hair slicked back and a pencil-thin mustache, John Dashby could have been a matinee idol to rival Rudolph Valentino. Instead, he was a flamboyant flying ace.

When Rodney jumped out of the plane, the reporters left Dash and ran up to him.

"No pictures please," Jack Jakes, the director said, stepping in front of the cameras. "Our stunts are confidential. Mr. Bell can take general questions though."

Short and bursting with energy, Rodney whipped off his wig and smiled, ready to be interviewed. With thinning brown hair, tiny blue eyes and a nose flattened from repeated breaks, his looks were comical, and the press loved him. He was quick-witted, fast-talking and loved the limelight.

"You were there too," one of the farmers said to Griffin as the crew unbuckled him from the plane. "How come they don't wanna talk to you?"

"They never do and thank God. I'd rather be left alone," he replied.

No reporters ever interviewed Gardner. No starry-eyed beauties came to kiss him. No children asked for autographs. Cameramen were of no interest to the general public. In fact, seeing a camera ruined all the fantasy. The audience wanted to believe they were witnessing everything first-hand. And it was exactly as Griff would have it. He wanted to deliver a dream, not be a part of it.

He pulled off his helmet and ran his hands through his curly auburn hair. Gardner was a tall, well-built man in his early thirties. His work demanded he stayd in shape, filming in all kinds of settings and under all sorts of circumstances, so although he was thin, he was strong. Clean-shaven with deep dimples, his light skin was constantly tanned from hours of work in the sun.

As he unbolted the camera from the plane, Jakes walked up to him. "Did you get everything?"

"Everything and more. You're going to love it."

Jakes never knew if Gardner was pulling his leg or not. His wicked grin was dangerously attractive, but not always square. Jakes asked cautiously, "No bullshit?"

"No bullshit. I even got footage of Rodney almost falling off."

"Great!" Jakes said, punching him in the arm. "Let's get to work."

As they walked back to the car, a woman came roaring up in a Kissel Gold Bug Speedster. Her hair was fashionably shingled, and she wore a chic car coat and driving gloves. She waved at Dash.

"Bitch," Griff muttered.

"You don't like Elizabeth Durant?"

"I used to until I got to know her."

They watched John Dashby break away from the two women and run over to the motorcar to kiss her.

"What's wrong with her?"

"She's nothing more than a party girl."

"Next to Max Factor, she runs the biggest makeup business in Hollywood. A party girl didn't do that."

"She still makes the rounds," Griff countered, putting his camera in the trunk.

"Gardner!" Dash called. "Nine o'clock tonight at Café Duval?"

"Thanks, but I can't."

Dash ran over. "What the hell? It's your birthday party." He looked hurt.

"I forgot. I've got a date--" The minute Griff gave the excuse, he knew it wouldn't be a good enough.

"Bring her along! That's not a problem. We have room at the table."

"I don't know."

"Good, then it's settled, nine o'clock," Dash said, slapping him on the back and running back to Libby.

Griffin slid into the motorcar and stole a look at the two of them. He hated Libby for dating Dash. Of all the men in California, she had to pick one of his best friends. She was the reason he didn't want to go Café Duval. She would be there, and not only would she make him uncomfortable, but she would bring back memories, memories he wanted to bury forever.

*   *   *

The Café Duval was the center of nightlife for anyone and everyone in the burgeoning film industry of Los Angeles. Frequented by the new celebrities, it was a gathering place, not only for dinner and dancing, but for meetings, making deals, and backroom gambling. The décor was lavish, resembling an Italian palazzo complete with chandeliers, brass and bronze metalwork, and plush carpets.

Griff arrived late and was just sitting down with his date, Vera Quinn when the waiter asked. "And what would the lady like?"

"What would you like?" Griff asked Vera. She was a well-dressed, sophisticated actress Griff had been dating off and on for two months. Although she was finely manicured with exquisitely coiffed hair, her eyes were too close together, and she was a cold fish in bed.

"I'll have a cup of Turkish coffee."

"I'll have the same but make mine extra strong please," Griff said.

Turkish coffee was the code word for Scotch at the Café Duval. It was 1925 and Prohibition was in full swing. Since liquor was outlawed, everyone was drinking.

Tonight Griff needed as much "brown plaid" as he could lay his hands on. Libby was sitting across the table with Dash. Rodney was with a buxom blonde.

When Dash stood up to lead Libby out onto the dance floor, Griff stole a look at her. He hated that she looked so good. She looked every bit as good as she did that weekend when they had been together over a year ago. He remembered everything about those three days with her, dancing in the dark, eating grilled cheese sandwiches on the fire escape, and riding the funicular to the top of Echo Mountain. Most of all, he remembered the hours and hours of intimacy. He had shared more of himself with Libby in three days than he had with anyone in a lifetime.

Griff hailed a cigarette girl and bought a pack of Lucky Strikes. After lighting one, he asked Vera about her new movie. She was more than happy to be talking about herself as he smoked and ordered refills of "Turkish coffee." Occasionally he would flash a smile at her, and that would please her.

He had a way with women. They said the way his eyes scrunched up when he smiled was irresistible and he looked like trouble. That was always his cue to lean in and say suggestively, "So you like a bad boy?"

When the band struck up, "Sittin' in a Corner," he put out his cigarette and took Vera out to dance. He was determined to show Libby he was having a good time.

"Those two make a nice couple," Vera said as they sailed past Libby and Dash.

"Yes, they do," and he swung away from them.

Rodney was out on the floor too with his date, Gracie, who towered over him. He was lined up perfectly with her cleavage and had a silly smirk on his face. He deliberately bumped into Griff and said, "Hey birthday boy, this joints alright but how about a change of scenery? I know a great place on Sunset. What do ya say?"

Griff shrugged. "Fine with me. Let's go."

After another drink and few more dances, the group headed downtown to the Sky Room, a restaurant, and nightclub on the top floor of The Admiral Hotel. A large circular room, lined with windows that overlooked the city, it had a revolving dancefloor and a jazz singer.

The room was crowded with guests dressed in expensive suits and gowns. Waiters moved from table to table serving elegant French cuisine.

As they sat down, Griff said to Rodney, "Pretty fancy."

"Nothing but the best for you, old pal," he said with a wink. Turning to the group, he announced, "If you want something stronger than a milkshake, you have to go to the restroom. The door to the bar's in there."

"What'll you have?" Griff asked Vera, as he stood up, pulling down his cuffs.

"A martini."

He laughed. "Oh boy, mixing your drinks. Should be an interesting night."

Griff, Dash, and Rodney headed into the restroom lounge. There were men sitting on divans and in chairs smoking. A stuffy attendant in a tuxedo stood by a closed door.

"I'm sorry, gentlemen the facilities are all in use."

"We just want to buy cigarettes," Dash said.

Hearing the code word, the attendant replied, "Right this way, gentlemen." He took them through the slick, green-tiled restroom lined with empty stalls, urinals, and sinks where he pushed a panel open.

"What happens to the poor suckers who really have to take a piss?" Rodney asked.

"We let them in, and they leave the usual way, sir," the man replied. "You will leave by a door at the far end of the bar."

They stepped into a dark, narrow room filled with people, laughing and smoking. There were three bartenders behind a long, highly polished mahogany bar, preparing cocktails. There were no tables or chairs. Guests were meant to obtain their drinks and return to the main dining room.

When their drinks were ready. Griff, Rodney, and Dash exited into the dining room through a different door, hidden behind some potted ferns off the dancefloor. They crossed the room, dodging dancers, waiters and revelers.

Holding a cigarette in his mouth, Griff cussed Vera for ordering a martini. It was hard to carry without spilling.

When they sat down and gave the women their drinks, Dash took Libby's chin and kissed her. "You look beautiful tonight," he said.

"Thank you, John," she said, smiled a crooked smile and looked away.

He scanned the room running his hand over his slick, black hair. When he spotted several women staring at him, he felt confident again. Vanity was high on his list of priorities.

Griff wondered what was going on with Libby. She was quiet and stiff tonight. If she didn't want to be here why did she come? He didn't want to be here either, but *he* had little choice. It was his birthday celebration.

She had always been a hard one to read. From the moment he met Libby, he knew she was hiding something, possibly many things. She was remote and unattainable, and her sultry good looks added to this allure. Griff knew one reason she was aloof was that she scoffed at love. She told him early on that she thought love was an overrated emotion, an overinflated phenomenon to promote procreation and sell movie tickets.

Rodney roared across the table, "Hey, Dash, I forgot to tell you, I almost fell off the Jenny today."

"What?" Dash said, straightening up.

"Ya, that air pocket we hit."

"I was wondering if that would give you trouble."

"I caught the whole thing on film," Griff added. "When his knees buckled, I thought he was a goner. I sure as hell didn't want footage of him buying the farm."

"What's the name of the picture you're working on?" Libby asked.

"*Final Curtain Call*," Rodney said, and everyone laughed. "Honest! That's really the name of it."

They laughed again.

"I don't understand you guys," Gracie slurred. Her hair had come loose, and one shoulder of her gown was slipping.

"Why do you take so many chances? Didn't you get enough death and dying in the war?"

Smiles faded, and the table grew quiet.

Gracie sloshed her drink onto the table. "Did I say something wrong?"

A waiter came up just in time with a birthday cake.

With mock surprise, Dash looked at Griff and said, "Who did this?"

Griff made an obscene gesture at him.

The cake was dark chocolate and covered with flaming candles. Everyone sang, "Happy Birthday" and some of the guests in the nightclub joined in too. Griff smiled, obviously embarrassed.

When they finished their cake, Rodney said, "Ladies, you owe Gardner a dance."

Griff made a face. He didn't want to dance with Libby. "You know I don't like to dance."

"Since when?" Dash declared.

"Since always. It's my birthday. Leave me alone."

"Come on, big boy," Gracie said, pulling him to his feet. "Let's cut a rug."

Griff glared at Rodney and Dash, and they laughed throwing ice cubes at him as he followed her out to the floor. It was a lively dance, and before he could sit down, Vera took him out for another.

As the song was finishing up, he noticed Libby going into the women's restroom. He knew she was avoiding a dance with him, and that was just fine.

But there was no escape. When she returned, drink in hand, Dash said, "Your turn, gorgeous."

"For what?"

"Get out there and dance with Gardner."

She ran her eyes over Griff coolly. "He looks a little worse for wear."

"I am. Those girls wore me out," Griff replied, quickly.

"Go on," Rodney said to Libby. "It's the only time of year he can get a woman to dance with him."

They all started coaxing and with an apologetic grin, Griff held out his hand to Libby. "Let's go."

Griff barely noticed Gracie or Vera when he danced, but he was keenly aware of Libby in his arms. He felt the warmth of her body and smelled her perfume. It was a slow fox trot, and they danced without looking at each other.

"Are you having a good birthday?" Libby asked in a disinterested tone.

"Swell," he replied flatly.

Griff kept picturing her with Dash. The longer he danced, the angrier he became. *And to boot she's here on my birthday, just flaunting it.*

"So why Dash?" he asked.

"I beg your pardon?"

"Why do you have to date my best friend? Or have you worked your way through every other guy in L.A.?"

"I *have* worked through all the guys in L.A. I did stupid and ugly ones first."

Griff clenched his jaw and looked away. "Still the bitch," he mumbled.

They went around the floor one more time and returned to the table. Rodney had just told a joke, and everyone was laughing.

Seething, Griff reached for a cigarette as the band struck up the Berlin tune, "What'll I do?"

"Gone is the romance that was so divine.
It's broken and cannot be mended.
You must go your way,
And I must go mine.
But now that our love dreams have ended--"

That's it, he thought. *I won't stay here another minute. Some goddamn birthday.*

"Vera," Griff said, "Time to go."

Chapter 12

"I won't be in the rest of the day," Libby called to the clerks at her shop. "Please contact me only if it is absolutely necessary."

"Yes, Miss Durant," they replied.

Libby put on her cloche and gloves and was out the door. Two women walking in the store stared at her. They immediately recognized Elizabeth Durant. Most women in Los Angeles did. They were familiar with her face and the magic her makeup performed on actresses *and* the ordinary woman on the street.

In the six years since coming to Hollywood, Libby had gained a reputation as one of the finest makeup specialists on all of the West Coast competing with the likes of Max Factor and the Westmores. With Clay Aberdeen's lighting expertise and her product innovations, she transformed faces in Hollywood from mere mortals to breathtaking screen legends. Gerta's name for her stuck and Libby became known as "The Goddess of the Looking Glass."

"Now if we could only teach them to act," Clay always joked.

Three years later, Libby embarked on yet another venture. She began marketing her makeup to *every* woman in Los Angeles, not just those in motion pictures. She was determined to enhance the looks and the self-esteem of every housewife and career woman in the city. After sinking every cent into a huge marketing campaign, Libby built a store called, "The House of Durant" on Sunset Boulevard to sell her "magic potions" to the general public. Her line of makeup called, Elizabeth Durant Cosmetics was an immediate success.

Her timing was impeccable. Women had just won the vote and were starting to throw off conservative attitudes about what it meant to be female, embracing new ways to express themselves. Hemlines went up, corsets came off, and makeup went on. They came in droves to the store, and Libby was able to expand the shop and product line several times. Now her prestigious makeup and accessories included wigs and hairpieces as well.

Although she catered mainly to women, men came too. There were private consultation rooms in the back of the store and word soon was out that Elizabeth Durant and her team were not only talented but discreet.

"La Grande Station, please," Libby said to her driver. After reading a letter from Uncle Owen, updating her on Durant family news, she opened a compact. There were rings under her eyes. After applying some powder and lipstick, she clicked it shut and looked out the window.

She had been exhausted all week. Seeing Griff on Friday night had been a bad idea, and it had sapped all her energy. She had acted like a petulant child trying to make him jealous, but she wanted him to know that she was happy and getting along just fine without him. She relished the fact that he had confronted her on the dancefloor about dating John. Always the wise guy and ever so cavalier, Griff seldom revealed his true feelings. When she angered him at last, Libby found it extremely satisfying. But over the next few days, she had regretted her actions. She found the stunt sophomoric and knew that she was too old for games.

Even though she had initially used John to make Griff

jealous, he was turning out to be a fun date. Although he was vain and superficial, he had a good heart. Libby knew he was seeing her because she looked good on his arm, but he treated her well and was creative in bed. She especially liked it when they went up in the Jenny. It was thrilling, and when they returned to earth, the excitement of the day made a lively romp in bed.

Libby's driver turned onto Santa Fe Avenue and pulled up in front of La Grande Station. It was a massive Moorish-style structure complete with a dome. A hodge-podge of connecting brick buildings, each one had a different roofline. Some were square, others were vaulted, and one was even cone-shaped.

Libby thought it was a hideous, jumbled mess, but today she wasn't critiquing the architecture. She had other things on her mind. She jumped out of the motorcar and rushed inside the depot, looking down the open-air concourse. It was jammed with people, but she saw a chic young woman in a blue twill suit pick up her bag and start running toward her.

"Pepper!" Libby yelled.

"Cuz!" she exclaimed, hugging her. "It has been too long. You've only been home twice in six years."

Libby stepped back and looked at her. "You look so damn gorgeous."

"It's the Paul Poiret suit. He can make anyone look good. And I love your shingled hair."

"Come on. I want to get you settled in at the house. We have a lot to talk about now that you'll be living here."

The moment they slid into the back seat of the Rolls, Libby lowered a shelf revealing a small bar complete with crystal decanters, barware, and olives. She made them each a martini.

Pepper leaned back and kicked her shoes off. "It looks

like you're doing well, Libs."

"I should be. I work all the time."

"What? No longer the party girl?"

"Well, maybe sometimes," and she laughed. "They work hard and play hard out here."

"Ha! You wouldn't believe what we hear back East about you movie people. They think it is one big orgy."

"Oh, sure it is," Libby said sarcastically as she lit a cigarette. "They also think we are out here only because we can't make it in legitimate theater. Heaven forbid we think for ourselves and create a whole new medium in show business."

"Now you must admit some of these people out here are questionable."

"How would you know?"

"Haydn told me," Pepper said.

"Ah, the famous Haydn Price, studio head extraordinaire. Tell me again how you met him. I know the movie convention at The West in Minneapolis brought him there, but I can't remember the rest."

"Yes, that was several summers back, shortly after I was engaged to Henry. I met him at Judge Greely's cocktail party."

"Oh that's right," Libby said. "And the love affair began. Was it hard to have a long distance relationship?"

Pepper shrugged. "I saw him more than you'd think. He came back every few months. He lived in St. Paul years ago and still has business interests there. But it wasn't enough. So here I am."

"What does Grandmother think? He is twenty years older than you."

"Grandmother still doesn't know."

"Ha! Well, that's probably just as well." Libby smiled a crooked smile. "But she'll have to know eventually--

especially if there are wedding bells."

"Yes, but first he wants me to settle in out here, see how I like it and try my hand at acting."

"Or is it *you* that wants to try acting?"

"Well, I *am* a teensy bit curious," Pepper said with a smirk. After sipping her martini, she added, "I've been taking acting lessons for over a year. Haydn thinks I have potential."

"Oh Lordy!" Libby exclaimed. "The man *must* be in love."

When they turned into the Hancock Park neighborhood of Los Angeles, Pepper whistled. "Well, look at you, pretty posh. My parents think you're living in some seedy apartment drinking yourself to death."

"Well maybe the last part," Libby said as the auto pulled in the driveway of her the brand new Renaissance Revival home. "It's modest compared to most houses in the neighborhood."

"Ah but it has your unmistakable style. I love the French doors running along the side."

Libby brought Pepper in through the pool area, an intimate patio surrounded by a hedge. The house was filled with archways, trimmed with mahogany, wrought iron and a large stained glass window over the front door illuminated the entrance. "That's the only bit of stained glass I allowed in here," Libby said, looking up. "I wanted plenty of natural light. Nothing like that mausoleum I was raised in."

Pepper looked around. The house was flooded with light from the floor to ceiling from French doors and the arched windows above. Instead of the heavy Spanish design currently popular in California, Libby had decorated the rooms with delicate furniture in light pastel colors and overhead there were murals depicting scenes from Roman mythology.

"Now go up and get ready to go out on the town tonight. My housekeeper, Mrs. Lockhart will get you anything you need."

"Is there a phone upstairs?" Pepper asked pulling her gloves off. "I want to call Hayden."

"Yes, tell him we have reservations at eight at the Hotel Hollywood."

Libby was not looking forward to seeing Haydn Price. She had heard mixed reviews about him. Some in the industry thought he was talented and charming, but most people thought he was nothing more than an ambitious businessman who saw motion pictures as a way to get rich quick. He had breezed into Hollywood, purchased several studios that were foundering and built an industry powerhouse in a matter of a few years. Even though it created jobs, it was at the expense of many.

The son of immigrants, Price had come up the hard way. Many believed he had underworld connections, and Libby wouldn't have been a bit surprised. She believed that he used and manipulated people and if Pepper suffered collateral damage in the process that was of no consequence to him.

After more drinks and laughs, they changed into evening clothes and were out the door again. "Wonderful to see you, Miss Durant," the doorman said at the Hotel Hollywood.

"Thank you, Bernie. It's good to be back."

Libby glided into the ballroom and ran her eyes over the crowd. She was comfortable here. After living at the apartment hotel for several years, it was her home away from home. It still housed many stars and people prominent in the industry, but many had left, building homes in Laurel Canyon and Beverly Hills.

"Hello, darlin'," someone said. It was Clay Aberdeen,

and he had a voluptuous woman on his arm. He had just checked his cowboy hat, and his red hair was a tousled mess. Nevertheless, his date clung to him possessively. She was a blowsy redhead with blue eyes and full lips, the kind of woman that turned heads. He straightened his tux and looked at Pepper.

"Clay," Libby said. "I want you to meet my cousin, Penelope Brennan."

"Charmed," he drawled and introduced his date.

"Call me Pepper."

"Are you here for a visit, Pepper?"

"I'm here to stay."

"Really? How brave."

"She's friends with Haydn Price. He believes she has acting potential."

His eyebrows shot up. "Well, well we could use someone who knows what they are doing in this town."

After they had found a table, Clay took his date immediately to the dance floor. Libby reached under the table and opened a bottle of liquor. Pepper watched her add alcohol to their drinks discreetly, "I didn't hear you ask for this."

"I didn't. It's a standing order whenever I come in. 'Golden Wedding' is nothing fancy, but it's a label that's always available."

Pepper lit a cigarette and looked at Clay. "He seems like a nice guy. Is that how he gets such a good looking girl?"

Libby shrugged. "He always dates beautiful women, and they all adore him. He *is* one of the nicest guys I've ever met."

"I apologize for being late, ladies," someone said.

Libby looked up. It was Haydn Price. A man in his early forties with thinning hair and glasses, Libby thought he looked more like an accountant than a studio tycoon. Even though he was well built, his round, Harold Lloyd glasses gave him a bookish, mousy appearance. Nevertheless, Pepper was taken with him, and she jumped up to kiss him.

Libby watched them embrace and thought, here is another one of life's great mysteries. But when Haydn Price started talking, she changed her mind. He was poised, confident and charming.

"I knew of you long before Pepper spoke of you, Miss Durant," he said, sitting down. "My congratulations on your success. It is no easy task to break into a man's world."

"It is not," Libby said, putting a cigarette in her holder. "Just as it is no easy task resurrecting three failing studios."

He smiled and looked at Pepper. "Here is my next project. I believe she has the potential to be a great star. May I count on you for help with makeup, Miss Durant? You and Clay Aberdeen are the best in the business."

Libby looked at Pepper. "Not much help needed there."

"Agreed," he said. "She's definitely one I won't let Thalberg won't get his hands on."

Pepper smiled.

Clay and his date returned from the dance floor, and Clay greeted Haydn heartily. They had worked together on several movies, and they immediately started talking about their current projects.

All night long Libby watched Haydn Price. He was gracious and amusing and had a sharp wit. It was such a surprise from someone who, at first glance, seemed so serious. Yet the longer she watched him, the more she began to realize what he was doing. He was orchestrating everything at the table from the topics of conversation to where people sat. When they danced, Libby kept her answers vague and unrevealing. She wasn't about to be manipulated by this smooth operator.

He did seem to worship Pepper though. Libby did not find that surprising. Pepper was truly adorable. She was the epitome of a perky, fun flapper, and Libby believed she may have a chance in pictures if she could translate that charm to the screen. She had the kind of personality the audience would love. A fresh face that was neither an ingénue nor a vamp, she was a true original. Libby knew Haydn saw that potential too and was determined to harness that appeal for his studio.

"So do you think your cousin is ready for Hollywood?" Clay asked Libby when they were dancing.

"Yes, she is certainly ready for Hollywood, but is she ready for Haydn Price? I don't trust him, Clay. What do you see that I'm not seeing?"

"I didn't just fall off the turnip truck, Miss Libby. The man's powerful and I have to get along with him. And I suggest you do too. Don't go interfering in their relationship. Let your cousin decide for herself."

"Alright," Libby said uncertainly.

As they danced past the band, the singer winked at Clay.

"You know Rebecca Lombard?"

"We dated for a while."

"Have you dated every gorgeous woman in Hollywood?'

"No, I never dated you."

"And why not?" Libby asked, pretending to be insulted.

"You're too classy. I like 'em trashy."

Libby laughed and shook her head. "You're one of a kind, Clay."

The song ended, and they returned to the table. The moment they sat down, the singer leaned into the microphone, looked at Clay and said, "This one's for you, darling," and started to sing, "You'd Be Surprised."

"Johnny was bashful and shy.
Nobody understood why
Mary loved him.
All the other girls passed him by.
Ev'ry one wanted to know
How she could pick such a beau.
With a twinkle in her eye
She made this reply,
He's not so good in a crowd but when you get him alone,
You'd be surprised.
He isn't much at a dance but when you takes you home,
You'd be surprised."

Libby looked at Clay, who was listening to the song, no expression on his face. She dropped back into her chair and exclaimed, "Oh my!" and she started to laugh. "Oh, of course!"

At last, she had the answer to *one* of life's great mysteries.

Chapter 13

"The milkman was just here, Miss Durant," Mrs. Lockhart said, heaving a rack of milk bottles onto the kitchen table.

"Oh good, thank you," Libby replied, picking up one of them. She walked into the living room where Pepper was sprawled out on the couch holding an ice bag to her head. "Good morning, cousin," she said.

"Too loud," Pepper mumbled.

"That must have been some party last night."

Libby took an empty decanter from the bar and poured the contents of the milk container into it. "Care for some hair of the dog that bit you?"

Pepper opened her eyes. "What the hell? That's not milk."

"Milkmen deliver all kinds of things nowadays."

"Right to your front door. Now that's service."

Libby mixed a sidecar and handed it to Pepper. "That'll help your headache. We've got to get going. We have to get you made up before Clay gets to the studio."

"The way I look today, you'll have your work cut out for you."

Libby walked over and moved her face from side to side, examining it. "It's going to be a long day."

"Shut up!" Pepper said, throwing a pillow at her as she walked from the room.

*   *   *

Even though it was early, Haydn Price's new studio was alive with activity. They were shooting a movie about

Cleopatra and extras dressed like Egyptians walked back and forth past the empty stage where Libby was doing Pepper's makeup. A trainer went by leading his horse all decorated in brasses, and Pepper saw a woman carrying a basket of snakes. Props were being wheeled over to the huge pyramid that had been constructed for the picture. Every time Libby saw a set carpenter, her stomach twisted with memories of Rudy.

She had just finished Pepper's makeup when a messenger handed her a note. "It's from Clay," she said to Pepper. "He was horseback riding last night, fell and sprained his wrist. He can't come today."

"What!" Pepper exclaimed.

The next moment, Griff Gardner walked up with a camera on his shoulder. "Well, hello there," he said to Pepper with a grin. "You need a cameraman?"

He hadn't seen Libby. When he turned around, the smile dropped from his face. "What are you doing here?" he asked.

"I might ask the same thing of you."

"Price cashed in on a favor, so I'm here to sub for Aberdeen," he growled.

Libby turned to Pepper. "We'll have to make other arrangements," and she started packing up her supplies. "This man is not qualified."

"Whoa! Hold your horses there, Princess Durant," Griff said. "The problem is that I'm *over*qualified to be doing your amateur makeover."

"Let's go," she told Pepper.

"But I have auditions tomorrow. It has to be today."

"Have Haydn reschedule them."

"No, I landed these myself," Pepper said, her eyes filling with tears. "I didn't want people to hire me just because they were afraid of Haydn, so I've been searching on my own."

"You have been out pounding the pavement this week?" Libby asked with surprise. She had been so busy she hadn't realized that Pepper had been out job hunting already. She sighed, dropped her arms and looked at Griff.

He looked back at her with his jaw clenched. "Make up your mind. My time is limited."

"We can do this without him, you know," Libby said, jerking her head at Griff.

"Not without footage of proper light and shadow, you can't," he snapped back.

"Oh, please Libby. I need all the help I can get!" Pepper cried. "I need to see what I look like on film."

Griff sighed and put the camera down. After rolling up his sleeves, he turned his flat cap around, so the bill was in the back and started setting up. "The shallow, superficial shit I have to put up with in this business," he grumbled just loud enough for Libby to hear.

Pepper jumped up and shook his hand. "I'm Libby's cousin from Minnesota. My name is Pepper Brennan—I mean Davis—Penny Davis. That's my new stage name."

"Griff Gardner," he replied. "You certainly don't look like a farm girl from Minnesota."

Pepper giggled. "We aren't farmers! What did Libby tell you? Our families--"

"Pepper, we have work to do," Libby interrupted.

Griff looked from one to the other. Rats so close, he thought. He had almost obtained information about the mysterious Elizabeth Durant.

Libby opened her kit to put finishing touches on Pepper's makeup. Her hands were shaking, and her mouth was dry. Of all the cameramen in Hollywood, why did Price have to bring Gardner in? She supposed it was because he was the best, and Haydn Price *always* had to have the best.

She stole a look at Griff while he took out his reflectors. She hated to admit it, but he was overqualified for this job. Gardner was one of the originals in cinematography and had been in it from the very beginning of photoplays, working with D. W. Griffith.

Clay told Libby that Gardner had been very young when he came to Hollywood and immediately D.W. had seen his potential, bringing him in as the second cameraman to Billy Bitzer. A year later though, he went to France to do air reconnaissance photography for the war effort. That's where he met John Dashby and Rodney Bell. Clay said that Gardner returned a changed man, more cynical but also a much more seasoned cinematographer.

"He has a love of the art and a love of storytelling," she remembered Clay saying. "And he still insists on being behind the camera even though he could direct other operators."

Clay had apprenticed with him several years earlier. "The first thing he told me was that you cannot learn cinematography. It is all instinct."

"Quit dreaming, Durant," Griff barked, waking Libby from her reverie. "I'm a busy man."

"What's the problem between the two of you, Libs?" Pepper whispered. "You act like you're going to tear each other's faces off."

"I would like to tear his face off."

"Well, will you try to restrain yourself? I'm nervous as it is."

Libby took a deep breath. "Alright, I'm sorry. I'll try to be civil."

"Did you two have a thing or something?"

"Yes, I'll tell you about it later."

For the first few minutes, Griff took footage of Pepper, doing mostly close-ups. After fussing with lighting and reflectors, he said to Pepper, "You know what? I'm going to get a grip. We're going to do this right," and he winked at her.

When he walked away, she said to Libby, "I think he's nice. When he smiles his eyes crinkle up."

"Oh, please. Next, you'll say his curly hair is cute too."

"Well, now that you mention it."

Minutes later Griff returned with a short, stocky man with tattoos. He was the grip and responsible for adjusting lighting and rigging. Griff had him retract the canvas overhead for natural lighting first.

A cigarette hanging from his mouth, Gardner started to roll the camera. He took footage of Pepper, turning this way and that with several close ups and at different angles. Next, he had the grip close the canvas and set up Klieg lights so he could take long shots and arc shots in the strong artificial light.

"Not too long under those lights today, Gardner," Libby warned. "She'll have eye burns."

"Oh really?" he replied, sarcastically.

With each shot, Libby would adjust Pepper's makeup and take notes. When they finished, Griff would have the film developed in the lab. Libby would study it and then fine tune Pepper's makeup. Later that day, Pepper would meet with a hairdresser, and Haydn had made arrangements for her to speak with the studio's fashion consultants. It was a huge day.

"I'm tired," Pepper said as they slid into a booth for a late lunch at Musso and Frank's Grill on Hollywood Boulevard. It felt good to be out of the glaring sun and in the cool darkness of the restaurant. With crisp white tablecloths, red leather upholstery and a long mahogany bar, it was obviously a nightclub rather than a luncheon spot.

"I'll take a look at that footage tonight and make notes of what to adjust," Libby said, opening a menu. "Stop by the shop tomorrow, and I'll make you up before the auditions."

"Libs," Pepper said, lowering her voice. "Is that Louise Brooks?"

"Yes," she replied, looking back at the menu. "All kinds of people in show business come in here. That new writer from St. Paul was here yesterday with his wife."

"Who?"

"I can't think of his name. He grew up not too far from where Grandmother lives on Summit Avenue. *This Side of Paradise*--"

"Oh, Fitzgerald?" Pepper said.

"Yes, Scott Fitzgerald. I think Grandmother knows the family."

"All the Irish know each other in that damn town," Pepper said. "I'm glad to be out here and anonymous for a change."

"Let's keep it that way. You almost slipped with Gardner this morning."

"I know it. Now tell me what happened between the two of you."

The waiter brought their lunch, and Libby explained.

She had met Griff well over a year ago at The Biltmore. Max Redmond, the actor, had been hounding her for weeks to go out with him, and at last, she agreed. He took her to an opening night party at the Biltmore to celebrate the release of the latest Douglas Fairbanks movie. Not yet a big star, Redmond was still clawing his way to the top taking bit parts. The party was in full swing, and at some point, Libby lost track of him.

When she walked over to the bar to get a drink, she heard someone ask, "No date on a Saturday night?"

She turned and looked. It was Griff Gardner. He

seemed to be laughing at her. This guy's fresh, she thought.

"I have a date," she replied coolly, putting her cigarette in a holder. "He's around here somewhere. And where's *your* date?"

"I can't find her either. A fine pair we are," he said, giving her a light.

When the bartender gave Libby soda water, she looked under a table for a bottle. When she didn't find one, she asked, "Is there a guy with pitcher pig somewhere?"

"The liquor's in the drink already," Griff said.

"Really?" and she took a sip. "You're right. So they're serving right here in front of God and everybody?"

"Pickford and Fairbanks can do whatever they want in this town. Did you work on this film?

"No, the guy I came with did though, Max Redmond. You know him?"

"Oh sure. I know Max. I'm Griffin Gardner," he said, shaking hands with her.

"Elizabeth Durant."

The band started playing "It Had to Be You," and the dancefloor filled.

Griff took a puff of his cigarette, running his eyes over the crowd. He was leaning on the bar, and suddenly he straightened up. "Well, I found Max."

"Where?"

"Right there, sticking his tongue down my date's throat."

Max Redmond was indeed on the dancefloor kissing the actress, Jeannette Blakely.

"Well, I'll be damned," Libby said. "And I didn't even want to go out with the bastard."

Griff shook his head. "I should have known." Tossing his drink back, he asked, "You hungry?"

"Not really."

"Good, let's get a hamburger."

They went to a late-night diner off Wilshire Boulevard and talked until sunrise, eating burgers and drinking coffee. The connection was immediate. He was witty and fun and had more substance than most of the movie people she had encountered. It was refreshing. The next day he asked Libby out again, and they dated for the next month until he went on location to shoot a Western. Unfortunately, the star of the movie was Jeanette Blakely, his date from the night at the Wilshire. Libby heard later they had reconciled and were seeing each other again. Then he was called out of town for several months.

"So is he still with Blakely?" Pepper asked.

Libby shook her head. "When he got back in town, he called me and wanted back."

"What did you do?"

"I told him the bank was closed."

*   *   *

Griff was exhausted. Spending the entire morning near Libby had put him on edge. He had balanced on clifftops, hung from buildings and photographed enemy arsenals but nothing had jangled his nerves more than working with Libby Durant. The entire morning, he had watched her when her back was turned.

She had the finest figure of any woman he had ever seen. Her curves were soft and understated, not coarse and exaggerated like so many of the women in Hollywood. And the way she moved, it drove him wild. Her every gesture was smooth and sultry, flooding him with desire. Best of all, she was unaware of her sex appeal. It was as fundamental to her as the color of her eyes. He covered his attraction with anger, but in reality, he felt a rush of lust every time she passed him.

He ground his teeth. He needed to forget her. When he

came back in town, she had made it perfectly clear that she had moved on. He wished he could tell her the truth about everything, but what did it matter now? He'd be damned if he'd grovel.

The most disturbing thing of all was that Libby had awakened feelings in him that were far beyond carnal yearnings. These were feelings he had never experienced, and they made him feel vulnerable. No one was going to have that kind of power over Griff Gardner.

*   *   *

The first auditions did not go well for Pepper, but she was not discouraged. She knew that she was just getting started and that competition was stiff. Every day hundreds of young women were pouring into Hollywood in search of fame and fortune, so she continued to audition. At last, she landed several small parts, and slowly gained acting experience. And then after several months, she was cast as a supporting actress in a Janet Gaynor movie.

"Haydn's not happy I took the part," she told Libby one morning. She was sitting on Libby's bed, hugging a pillow, watching her dress for work.

"I thought he wanted you in photoplays," Libby said as she dropped a slip over her head.

"He wants to save me for just the right "vehicle" as he calls it. I told him I wanted to do it my way. I need to work."

Libby took a puff of her cigarette, sat down on the bed and rolled up her silk stockings. When she stepped into her dropped waist dress, Pepper said, "Hey, that hemline is alarmingly short, Miss Durant. May I borrow it sometime?"

"Sure," Libby said, brushing her hair. "Are you coming by for makeup this afternoon?"

"Yes."

"I won't be at the shop. Have one of the girls do it."

"Where are you going?"

"They need help on *The Phantom of the Opera*."

"You're helping Lon Chaney?"

"Yes, and some of the cast. You should see his makeup in the final scene, Pepper. It's going to scare the hell out of audiences. In my world, this man is a god."

"You helped him on *The Hunchback of Notre Dame* too, didn't you?"

"He was in charge of his own makeup. I only assisted. He used a lot of prosthetics, and some of them were heavy. He truly is a miracle man," Libby said, grabbing her handbag. "I have to run! See you tonight."

As Pepper was dressing, Mrs. Lockhart told her Haydn was on the phone.

"Hello, darling," she said.

"I have good news and bad news," Haydn announced.

She frowned, "What?"

"The bad news is you won't have time to be in *Gentleman Jim* with Gaynor. The good news is that you'll be starting in *Good Time Charlie* the end of the week. You'll be the leading lady."

Pepper was dumbfounded.

"Pepper, are you there?"

"Yes, I'm here." Her heart was pounding so hard, she thought she would faint.

"It'll be your breakout movie. Your co-star will be Billy Arnold."

"Billy Arnold! You can't be serious. I'm not ready for this."

"Yes, you are. It's a screwball comedy--perfect for you. You're going to be a big star, kid."

"Oh, Haydn, thank you, thank you, but I'm scared."

"I know. I'll be there every step of the way. Dinner tonight to celebrate?"

"Absolutely," she said. She was so excited her knees

were shaking.

"Are you happy?"

"Happy? Hell, I'm over the moon!"

*   *   *

Haydn was right. Penny Davis did become a big star. *Good Time Charley* broke box office records and launched her career overnight. Audiences adored her image of the loveable flapper, and overnight she became the toast of the town. She was the latest trendsetter, and all the magazines ran stories on her "style." Women wanted Penny Davis hairstyles, clothing and makeup. They walked like her and even talked like her, and through it all, miraculously, Pepper remained grounded. She found the fame and adoration amusing but knew it wouldn't last.

She gave credit to Haydn Price for mentoring her, but everyone knew she was the one with the talent. She was a born comedienne. Much of her humor was physical comedy, and audiences found her facial expressions hilarious. But above all, she had impeccable timing and an instinct for new takes on old gags.

There were invitations to parties, dinners, and guest appearances and Pepper went to them all. The ultimate Hollywood party girl, Libby didn't know how she could cram it all in. Yet even with all the late nights, Pepper never let work slide. She worked hard, and in a few months, she had enough money to take a suite of rooms at the prestigious Beverly Heights Hotel.

Work had been escalating for Libby as well. She had been talking to financial planners about expanding her products across the country. Max Factor had launched his line nationally, and Libby believed Elizabeth Durant should do the same.

"Dinner at seven tonight before it gets too wild at the 510?" Pepper asked Libby on the phone.

"I'll try. I've been meeting with investors all day and still have to get over to the shop to do some bookwork," Libby replied.

"Alrighty, when you get there the password is, 'The mayor sent me.' Are you coming with Dash?"

"Yes."

"See you tonight."

Libby would rather go home and just soak in the tub, but it had been weeks since she had seen Pepper. She knew it would be loud and crazy at the 510 Club too. It was not only a popular, exclusive club with the best liquor in town, but it was also New Year's Eve.

She couldn't believe it was going to be 1926. It had been a whirlwind since she had arrived in California. In six years she had accomplished all her goals. She was glad she lived in a time where a career was possible for women, even though it was unusual. Grandmother and Uncle Owen had both written to her saying they were proud of her. She missed them both. During quiet moments, she would think about Jennie and Rudy too. She knew that the grief would never subside, but hopefully, it would dull with time.

She had to rush through her bookwork, but she made it home just in time to change for the celebration. She put on her gold beaded evening dress with a hemline that was short but fashionably uneven. The back of the dress was cut dangerously low too, so she wound a long string of pearls around her neck, and let them drape down her spine. Dash rang the doorbell just as she was pulling on her long white gloves. Her relationship with John Dashby had cooled the past months. Now they saw each other only occasionally. Nevertheless, he made her laugh, and she liked his light-hearted attitude. He was the epitome of the devil-may-care flyboy.

"The mayor sent me," he said when she opened the

door.

"Wrong address," she said. "No fun to be had here."

He put his arm around her and pulled her close. "There could be."

"We're late," she said, laughing and trying to wiggle free.

"I usually take it slow, but I can be quick too," he said kissing her. As he ran his lips down Libby's neck, he stroked her back lightly.

His warm hands on her skin felt delicious, but she pulled back. "We want to save something for later."

"Oh, I have plenty to spare, at least for two or three times tonight."

She laughed and grabbed his hand leading him out the door.

Loud music blasted out of the 510 Club when the doorman opened the peephole. Dash gave the password, and they walked into a party that was already in full swing. The room was crammed with revelers, dancing, laughing and drinking champagne. Although the lights were low, the nightclub was filled with color. The women's dresses were every shade of the rainbow from soft pastels to bright reds and greens. And everywhere there were balloons.

The air was thick with smoke and music as Libby and Dash wound through the room. A woman was doing the Charleston on a table, and when she kicked her legs up, she had no undergarments. No one even noticed.

They found Pepper and Haydn at two large tables with other couples. Most of them were friends from the industry. Although there were two actors, most of the group worked behind the scenes. One of them was a set designer, another worked in wardrobe, two were screenwriters, and one was an aspiring director. Haydn included a few of his friends as well. After several drinks, dinner was served.

"Any luck today with investors?" Pepper asked Libby, as she cut into her steak.

"No, it has been nothing but nay-sayers," she replied. "It may not happen. At least not now." She was trying hard not to sound upset. But she was downhearted. Libby had met with six different investors, and they had all rejected her. Any feelings of disappointment she tried to squash, telling herself that she was spoiled. But with her high level of tenacity, she would not give up and was starting to feel desperate.

"What are you trying to do?" Haydn asked.

"I want to market my line of cosmetics nationwide."

"And no one will invest?"

"No, I have suspected all along they don't think I have a head for business."

"Because you are a woman?" Haydn asked.

"I know that's part of it. In fact, the investor I met with today came out and said he was not comfortable being a backer for a woman." She chuckled. "At least he was honest. The other part is that the cosmetic industry is so new."

Pepper chuckled cynically. "That's what they said about moving pictures."

Haydn put his fork down. "My money is all tied up right now in my new studio, but I may be able to offer a little assistance. Perhaps they have a concern that you are a free agent."

"Well, yes. They said that too, but they are ignoring the fact that I have been working independently for six years, making a go of it all by myself."

"I have seen your work Elizabeth, and it is no secret that I am in awe. I've been wanting to ask you this for some time, but I always thought you would refuse. I could offer you a contract with Mirador as head of the makeup department. It is not a cure-all, but it may allay investor's fears about guaranteed income." He watched Libby closely and added, "To have you on our team would be an honor."

Libby was stunned. This would definitely make her more appealing to the investors and be an easy fix. But to be an employee?

"Your makeup line and shop would, of course, be completely independent from the studio," Haydn added. He shrugged and started eating again. "It's just a thought."

"It certainly is," Libby said. "Thank you."

They finished their meal, but Libby was preoccupied. She wanted to go home where it was quiet and consider Haydn's offer. It was most appealing, and studio contracts seemed to be the way of the future.

When dinner was finished, they did some dancing, and when everyone was sitting back down, Haydn stood up. Two waiters immediately started filling everyone's glasses with champagne. "Please drink a toast," he said, looking at Pepper. "To the future Mrs. Haydn Price."

Everyone cheered except Libby. Twice in one night, she had been dumbfounded. She jumped up quickly though and kissed them both. Pepper was blushing. In all the years, Libby had known her, she had never seen her cousin blush. She must truly love him, Libby thought tenderly. *Poor kid.*

Chapter 14

Libby couldn't sleep, and part of the reason was that the sun was up. They had stayed at the 510 Club well after midnight and then Haydn had them all over to his home in Beverly Hills for an engagement celebration. This was his second marriage, but he told everyone he was determined to treat it like the first. They had more champagne with caviar and Libby ended the night at Dash's apartment. At sunrise, she slipped out of bed and took a cab home.

After tossing and turning, she finally got up and fixed herself some coffee. Mrs. Lockhart was off for New Year's Day, so Libby fixed herself some breakfast and brought the milk in. As usual there bottles of milk and bottles of liquor. She considered having a morning "eye-opener" but cast off the idea. She had to think clearly today and sort things out. She was confused about Haydn. The longer she knew him, the more she liked him. He was helpful but never pushy, a talented businessman, and best of all, he was good to Pepper.

As she sat in the breakfast nook, staring at the pool, she wondered if she should sign with Mirador Pictures. It could open all kinds of doors, but she would lose her freedom. Would she revert back to her rebellious school girl ways?

Haydn told her not be in a hurry to make a decision, so she took the next few days to consider it. And then late one afternoon at the shop, one of her employees said, "There is a gentleman having his nails done who would like to meet you. He says he's a friend of Mr. Harold Thompson."

"The banker?"

"Here is his card."

Libby looked at it, put her pen down and walked into the gentleman's section of the salon. "Welcome to our salon, Mr. Grieves."

He was a man in his middle years, slightly overweight with a thin mustache. "How do you do, Miss Durant. I'd shake your hand but--" and he nodded at the manicurist, smiling. "I know you're busy, so I'll be brief. Harold Thompson thought I should speak with you. He said you are looking to expand your business. I specialize in--" and again he looked at the manicurist.

"You may speak freely, Mr. Grieves."

"I specialize in investments that are a bit unorthodox. Shall we call them creative ventures? I have found many of them to be most worthy though. Everything is exciting and new out here in Hollywood, and I am willing to consider fresh ideas for investments. Nothing ventured, nothing gained."

Libby smiled slowly, trying to remain poised, but on the inside, she wanted to do the Charleston. "Would you have time to talk after your manicure?" she asked.

"Certainly."

"I'll be in my office."

Off and on that entire week, Libby met with Douglas Grieves. It was no surprise that the interest rate on the loan was somewhat inflated, but the other terms seemed reasonable. To increase her chances of obtaining the loan, she told him that she was signing a contract with Mirador Studios. He said that would definitely help.

By the end of the week, they agreed to terms. She would take a one-year contract with Mirador and the loan from Grieves.

The next morning as she was about to leave for work, the phone rang. It was her Aunt Bertie Durant. "Elizabeth, I have bad news. Your Aunt Grace died suddenly last night."

"Oh no. How is Uncle Owen?"

"He is holding up well."

"What happened?"

"We think it was a heart attack."

"When is the funeral?"

"That's part of the reason I'm calling. We won't decide anything until we know if you coming home."

Libby hesitated. She had a multitude of work obligations and the contract to sign, but it must all wait. She had to see Uncle Owen. "I'll return immediately."

She took a private compartment on the train, and several days later she was back in Minneapolis. The night before the funeral, Libby stayed with her Aunt Lavinia and Uncle Grayson Durant in their palatial home on Lake of the Isles, but she couldn't wait to leave. They made it apparent they thought she was nothing more than Hollywood party girl, so she telephoned Grandmother Brennan to stay with her instead.

Her first stop after the funeral was to see Zappy and Tante at the house on Grove Avenue. They were doing well and were delighted to see her.

"Whenever you are ready to retire, you tell me," Libby said. "And I will make all the arrangements." But both women declined, saying, for now, they were still willing to help with the children.

Next, she went the attorney's office to check on the status of the foundation, and once she found everything in order, she walked several blocks down to the newly built Young Quinlan Department Store to meet Grandmother Brennan for lunch. Grander than the first one, it was a large, graceful establishment with rich carpeting, crystal chandeliers, and brass fixtures. A gloved elevator operator took Libby up several floors to the dining room. Looking more like a tearoom than a restaurant, the Fountain Room was filled with well-dressed women, eating dainty finger sandwiches. In the center of the dining area was a stone pond with a cherub and a swan fountain, and a stage for fashion shows.

"You look well, Elizabeth," Olivia said when she sat down. "There's just enough time for us to have lunch and see the modeling."

Libby was alarmed when she saw her grandmother. Although she still looked chic in her green Chanel suit, she had lost a great deal of weight, and her face looked haggard.

While they ate their salads, Olivia informed Libby that Pepper had told her of the engagement. "What do you think of him?" she asked.

"He seems to adore Pepper," Libby replied.

"Yes, but what do *you* think of him?"

Libby hesitated. "Well, he's growing on me. I wasn't sure at first."

"I haven't even seen a picture of him yet, but I understand he is a good deal older than Penelope. What on earth does she see in him?"

"He is a charming Irish-American, Grandmother. Need I say more?"

Olivia raised her eyebrows and sipped her tea. "There's plenty of *young* Irish Americans too. How is your Uncle Owen?"

"I haven't talked to him yet. He was so busy at the funeral. But everyone says he's doing well."

"There was no love lost between the two of them, you know," Olivia said, referring to his marriage. "But it is still hard."

With nothing more to add, Olivia went back to her salad, and for the first time ever, Libby noticed the conversation drag with her grandmother. Something was definitely wrong. She was usually so quick and witty, but now every movement seemed to be an effort, and she had lost her sense of humor.

"Is everything alright with you, Grandmother? You seem tired."

She looked up at her and then dropped her eyes again. "Honestly, Elizabeth, stop with the doleful expression. I'm getting older. That's all. Perhaps I am tired. Oh look, they're starting the fashion show."

*   *   *

The next day Libby went to have lunch with Uncle Owen. It was a bitterly cold day, and Owen was sitting by the fire in the library. The staff set up a small table in front of the blaze for them and served them soup and popovers. Libby thought he looked good. His hair was grayer, but he had very few wrinkles and still retained his distinguished good looks.

"You seem well, Uncle."

"I am doing well," he replied. "Although it will be strange without Grace. It will be an adjustment not seeing her across the table each morning." He looked up at Libby. "You know that we were never the best of friends."

"I always suspected that."

"But she was never unkind, only disinterested. She had her garden club and bridge club. How about you?" he asked. "Any suitors in your life?"

"Suitors? Really, Uncle Owen, are you two hundred years old?"

Owen always liked his niece's irreverence. It made him laugh. "I'm an old fool. What shall we call them?"

"I don't know, but whatever we call the men in my life, there is no one special."

"You are too busy with that business."

"Which brings me to something I want to ask you," Libby said, putting her spoon down. She told him how she wanted to make her line of cosmetics national, but that it had been difficult finding investors. When she asked his opinion of Grieves' offer, he frowned.

"Is there a problem with it?"

"No, no. It all seems quite straightforward."

"Then what?"

"No, no nothing. It sounds solid."

But after that, he changed the subject asking about Pepper's career and upcoming marriage. He was also anxious to hear Hollywood gossip since he was a fan of the movies. They spent the entire day together talking and laughing, and that night Libby caught the train back to Los Angeles.

When she arrived home, there was a telegram from him.

"Do not sign that contract," it said. "I would like to be the sole investor in Elizabeth Durant Cosmetics."

*　　　　*　　　　*

So much had been solved with Uncle Owen's offer. They spoke several times over the phone, and after their attorneys had drawn up the papers, everything was complete.

Owen Durant had been following his niece's career closely, and he could see she had the Durant head for business. Always looking for a good investment, he was delighted when she told him she was expanding. He slept on it only one night before calling her and leaving the message.

Libby thanked Douglas Grieves' for his offer but politely

declined. Haydn was disappointed that she was not going to sign with Mirador, but he said he understood completely. She thanked him for offering to help, and he countered immediately with a request. He needed Libby's makeup expertise on his next film entitled, *Jack the Ripper*, and he wanted her on the set to help Pepper relax too. It was her first serious role, and she was feeling unsteady. Libby agreed without hesitation.

When Libby arrived on the set the first day, Pepper told her she had requested Griffin Gardner for cinematography.

"What! I would have thought twice about taking the job had I known."

Pepper winced. "That's why I didn't tell you until now."

"Damn it. He is so arrogant."

"Oh, he is *not* arrogant. He makes me laugh."

"Tell it to Sweeney," Libby mumbled.

In spite of Libby's reservations, the first week went well. Griff stayed away from Libby, and Libby stayed away from Griff.

He spent a great deal of time laughing and joking with Pepper, along with the director, both of them trying to put her at ease. Gradually, with a little coaching, she delivered her lines convincingly, and by the second week, she was delivering an exceptional performance.

Libby had little time to be uncomfortable around Griff, her team was so busy. The setting was Nineteenth Century London, and most of the characters were street people and prostitutes. Makeup, wigs, and wardrobe were key elements. They had to make the actors look dirty and haggard, and age many of them, or make them look sick, and Griff had to work closely with her team, lighting everyone properly.

His creative use of light and shadow gave the film an eerie atmosphere. He experimented with backlighting and side lighting, and when filming Pepper, he put gauze over the camera to soften her look to make the audience sympathize with her.

"Some of those shots look like paintings," Libby heard one of the extras say.

Griff laughed. "I suppose. My parents pushed art on me from a young age."

"They liked art?"

"That's how they earned a living."

"What kind of art?"

"They did murals and large paintings in train stations, restaurants, lobbies, that sort of thing."

"Oh, I bet I've seen some of their work," the actor said.

"Maybe."

"Did you grow up in New York?"

"We lived nowhere," Griff said, putting out his cigarette. "We traveled wherever there was a contract."

"Same thing here. But we were vaudeville."

When Griff turned to adjust a light, he saw that Libby had been listening, and he locked eyes with her. A jolt of pleasure passed through her body, and she looked away quickly.

Weeks passed, and makeup became more challenging. There were many violent scenes, involving blood and lacerations, so artificial wounds were needed, along with prosthetics.

"We shoot the scene today where you are attacked," the director said to Pepper.

"I'm ready," she said as one of the wardrobe women put a hat on her head.

Griff and his cameramen took their places. The director called, "Action," and they started to crank the cameras.

"Start walking," the director said to Pepper. "Now look over your shoulder. You're nervous. Is someone following you?"

Libby stood rigidly and watched. Pepper was a master of pantomime. The director continued to coach. "Now Jack, come to the door. You are ready to strike."

Libby knew it was just a photoplay, but the scene was unnerving. Her mouth went dry, and her heart began to pound. Memories flashed before her eyes. The actor playing Jack the Ripper grabbed Pepper, raised the knife, and Libby jumped. She couldn't watch anymore. The violence of the scene was too much. She was going to vomit. Her foot caught on a cord, and she sent a ladder crashing to the floor.

Running off the set, the first thing she saw was a garbage can in between two buildings. She dashed over to it, starting to retch. Over and over she vomited, tears streaming down her face until she could barely stand any longer.

Panting, she pulled her gloves off to wipe her lips, and there was Griff. He was staring at her, wide-eyed. He looked at the scars on her arms, and up at her face again. "I—I was worried about you," he said. "When the ladder fell, I looked over, and I saw you running."

"What ladder?" Libby mumbled, pushing the hair from her face.

"Never mind. Are you alright?"

"Yes, just too much to drink last night."

He handed her his handkerchief. "Maybe you should go home."

"No, there's too much to do. I'll be fine," she said and put her gloves back on.

*   *   *

Griff knew why Libby was sick and it wasn't a hangover. It had something to do with those scars on her arms. When they were dating, she told him they were from an automobile accident, but judging from her reaction today it was from something else.

When he went home that night, he tried to put the incident out of his mind, but it nagged him. He told himself that her problems were not his problems and that their relationship was over, but he had to know the truth. What was she hiding?

*   *   *

Jack the Ripper was complete, and Griff was back to work again shooting a chase scene in another Mirador picture. He was sitting with his camera on a wooden platform attached to the front of an automobile. He had on his old aviator jacket, knickerbockers, and high boots. His friend, Rodney Bell was in another car doing the stunt work.

"Ready!" Griff called to the director.

"Alright."

"Is the road blocked off?" Rodney asked.

"We have it to ourselves," the director called back to him.

Everyone settled into place, and director yelled into his megaphone, "Action!"

Griff started cranking as the actor started the automobile. They drove down the dirt road at top speed with Rodney driving alongside them in his motorcar. Griff was to get shots of the actor behind the wheel and then footage of Rodney as his stunt double next to them. The climax of the scene was to be Rodney jumping from his motorcar just before it careened down a hill.

At top speed, they went around one curve and then another when suddenly a farmer driving a pickup full of fruit came down from an orchard and turned onto the road. There was no time to stop. Rodney who was on the outside was the first to swerve. The tires on his automobile caught on some rocks, and he tumbled down the hill. The last thing

188

Griff saw was the look of horror on the actor's face before they too went over the edge.

*   *   *

Rodney Bell did not survive the crash. His neck was broken when the motorcar rolled down the hillside. Griff and the actor survived but were in serious condition. The driver of the fruit truck escaped without injury.

"It's a dangerous proposition surviving a war," Clay said as he sat on the edge of a chair in Libby's living room. He had just given her the news. He was holding a low ball glass, swirling the liquor around and around. "Sometimes when you escape death so many times you think you're invincible. Sometimes you even invite it to a duel."

Libby was standing by the fireplace, clutching herself tightly with her arms crossed over her chest. She swallowed hard. "Surely you're not blaming them?"

"No, I'm just saying taking chances over and over again can be a byproduct of war. That's why so many of them are barnstormers. Not many survive that either."

"Is it like that for you?"

He shook his head. "Everyone reacts differently."

Libby walked to the window and looked out. "Will the hospital allow visitors?"

"I'd wait. They were both pretty out of it when I saw them."

But Libby couldn't wait. Before Griff was awake, she visited. He was unconscious, and his head was bandaged. His face was purple with cuts and bruises, and one arm was in a cast. She visited George too who was awake but groggy and in pain. Both his legs were broken.

Clay called the morning after Rodney's funeral and said he had just been up to see Griff. "He's awake and doing well. Crabby as hell which my mama always says is a good sign. George has gone home."

"This is good news. I'll go and see Griff today."

That afternoon when Libby arrived at St. Vincent's Hospital, she stood outside the entrance to the ward, uncertain how to act. She wasn't sure she should be going to see Griff at all. Their relationship had been so hostile that he may just have the staff toss her out.

She took a deep breath and walked down the aisle to his bed. He was dozing, and Libby stared down at him. He was thin, and his head was still bandaged, but his eyes were no longer purple and swollen. She cleared her throat, and he opened his eyes.

Tossing a box of candy on the night stand, she said, "I know you like candy, so here."

A smile flickered on his lips. "Why hello, Durant, you warm, loveable person."

"I know," she said, rolling her eyes. She sat down on the bed, lit a cigarette and said, "Well, what the hell happened?"

"I don't remember a goddamn thing."

She frowned. "I'm truly sorry about Rodney."

Griff looked down and nodded.

There was a painful silence. Struggling for something to say, Libby asked, "Has Dash been up to see you?"

"He has. Don't you two talk anymore?"

Libby shook her head. "Clay has been keeping me up to date on everything."

A nurse brought in a tray of food and helped Griff sit up. She brought Libby a chair and pulled the white privacy curtain around the two of them.

"I don't have to feed you, do I?" Libby asked.

"Would you?"

She answered him by handing him his fork.

"When will they let you go home?"

"I don't know. Not soon enough." He pushed the food

around on his plate, inspecting it with a scowl on his face. "So what have you been up to? Any movies?"

"I have a few, but the big news is that I'm taking my cosmetic line national."

He raised his eyebrows. "Really? Congratulations. That is big news. So you are a busy businesswoman now."

"Yes, and speaking of business, I better get back," she said, standing up. "I just wanted to bring you that candy."

"Thank you. Hey, would you--" He looked at her as if he was unsure and then said, "Would you have time to come back and play gin with an invalid?"

Libby's stomach jumped. He wanted her to come back. She smiled. "Do I have to let you win since you're sick?"

"Yes."

"Alright." She pulled the curtain back and said, "See you tomorrow?"

"Bring more candy."

She nodded.

He listened to her walking away, her high heels clicking on the ward floor.

*   *   *

Libby came back every day for a week straight. She always came late in the afternoon when she was done on the sets, and things slowed down at the shop.

"What have you got for me today?" Griff said when she walked up.

Libby pulled the curtain closed, slid onto the edge of the bed and handed him a package. "A ham sandwich."

"With mustard?" he asked, grabbing it and taking a bite.

"Yes, and you're welcome."

"Thank you," he mumbled with his mouth full. He swallowed and said, "No more tuna. The nurse smelled it yesterday. She's getting suspicious."

Libby laughed. "Alright, what do you want me to bring?"

"Corned beef and I want you to bake me something for dessert."

"That will not happen."

"Have you *ever* baked anything?"

Libby put her fist to her mouth, pretending to think and said, "Um, no."

Griff started to laugh and then grabbed his broken ribs. "Ouch," he exclaimed. Taking a breath, he continued. "You are pathetic, Durant. When I get out of here, I am going to cook you a meal and teach you to bake you a cake."

The thought of dating Griff again flooded Libby with excitement. She covered her elation by pulling out a deck of cards and started shuffling. "No more letting you win at gin anymore."

"If you think I haven't been winning on my own, you live in a fantasy world."

"I work in Hollywood, don't I?"

"Hey, how's the cosmetic campaign going, Oh, Goddess of the Looking Glass?" he asked as she dealt.

"Speaking of another fantasy world--"

He laughed. "I didn't say that."

"Well, makeup is an illusion," she conceded good-naturedly, "Anyway, I hired an advertising agency to help me wade through it all. We're thinking of putting ads in magazines, approaching department stores—that sort of thing."

"You need to make women feel like that can't live without it."

"True, but it will be tough. There are still a lot of people that think cosmetics are for Jezebels."

Griff fanned his cards out. "We know about *that* attitude. Not only do we have Prohibition but the Hayes office now too."

They went back and forth, drawing and discarding.

"So Dash was in this morning."

"Really?" Libby replied, uninterested.

"He has a new girl," Griff said, and he stole a look at her.

"That's nice."

"He asked me if you have someone new."

This time Libby stole at look at him. "Too busy bringing sandwiches to invalids," she replied, discarding.

Griff looked pleased and then said suddenly, "Oh look gin!"

Chapter 15

Taking Elizabeth Durant Cosmetics to a national level was a lot of work, but at last Libby and her team had developed a strategy for expansion. It was costly but a necessary risk. They would put ads in all the big name magazines, purchase space on billboards and obtain air time on the latest innovation, the radio. It would involve designers, copywriters, models and voice talent.

Although Libby was overwhelmed with demands on her time, knowing she would see Griff at the end of each day kept her going. One afternoon when she walked into the office, her secretary handed her a message from him. He had been discharged from the hospital, and once he was settled back at home, he was going to have her over and teach her how to bake a cake.

Libby smiled. She sat down behind her desk and thought about him. Seeing him recently was just like old times. They laughed, teased each other and flirted outrageously.

Only now would she allow herself to think again about their intimate moments together a year ago. She could still feel his urgent caresses. There had never been anything tentative or shy about Griff's passion. When he pulled her into his arms, she knew what he wanted. It was as if he was starving for her. She remembered the heat of his hands and the rough stubble of his whiskers chafing the tender skin on her face and breasts. She remembered the slow, sultry nights where they teased each other until they were both frenzied with excitement ending it all in rapture.

Would it all happen again? The thought of it warmed her. Seeing him day after day at the hospital had rekindled her desire. She chuckled. *Even in a hospital bed, that man looks good.*

*   *   *

Libby had been so busy she hadn't seen Pepper in weeks, so one night she had her to the house for supper.

"Mrs. Lockwood left us a roast and baked potatoes," Libby said, opening the oven door.

"It smells divine, cuz."

"I want to hear all about the wedding," she said, pulling the roast out.

"Well, we're going to honeymoon in Havana."

"I hear it's beautiful there."

"Yes, and apparently horse racing is popular. Haydn's going to race his thoroughbreds." Pepper said, sitting down at the table.

"Are you going to get married here or in Havana?"

"I don't know. He's going to surprise me with the location."

Libby dished up their meal and sat down. "You really love him, don't you?"

"I do. The age difference shocks everyone, most of all my parents, but he treats me like a queen. I feel like I have everything I ever wanted. Now maybe children too."

"You think right away?"

She shrugged. "I don't know. My career is just getting started. Maybe I'll just settle down and become a housewife."

"That'll be the day."

Pepper laughed. Taking a bite, she said, "Yum, home cooking. I'm tired of all the restaurants and take-out joints. Now tell me about you and Griff Gardner."

"Nothing to tell except that we've called a truce."

"Going to see him every day in the hospital sounds like more than a truce. Do you think you'll date again?"

"If you call him teaching me to bake, dating, then yes."

*   *   *

Griff called, at last, inviting Libby over for dinner and baking lesson.

"But I don't want to learn to bake," she complained.

"You're going to learn. Come over at five on Friday and bring your apron."

All week long Libby looked forward to seeing him again, but the morning of the date, he sent a note canceling. He had been called out of town suddenly.

Libby was disappointed, but she was determined not to jump to conclusions, so she waited. A week passed, and there was no phone call or letter. By the end of the second week, she was getting angry and decided to find out what was happening. She contacted Jack Jakes, the director who was one of Griff's closest friends, and he told her that Griff was called away to Paris.

"Paris!" Libby exclaimed.

"He has family there."

"He does? Who?"

"I don't really know."

Jack seemed reluctant to say any more, so she hung up. The familiar knot returned to her stomach. A long, unexplained absence is one of the things that killed the affair last time. *What is going on? Does he have a woman in every port? Just who is it he seeing when he leaves?*

She spent night after night tossing and turning, hating Griff for ensnaring her again. She felt tricked and cursed herself for allowing him to play with her heart once more.

One morning after a particularly restless night, she looked in the mirror and was startled. She had lost weight, and there were dark rings under her eyes. Thank goodness you know makeup, she thought. But it was more than her appearance that alarmed her. It was the constant inner turmoil. She must forget Griff Gardner and move on with her life before it made her sick.

She threw herself back into work and forced herself back into a social life. She started dating again, and after a month, the anxiety loosened. Her sleep improved, and although she was still hurt and confused, she carried on.

And then Griff returned. She overheard a crew member say that he was on the set of *The Cask of Amontillado.*

Libby's heart started pounding. So he was back and hadn't bothered to call. "When did they start filming?" she asked.

"Over a week ago."

Libby nodded and turned away. Well, that was that she said to herself. It's over before it even got started again. She straightened her back, raised her chin and returned to the set. At least work was going well. She was supervising makeup on *The Black Pirate* with Douglas Fairbanks and starting *The Scarlet Pimpernel* with Gerta Linden. Clay was doing the filming on both pictures, and it was the best thing that could have happened to Libby. It was good to be around old friends.

The first day on the set of *The Scarlet Pimpernel*, it was chaos. Crew members rushed back and forth carrying drapes, gold painted tables and crystal chandeliers for a scene at a French palace. When Libby arrived with her team, Gerta swept over to her immediately. She was the epitome of a great star, confident and beautiful, self-centered and arrogant. Dressed in a long Japanese wrap, ready for makeup and wardrobe, she cooed in her thick German accent, "Elizabeth, my *leibchen*, so good to see you, but I am angry with you, my beauty."

"Why?"

"Because you don't do my makeup anymore."

"I'm sorry, Gerta. Is Paul not following my instructions?"

Gerta shrugged. "He is, but he does not have your careful eye."

"I tell you what, for old time's sake, I'll do your makeup today. It'll be fun. We'll catch up."

"Darling, that would be wonderful. I do love you."

Libby was just starting on Gerta's makeup when Clay came into the dressing room telling her that Griff Gardner was asking to speak with her.

Libby was speechless. Clay stared at her, waiting for her reply. "Tell him I'll be right out."

She took off her white coat, squared her shoulders and went out onto the set.

"Griff! So good to see you," she called as she walked toward him.

Dressed in work clothes with his sleeves rolled up, and his flat cap on, he looked frazzled and tired. Although he had returned to his normal weight and robust build after the accident, his smile seemed forced.

"Where have you been doing? I'm still waiting for my baking lesson," she joked.

He seemed surprised at her pleasant demeanor. "I—I was called out of town. I was in France."

"That's what I heard. What is it like after the war?"

"It was rough," he mumbled.

"May I help you with something?" she asked as if she was addressing a customer.

"Well, I--" he stammered. "I have a favor to ask. Would you be able to come by my house some evening this week? I need your expertise on something."

Libby reached into her pocket, pulled out a business card and handed it to him. "Of course. Just give Catherine a call, and she will set something up.

Clearly surprised, he searched her face. Libby returned his gaze with her professional mask in place.

"Very well. I'll make an appointment."

Libby smiled and turned away. As she was walking back to the dressing room, she thought to herself, "Behold my best makeup job ever, Griff Gardner. But this disguise was not applied to the skin."

* * *

A few nights later, Libby went to Griff's bungalow. A year ago, he had purchased an unassuming two bedroom home a few blocks off Sunset Boulevard.

For being the highest paid cinematographer in the industry, Libby thought that he was certainly living below his means. She parked her Kissel Gold Bug and walked up to the front door. It was a hot night in late autumn, and the neighborhood was alive with activity. Children were laughing and playing on the lawns, and motorcars rattled up and down the street.

She took a deep breath to steady her nerves and knocked.

Griff opened the door. He smiled and said, "Thanks for coming, Libby."

She stepped inside and looked around. The house was decorated with the Mission Style furnishings she had seen in his apartment.

"I like your new home, Griff," she said.

"Thanks, how about a drink?"

"Sure."

Is scotch alright?"

"Fine but just two fingers," she said, sliding onto the edge of a chair.

"I'm sure you're pressed for time, so shall we get started?"

"Yes, you certainly have me curious," she said.

"Claire?" he called.

Libby heard a door open, and a little girl about the age of seven came into the living room. She was small for her age with thick dark hair and big, brown eyes. She was a gorgeous child except that the skin on one side of her face was red and disfigured.

"This is Claire, my daughter," Griff said.

Libby's jaw dropped. *Daughter? Griff has a child?* She was so stunned, she couldn't find her voice. She stared at the little girl. At last, she said, "Hello, my name is Elizabeth."

"*Bonjour,*" Claire murmured.

"We are just getting to know one another. Aren't we Claire?" Griff said in French.

Claire nodded.

Libby ran her eyes over the girl's face. The scarring appeared to be burns, and they ran down the left side of her face and onto her neck. They were slightly raised, and although they had not affected her eye, her left eyebrow was missing most of the hair.

Griff saw Libby's reaction and handed the scotch to her.

"Does she speak English?"

"A little."

"Welcome to America, Claire," Libby said in French, pulling her gloves off.

Claire looked down at scars on Libby's arms, and then up into her eyes.

"We have been getting settled in these past few weeks," Griff said. "Claire will be starting school here."

"How do you like it here?"

"*Pardon, mademoiselle?*"

Libby repeated her words slowly. Her French was rusty. She had not used it since school.

"Yes, I like it," the child replied. When she smiled, Libby noticed she had her father's grin.

He asked Claire if she would go to the kitchen and draw a picture for Mademoiselle Durant. When the girl left, Libby said, "Your French is good, Griff. I had no idea you spoke other languages."

"Just French. I learned it during the war. Thank you for showing her your arms," he said, nodding towards Libby's ungloved hands. "Is there anything you can do for her scars?"

"Certainly, it won't be difficult. Most of it will be about training *you* to apply the makeup until she gets older."

"She starts school in a week."

"Very well. I will need a few hours every night to train you properly. The most important element will be to blend it perfectly."

"I understand. I don't want her to be a target. The adjustment and language barrier will be hard enough."

"Where is her mother?"

Griff lit a cigarette and started to pace. "She's back in France, extremely ill. When the doctor told her there was no hope of recovery, she contacted me to take Claire. I had no idea the girl even existed. She was the result of a weekend fling during the war. Giselle, Claire's mother, and I lost contact, but she knew I was a cameraman in Hollywood, so she had a girlfriend find me by going to the movies and reading the credits. At last, the girlfriend saw my name and wrote to the studio. They, in turn, contacted me." He stopped pacing and looked at Libby apologetically. "The letter arrived a few days after I got home from the hospital."

Libby nodded slowly.

"When I arrived in Paris, Giselle was still in the hospital barely able to speak. It was still unclear if she would live. Claire was staying with the friend."

"How was Claire burned?"

"A fire during the war," he murmured.

All of a sudden he turned and walked to the kitchen. He was a nervous wreck. She heard him say, "That's good. She'll like that."

He returned, sat down on the edge of a chair and puffed his cigarette. He blew out his smoke and said quietly, "My buddy Jack Jakes warned me against going. He said European women would say anything to get their kids over here. He told me Claire could belong to any doughboy, but I wasn't taking any chances. I wasn't going to make that mistake again."

"What do you mean?"

He tossed his drink back and shook his head. "*That* story is for another time."

"She looks like you, Griff."

"I see it too. I was right to go and get her. She's really a nice kid."

"I can tell."

"Will you?" and he swallowed hard. "Will you help me?"

"Of course, I'll help you," Libby replied.

*   *   *

All week long, for a few hours every day, Libby and Griff worked together on Claire's face. They changed the lighting from overhead to side, going from direct sunshine to lamplight. They tested how the makeup would last in the heat, and the time it would take before fading. They even considered how the makeup would transition from outdoor to indoor, experimenting with shading and contouring.

Claire seemed to enjoy every bit of the attention. She

said little, sitting patiently for hours, never complaining. She would stare up into their eyes obediently waiting for her next directive. At first, Libby thought it was the language barrier, but after a while, she realized that the child was naturally quiet.

She was also very observant, which made Libby sorry for her. She couldn't imagine how terrifying it must have been growing up in a war-torn country and then having to leave her mother and start over in a new country. She was lucky she had such a good father.

At last, Libby and Griff decided what technique was the most effective, and it was time to pull it all together. When she was done, she turned Claire around to look in the mirror.

Silence.

Libby saw Griff swallow hard.

"What's wrong?" she asked frantically.

Claire mumbled something in French and looked at her father.

"That's *just* it," Griff said. "There's nothing wrong at all."

*   *   *

"Alright, *Papa*, tonight you are applying the makeup yourself," Libby said to Griff the next evening. "I will do nothing but watch."

Griff grimaced, and Claire giggled. He took a deep breath and draped a cape over Claire's chest. Opening Libby's makeup box, he reached for a tube and then stopped, looking up at Libby uncertainly. She nodded, so he applied the base.

"Too thick there," she said abruptly.

"Alright," he mumbled and adjusted it.

When he reached for the next tube, she raised an eyebrow, and he put it down quickly. Choosing the correct color, he blended and smoothed, and successfully applied the eyebrow.

But when he started shading, Libby said, "Absolutely not."

He corrected it.

When he reached for a brush, and she barked, "Wrong!" he threw his head back and gasped, "My God, how the hell do you keep employees?"

"Watch your language," she warned, looking at Claire.

Griff sighed and picked up another brush as Libby watched, cigarette smoke curling around her head. She said nothing, so he assumed he was right.

By the end of the lesson, Griff was exhausted, but he had completed the makeover, and the work was satisfactory.

"Would you come by the first week of school to help me until I get it right?" he pleaded.

"Ouch, that's early. It will cut severely into my fabulous social life."

"I promise I'll make it up to you," he said. "I'll take you anywhere you want to go for a week."

"Done."

* * *

The first week of school went well for Claire, and Griff was relieved. "She told me that she already has made some friends," he told Libby as they drove along the coast in her speedster one afternoon. It was a beautiful day in November, and they decided to go the beach.

"She's so quiet. I'm surprised it happened so fast," Libby said as she pulled off the road.

"I know it. She wants to have a friend over on Saturday already. What should I do with them?"

"Don't ask me. I don't have kids." She took her scarf off, put it on like a headband and tied it at the back of her

204

neck.

"Well, you were a little girl once. What did you do at that age?"

"I don't know, books, paper dolls. My childhood was— unusual though."

Griff jumped out and opened her door. "You've told me barely anything about your past, except that you lost your sister. What did your father do again?"

"Hardware and lumber," she replied as they started down the beach.

"I thought you said he was a farmer."

Libby didn't answer.

"So he had a hardware store?" Griff asked.

"Um—well let's say he had a lot of hardware."

"So he had several hardware stores," Griff stated. "Nothing unusual about that."

Eager to get the focus off of her, Libby asked, "You lost your sister too, didn't you?"

"Yes, the Spanish Flu."

"Did you get it?"

"No."

"I had it," Libby said. "My friend Rudy took care of me. I'll always wonder if I gave it to him." She looked down. "He didn't make it."

They fell silent, walking side by side. The surf swept up near their feet and receded. Griff asked at last, "Was he your first love?"

"No," Libby said, chuckling. "But we were certainly much more than pals. Rudy changed my life. He too had scars--from the war and taught me how to use makeup to cover mine up."

Griff stopped and looked down at her arms. "You didn't wear your gloves today."

"No need to with you," she said.

Griff picked up her hands and looked closely at her arms. "Will you tell me about the accident?"

Libby froze. She had told him once that they were from an auto accident, but she didn't want to go into too much detail. She had already made mistakes in her lies about the family business. "Griff, I don't like talking about it. It's—it's like reliving it again."

"I understand. It's like that for me with the war."

*   *   *

Griff and Libby continued to spend time together, but Libby was determined to keep her guard up. *I must not allow him into my life. He says I tell him nothing about my past? Well, I know nothing about his present.* But slowly she felt herself losing the battle. He was smart and engaging and made her laugh. His charm paired with his good looks and wicked grin proved irresistible. Libby was feeling herself slip.

One afternoon after a late lunch with friends, Griff asked Libby to come to work with him. "I need to do some sunset lighting adjustments. Jakes wants me to shoot some footage of Mae Langford for *All her Own,* and I need to be ready for her before she arrives. Since Jakes can't be there, will you help?"

"What do I have to do?"

"Just stand there while I work with the lighting."

"Alright."

They wound their way through the busy streets of Hollywood. No longer a sleepy little community outside Los Angeles, it was now a city with large studios, shops, and office buildings, all devoted to the film industry. And every day it was growing. The surrounding area was filled with housing for actors, screenwriters, accountants and everyone in the business. Gone were the days of adapting warehouses and abandoned buildings to fit the needs of evolving studios. Now moving pictures were big business and worthy of new development.

They parked and walked down a trail to an open field. Griff set up his camera and had Libby stand by some trees. The setting sun was streaming through the leaves, backlighting her.

Griff adjusted her position, turning her this way and that, so the light framed her head properly. When he was satisfied, he turned his flat cap around so the bill would not hit the camera, adjusted the lens and started cranking.

"Now reach up to the tree as if you are taking a piece of fruit."

Libby reached up to the tree.

"Now look at me, you gorgeous doll."

Laughing, she looked at him. Griff knew just how to get people to relax in front of the camera.

"Alright, take a break for a minute," he said.

Libby sighed and rolled her shoulders. She sat down on a stump and watched him dash around making adjustments. He was hanging a mirror from a tree, so it reflected the rays of the sun in just the right way. There was something so desirable about him when he was at work.

"What time is Mae coming?" she asked.

"She should be here any minute."

Libby didn't like Mae. She thought she was shallow and vain and didn't want to watch her flirt with Griff.

"Shouldn't you be writing this down?" she called over to him.

"It's all right here," Griff said, tapping his head.

He backed away, returned to the camera and took some more footage. "Turn and look at me," he said.

Libby looked at the camera.

"Now walk away, slowly toward the trees."

"Come back now," he called to her.

This time he put his hand on the back of her head and tilted her chin up as if he was going to kiss her. Libby swayed slightly toward him, but instead of kissing her, he inhaled sharply and stepped back.

"Where the hell is Mae?" he barked going back to the camera.

After filming, they waited a few more minutes, and at last, he said, "Well, we've lost our light. Forget it. Let's take the footage back to the lab. At least I can see if the effects worked."

Libby was relieved Mae hadn't shown up. When they arrived at the lab, it was late, and they were the only ones there. It was a large room filled with work benches, tools, reels, and projectors. Film cans lined the shelves along with bottles of chemicals. There was discarded film scattered everywhere, and Griff swept it aside.

"Have a seat. I'll just be a minute."

He fussed with the footage while Libby waited.

"Alright, let's go in here."

Libby followed him into the projection room. She was nervous. She had always wondered what she would look like on camera. She was afraid she'd hate what she saw.

Griff threaded the projector and turned out the lights. When he started to crank, Libby's heart jumped. There she was, and it wasn't as bad as she thought.

"What do you think?" Griff asked.

"I think the lighting is nice." The sun streamed through the trees and sent rays through her hair almost like a halo.

Libby watched herself reach up to the tree and pretend to take fruit. And it was followed by Griff making her laugh, the close-up and the shot where she was walking away. All the footage illuminated her with the backlighting of the soft sunset.

"It's really pretty," she said.

"We call it magic hour light."

"It does seem like magic," Libby echoed.

The film ended.

"I always wanted to capture you in that light."

Libby turned to him, looking confused. "What?"

"Mae didn't come today because she wasn't invited," he murmured.

Griff stepped up, tipped her head back and kissed her.

Chapter 16

Griff promised himself he wouldn't do it, but the temptation had been too great. For months he had wanted to capture Libby in the magic light, but he knew he would lose control. As predicted, he did.

Camera work had always been an intimate experience for Griff, and having Libby as his subject proved to be too much. Touching her and studying her in that special light had been unwise. Looking at her through the lens and capturing her on film had been far too moving. In the end, he yanked her into his arms and kissed her, and for hours after that, they buried themselves in passion. He had to leave early that evening to pick Claire up at a friend's house, and he found it fortunate. It forced him away from Libby before he overplayed his hand and said something he shouldn't. He could not get involved with her. He may be called away unexpectedly again, and the relationship would only end in disaster. He wished he could tell her the truth, but it was too risky.

All of his old feelings returned with a vengeance, the grinding lust, the uncertainty, and that strange yearning deep inside that shook him to the core. And what about Claire? He had a child now to consider and couldn't leave her at the drop of a hat either. Life seemed to be a jumbled mess.

The fact that he was a father was completely overwhelming. It had come upon him overnight, and his head was spinning. He didn't know the first thing about fatherhood and fumbled through the job blindly. Several neighbors helped out, and he questioned them about parenting, but it just wasn't enough. One thing was perfectly clear at least, Claire was an amazing little girl, and he adored her.

"I'm going to have to cut back on the dangerous stunts," he told Dash one afternoon after some aerial work.

Dash took off his helmet and said, "Why?"

"Claire. I may be all she has left."

"Any news of her mother?"

"They tell me she's improving, but she looked like a corpse when I saw her."

"So I suppose you'll say no to my next question."

"What?" Griff said, putting his camera in the auto.

"I'm going to be doing some flying for Haydn Price."

"A movie?"

Dash lowered his voice. "Rum running on the Great Lakes."

Griff's eyebrows shot up. "Haydn Price is into that?"

"Oh ya, and on no small scale. He works with Izzy Bronstein--nicknamed, 'The Kid.'"

"Never heard of him."

"He's a big-time racketeer in Minneapolis and Detroit. He runs liquor down from Canada. I'll be picking up hooch in Port Arthur and making deliveries all over the shoreline of Superior. He already transports on water. Now he wants to use the air too."

"Port Arthur? You'll be back home."

"That's all part of it," Dash said with a smile. "I'll be back with the old gang in Canada. Price said he'll get you your own Jenny if you're interested."

"I assume it pays well," Griff said, starting the car.

"Damn right it does. Are you in?"

Griff shook his head. "I would have been interested a few months ago but not now."

*   *   *

Libby's life was turned upside down again, and it was all because of Griff Gardner. She knew that she shouldn't see him, but she didn't care. Most certainly he could and would disappear again, but she was prepared for it. She would take each day as it came.

Griff made her deliriously happy. She couldn't stay away from the man. Together in her room, with the door closed, they were at their best. They were connected by something intangible and visceral, linked somehow, in their own private world.

Their moments of intimacy were like nothing she had ever experienced. For the first time in her life, Libby felt warm and protected, and she believed at those times she was everything to Griff too. Instead of a hedonistic rush of passion, their lovemaking was a slow, careful expression of deep affection. When he held her in his arms, she felt something burn deep within her, and when he left, it turned to pain. It was a feeling so intense that it frightened her, so she covered her fear by joking and taking a cynical view of love.

"I don't believe in love stories," she told Griff one night when he wanted to see the movie, *Seventh Heaven*.

"What? How can you say such a thing?"

"Oh, come on, Griff. You know as well as I do that love is an overrated emotion. No one really ever feels like that."

He stared at her, dumbfounded. "You've got to be kidding me. So according to you, people don't really fall in love?"

"Not like that," and she laughed. "Don't get me wrong. I believe in love, but it certainly can't move heaven and earth."

Griff opened his mouth to say something and changed his mind. She noticed he was quiet the rest of the evening, but she didn't care. He might as well know right off how she felt.

They spent several evenings a week together, many of them with Claire, almost as if they were a family. They took drives, went to the beach and attended movies, but only the films without romance. They even had Christmas together which they celebrated at Libby's home. Claire thought it was the most beautiful house she had ever seen and on several occasions, Libby had her over to spend the night so just the two of them could spend time together.

Libby adored Claire, but the shadow of the girl's mother haunted her. Was this woman important to Griff? She tried not to dwell on it, but it nagged her. And the fact that she was French galled her. She was probably chic and sexy with an enticing accent. And is that where he was going when he disappeared for long periods of time?

One afternoon in Westlake Park, as they were watching Claire play on the monkey bars, Libby said, "Claire's athletic like you."

"Dear God, don't let her go into stunt work," he replied.

An old couple walked past them and nodded a greeting.

Griff leaned in with a teasing smile in his eyes and said, "You know we look like an old married couple sitting here in the park."

"Don't get used to it, Gardner," Libby said, pushing him away in jest.

"Why? I'm the quintessential family man."

"Oh, yes, just a normal father who hangs from buildings, straps himself to airplanes, fast motorcars and--"

"Mademoiselle Durant, look!" Claire called as she hung

upside down.

"See? You set a bad example," Libby said, laughing. She called to Claire, "You are very brave, darling!"

Claire and Libby were good friends. Libby was Claire's first friend in America. The day she revealed her scars to Claire, there was an instant connection.

"Is Pepper back from her honeymoon yet?" Griff asked.

"The end of the week. I'm anxious to hear about Havana."

"How are you feeling about Haydn?"

She shrugged. "As long as he's good to Pepper, I don't care. Heard from Dash?"

"Not a word."

"I wish he wasn't doing it. It's dangerous flying over those lakes. They're like oceans.

"Speaking of the Great Lakes, I'll be seeing Lake Michigan soon," he announced.

"Why?"

"I'm taking Claire to join her mother in Chicago."

"What?" Libby's heart started to pound. She knew Giselle had recovered, but she had no idea she was in America. "She's living *here?*"

He nodded. "She has friends in Chicago who helped her find work."

"Well this is news," she said, glaring at him.

He looked down at his hands. "I've been helping her settle in."

"You helped her come over here?"

"Yes."

Libby's jaw dropped. "Griff, you could have told me. Are you—are you serious with this woman?"

"No! There's nothing between us. But Libby, I have an obligation to her and to Claire."

"Damn it, Griff, you have an obligation to me too—to

tell me the truth." she barked, jumping to her feet. "Who the hell are you anyway? You never tell me a thing about yourself. I'm sick of it."

His eyes flashed, and he grabbed her wrist. "Don't lecture me about secrets, Mademoiselle Durant. Let's talk about these scars. They're not from any goddamn automobile accident."

Libby stared down at him, panting. Abruptly, she turned on her heel and left.

* * *

Griff called Libby a week later asking her to come and say goodbye to Claire, but he offered no apologies or any signs of reconciliation. She stopped by just long enough to hug the little girl and reassure her she would see her again very soon. But down deep, Libby wasn't so sure. Things were stiff and uncomfortable with Griff all over again.

When he returned from Chicago a few weeks later, he didn't call Libby. She heard he was on the set of a comedy being filmed outside of town, and even though she had a makeup crew out there, she avoided being on the set. The two of them were back to their old ways.

One afternoon, she had to drive out because her artists had some issues that needed immediate attention. Clay was there getting ready to shoot a chase scene involving a train. "Where have you been, darlin'?" he drawled. "I miss my baby."

"Busy getting ready to launch my new line," she said, kissing his cheek.

"So it's time. What happens now?"

"We flood the media with advertising, and I go to Minneapolis and New York to promote it at department stores. All starting next week."

"Whew! Will I ever see you again?"

"Probably not," Libby said.

Reaching for his cigarette, she took a puff.

"Still seeing Gardner?" he asked.

"No. I feel like a damn fool all over again."

"Why?"

"He filmed me in what he called the 'magic hour' light one afternoon, telling me he'd been wanting to do it for months. I fell right into his bed again. I suppose all you cameramen use that line."

"That's the first I've heard of it," he said. "But it is a good--"

Libby laughed and cuffed him on the arm. "Let's talk about something else."

"Alrighty, how's Pepper?" he asked.

"She's fine, happily married."

"Recovered that fast?"

"What do you mean?"

"You don't know?"

"Know, what?"

"She took a tumble."

"She did!"

"Oh, she's alright. Up and working, but she has some nasty bruises. When I came into her dressing room on *A Kiss for Luck,* her chest and back were covered in bruises. Makeup was working on her."

"No, I didn't know."

Clay raised an eyebrow. "She *said* she fell down the stairs."

Libby stared at him. "That's what she told you?"

"She said she'd been drinking and laughed it off."

The train started clanging its bell and Clay said, "That's my cue. I have to shoot this."

He ran over to the tracks. That's when Libby saw Griff. He was climbing up the side of a boxcar, his camera fastened to the top of the train. Two stunt men climbed up behind him as a Jenny circled overhead.

"So much for his vow to quit dangerous shots," Libby muttered.

The director brought his megaphone up and roared, "Action!"

The train started to roll, and Griff started to crank his camera. The engine picked up speed, and the stunt men started the chase scene, jumping from boxcar to boxcar. The train chugged across a flat open area with Griff sitting on top, unsecured.

The pilot swung the Jenny low and soared down to the train, trailing a rope ladder. One of the stuntmen reached but missed it. The Jenny roared back up into the sky and circled for another take.

"I can't watch this," Libby said, and she turned to her automobile. "What the hell kind of crazy business am I in?"

Without delay, she headed for the set of *A Kiss for Luck*.

*   *   *

Pepper was just finishing a scene and heading back for a costume change when Libby caught up with her. "I just saw Clay, and he told me you fell down the stairs."

Pepper pulled off her wig, shook her hair and laughed. "Yes, did. I got a little tight and missed my footing. I'm fine though."

Libby followed her into the dressing room. Two wardrobe women came forward and helped Pepper step out of her gown. Libby saw bruises on her back, chest, and breasts. They were purple and obviously tender because she jumped when one of the dressers brushed against her.

Wardrobe went out, and Libby asked, "Did you go to the hospital?"

"Of course not. Nothing's broken."

Libby saw dark circles under Pepper's eyes when she

wiped off her makeup. She looked frazzled and anxious.

"What's wrong? You look tired and upset."

"Nothing, Libs," Pepper said, but her eyes filled with tears. She turned away so Libby couldn't see. "Damn it. I need to get ready for my next scene. Where the hell's makeup!"

"I want to know what's going on," Libby demanded.

"Nothing more than a wild night. I told you."

She grabbed Pepper's arm. "No doubt it was a wild night, but it wasn't fun-filled."

Pepper jerked away. "I don't like what you're implying."

"You fall down the stairs, and there are no bruises on your arms? This is Haydn's work, isn't it?"

"How dare you!"

Just then the makeup specialist came into the dressing room.

"When you're ready to talk, you know where to find me," Libby said and walked out.

*   *   *

The more Libby thought about it, the more furious she became. How convenient the bruising was not visible. They had been inflicted in areas that would not prevent Haydn's precious investment from performing. Libby found this to be even more disturbing than an attack committed in a moment of passion. It was devious and smacked of premeditation.

And the family crises continued. She received a letter the next day from one of the cousin's informing her that Grandmother Brennan was in serious financial trouble. She told Libby that the Brennan's long time financial advisor, Arthur Harrigan was caught embezzling money. He had been making questionable investments and channeling funds into his own account for several months. It was all very surprising since he had been a dependable, trustworthy friend of the family for years.

"Grandmother has sold the lake home in White Bear, and she may have to sell the house on Summit Avenue too," her cousin said in the letter. "She owes a great deal of money to many people. She has lost a lot of weight and suddenly looks very frail."

So that's why she looked so exhausted the last time she had been to Minneapolis, thought Libby. Immediately she called Pepper. Things had been icy between them since that day in the dressing room, but Libby put that aside. This was more important.

It was early Sunday morning, and Pepper told her to come to the house. When she pulled up to the Price residence in Beverly Hills, she chuckled. Every time she came here, she was amused. Haydn had it built shortly after he moved to California. A sweeping estate with manicured lawns and a massive Tudor-style home, Libby found it ostentatious and overdone. To her it seemed as if he was trying to prove something, or better yet, trying hide from something behind those gates.

Pepper came down the front steps holding a letter. "I got one too," she said. "I just opened it. What the hell is going on?"

They walked around to the pool and sat down. The sun was already heating everything up, and they sat in the shade. "This is all so shocking," Pepper said. "Does your letter say the same thing as mine?"

Libby handed it to her, she read it and nodded. "I am flabbergasted that Arthur Harrigan could do such a thing. He was always so staid and conservative, and most of all honest."

"There must have been a dark side to him we never knew."

Just then Haydn came out to join them. He was in swimming trunks and had on a lightweight robe. He was tan, and his physique was fine. Nevertheless, Libby thought he looked too old for Pepper.

He came over and kissed Libby on the cheek. He was pleasant and hospitable. It was obvious Pepper had not informed him of their argument in the dressing room.

"Hello, Hayden," she said with a smile. "I hope I didn't wake you. It's early."

"Not at all. I get up every morning and go for a swim. Is everything alright?"

Pepper made a face. "Well no. Take your swim, darling. After Bonita brings coffee, we'll fill you in."

"Very well," he said, walking to the edge of the pool and diving in.

"So what now?" Pepper asked. "Can't Uncle Roger buy her out of the Summit house? They live there already."

"He doesn't make enough money."

Pepper sighed. "So few options. Bridget said in her letter that none of the Brennan's are doing well right now, to say nothing of those with the family illness."

"What about your parents?" Libby asked.

"Father is still recovering from his financial losses earlier in the year."

"Good lord. It looks like it's up to you and me."

The housekeeper came out and set down breakfast on the patio table. Pepper poured Libby a cup of coffee and handed it to her.

"I can give her *some* help," Libby said. "But the entire amount is out of my reach."

Pepper nodded and looked over at Haydn as he did laps in the pool. "I'll talk with Haydn," she said.

Libby's stomach twisted. She did not want him involved with the family business. "No, Pepper."

"Why not?" she asked, instantly defensive.

Trying to be diplomatic, Libby said, "Why should he bail Grandmother out? This is a family problem."

"Haydn *is* family now. He's my husband, Libby. Do you have a better idea?"

Libby stared at her, trying to hold her tongue. She knew Haydn's underworld connections would add to her grandmother's problems.

Haydn finished his laps and climbed out of the pool. Toweling his hair off, he walked over and sat down.

"So ladies, did you solve everything?"

"No," Pepper said, handing him one of the letters. "Is there anything we can do?"

When he finished reading, he whistled. "That is a great deal of money. I'll need to take a look at the books."

"Maybe we should exhaust all possibilities before we impose on Haydn," Libby suggested.

"This is *my* money too, Libby."

"Yes, but--"

"Would you deny this to Grandmother?"

"Ladies," Haydn said, standing up. "I don't even know if I can help. Give me a few days, and I'll see what I can do."

*   *   *

Libby had a bad feeling about Haydn becoming involved in family finances, but Pepper was adamant. Despite her protests, in a few days, Pepper and Haydn stepped forward with the money. Libby offered to contribute, but Pepper said coolly, that it would not be necessary.

It took weeks to sort through all the mess. There were conferences between Haydn's attorneys, his financial advisors and the lawyers representing Grandmother Brennan's estate. Eventually, Olivia Brennan was saved from ruin, but Libby believed it was a high price to pay.

"Are you sure you can't come back to Minneapolis with me?" Libby said to Pepper on the phone before she left for her promotional tour.

"I would love to, but I'm starting a new movie. Haydn and I have to get out there soon. Do you know he's never met, Grandma Brennan? I know she wants to thank him personally. He'll be going up to the North Shore soon, so maybe I can go back then."

"The north shore of Lake Superior?"

"Yes, he's opening a lodge and several resorts up there."

Libby knew instantly this was related to his rum-running operation.

"Well, if ever you want to join me," Libby offered. "I'll be going back and forth to the Twin Cities frequently on business. It would be fun."

"Alright, I'll try."

When they hung up, Libby felt unsettled. She hated leaving Pepper. Although she presented a happy face, she knew there was something terribly wrong.

Chapter 17

Even though Libby was worried about Pepper, it was Griff who truly robbed her of her peace of mind. Ever since their parting, the familiar ache had returned to her stomach and loneliness haunted her like a phantom. All the way back to Minneapolis, she fought memories of him. Until now it had been easy to distract herself with work, but with hours and hours of free time on the train, it was impossible not to think of him. Continuously she would go over the rubble of their relationship, trying to make sense of it, but there were too many unanswered questions, and in the end, she had to quit or go mad.

She found comfort in *Enough Rope*, a book of poetry by Dorothy Parker. Everyone was talking about the collection by the New Yorker columnist, so Libby picked up a copy at the station before she left Los Angeles. The satirist's caustic wit and wry, cynical views on love appealed to Libby and was the perfect balm for her wounds.

When she finally arrived home, she surprised herself; she was glad to be back. Time had softened the childhood memories and blurred the pain. So much had changed in the past few years. There was a building boom going on, and scores of motorcars roared up and down the streets. Only an occasional horse and wagon was seen, and it looked out of place and old fashioned.

Libby couldn't believe she was twenty-seven years old. The years in Los Angeles had flown by, and in that time the movie industry had gone from a crazy, precarious experiment to a solid multi-million dollar industry. And now there was the possibility of sound. Many thought it was a passing fancy, but Libby felt differently. She remembered those words once describing motion pictures themselves.

Everywhere there was the talk of Lucky Lindy as well, the hometown boy who had just crossed the Atlantic in his single-engine plane. Libby was flabbergasted at his courage. Every time she heard someone speak of the young man from Little Falls, Minnesota, she thought of Dash flying his Jenny back and forth across Lake Superior, a feat almost as daring.

After settling in at the Hotel Leamington, Libby went to see Zabby and Tante.

"Our little girl!" Zabby said, wrapping her arms around her. She looked older and had put on more weight, but she looked happy.

"Where's Tante?" Libby asked.

"At her sister's for the afternoon, but she'll be back in an hour of so."

Libby ran her eyes over the kitchen. Everything was different in the house on Grove Avenue. It was now geared to running a large facility for many children. There were several iceboxes, a new electric refrigerator and three women cooking. "A busy place," she said.

"It is. Would you like to look around?"

"Has anything changed since my walk through last time?"

"Yes, we have made room for six more little ones," Zabby said, patting a little boy's head as they walked through the dining room. "Most of them are in school right now."

The plush furnishings downstairs had been replaced with durable furniture suitable for children, and the large upstairs bedrooms had beds lined up in rows with closets full of schoolbooks, clothing, and toys. Gone forever were Libby's fancy hat boxes and Chanel suits, replaced with tiny skirts, blouses and old button-up shoes.

One thing remained unchanged though, and Libby laughed when she saw it. The children still covered the naked cherub at the top of the stairs with doll clothes.

That evening Libby, Zabby, and Tante had supper together in the carriage house. They laughed and reminisced about the old days, sometimes with laughter, sometimes with tears.

"Any good moving pictures coming out?" Zabby asked.

Libby thought a moment. "There's a scary one coming out with Lon Chaney. You should see what he does--"

"We like love stories," Tante interrupted.

"Oh, really you two. They are so silly."

"No, they aren't. Why isn't our girl married?" Tante asked.

"Durant Cosmetics takes all my time. Come to the unveiling of my new line next week," she said, changing the subject.

"Where will it be?"

"Dayton's, Powers and Young Quinlan."

"We will certainly come if we are not needed here," Tante replied.

"Have you seen your grandmother?" Zabby asked.

"She's in Asheville at the Highland Hospital again."

"Seeing your Aunt Mary?"

Libby nodded.

*   *   *

In the following days, Libby prepared for the unveiling of Elizabeth Durant Cosmetics. Her first order of business was to meet with an employment agency and hire two assistants. She also trained cosmetic counter employees at the three department stores to be Durant representatives. They would assist in displays, demonstrations, and sales.

After a week, she scheduled a conference at the Leamington Hotel tea room with columnists from all of the local papers. Dressed in a blue suit that was belted at the hip and wearing a red beret, she looked chic and professional. But Libby was nervous. She knew the real reason the newspapers had flocked here today. They had come to meet Elizabeth Durant, daughter of the beautiful but mad Lillian Durant. They wanted to satisfy their morbid curiosity about the hideous assault twenty years earlier.

Long before the press conference, Libby knew what she was going to do. The reporters started off feigning interest in the makeup line but then the real questioning began. She took off her gloves, held her arms up and said, "Behold the magic of makeup. This is what you really came to see today. Is it not?"

They stared at her, dumbfounded. "The story of how I obtained these scars is no secret. But *today* the real question is," and she raised her eyebrows. "How do I conceal them?"

They shifted in their chairs.

"From where you are sitting, ladies and gentlemen, are these scars visible?"

"No," they murmured, shaking their heads and looking at one another.

"If," and she paused. "I can cover this gross disfigurement with powders and creams, what can makeup do for ordinary aging?" Libby stepped among them, holding out her arms for inspection. "Up close the scars are apparent. But only," and she hesitated. "Only if you are looking for them."

She walked back to her table, buttoned her cuffs and said, "*This* is the miracle of makeup. But the intention of

Elizabeth Durant Cosmetics is not to cover up flaws. It is to enhance a woman's attributes and allow her real beauty to shine through."

When Libby finished, the columnists flooded her with questions, fascinated with technique, the variety of the line, and her Hollywood connections.

Once and for all, Libby had successfully put to rest the morbid curiosity about the assault so many years ago. The next day the papers applauded her as a talented and committed businesswoman giving their stamp of approval to Elizabeth Durant Cosmetics. The unveilings that followed were a huge success.

"I couldn't be happier," she told Uncle Owen at supper a few nights later.

"It's obvious you are a Durant," he said proudly.

"The Brennans did alright for themselves too," she said with a smile.

"*Touché*," he said.

They were dining at his favorite restaurant, The Nankin, a Chinese establishment in downtown Minneapolis. Dimly lit with Chinese lanterns overhead, they sat in the busy dining room with oriental waiters in white aprons darting back and forth.

Uncle Owen was dressed in a sharp pinstripe suit and tie. He was just coming from his favorite haberdashery. Even though he was in a wheelchair, he went everywhere. "Hell, I've got the money. Why not pay someone to push me around," he always said.

"We'll both have the chow mein," he told the waiter. "And an order of egg rolls please."

"When do you leave for New York?" he asked finishing his cocktail.

"Tomorrow, but I'll only stay a few weeks. After introducing my line, I'm coming back here to set up an office and take an apartment."

"My favorite niece is coming back to stay?" he said excitedly.

"Sort of. I'll have a flat in New York and my home in Los Angeles too."

"Where will you live?"

"At a residential hotel near the St. Paul Cathedral called, The Commodore. I've hired a decorator so when I return it should be all ready." Libby smiled. "If things keep going well, I think you'll have a good return on your investment, Uncle Owen."

"I never doubted it for a minute."

*   *   *

After introducing her line in New York, Libby was back in the Twin Cities within a month. Anxious to be out of hotels, she moved into her apartment immediately. Libby loved the new flat in the posh residential hotel near downtown St. Paul. A large brick building with all the amenities, it had an elegant supper club on the main floor, a small in-house grocer and a speakeasy that was hidden downstairs.

Libby hired one of the best interior decorators in St. Paul, and he did not disappoint, delivering exceptional work. All of the furnishings were in the Style Moderne, a sleek, geometric design reflecting the latest fascination with ancient civilizations. The chairs and divan were low-backed with sweeping lines and curves. The tables were angular and lacquered black. The decorator splashed the ebony and ivory palette with colorful accent pieces and fabrics from around the world.

Libby loved it. She was tired of the heavy furniture and thick drapes from her childhood. This was fresh and new, entirely suited to someone who was introducing a modern lifestyle to women.

"I'll have a Gibson," Olivia Brennan said as she walked through Libby's new apartment looking around. "I've been craving one of those since I got back from Asheville. I'm sick to death of juleps."

Libby was glad to see her grandmother looking well again. Although a bit thinner, she was back to her saucy attitude.

"How do you my new place?" Libby asked.

"I adore it. The best part is that it's only a few blocks away from me."

"Handy, if you ever stayed home."

Olivia slid onto the edge of the chair. "I know, but I just had to check on Mary."

"You need to slow down, Grandmother," Libby said walking around the bar and handing her a drink. "Is everything back to normal? Do you need any more financial help?"

"No, it's all taken care of. Penelope and her husband saved me, and I am eternally grateful. My lawyers tell me that in a short amount of time the estate will be stable enough to start reimbursing them."

Libby sat down across from her. "Were there any--" and she hesitated. "Were there any strings attached?"

"No, why?" her grandmother asked.

She shrugged and sipped her drink. "No reason. I'm just glad it's over."

"I am too. I kept telling myself, 'You came from nothing, you can leave with nothing, but the whole thing scared the hell out of me."

"They haven't found Arthur Harrigan yet?"

"No, I have a feeling he's gone forever. I can't understand it. For years he was a trusted friend of the family."

"Do you suppose it was gambling?"

"I suspect."

Olivia finished her drink, held out the glass. "I'll have another one, Elizabeth, and this time don't forget the onion."

* * *

One morning as Libby was getting ready to go into her office, the phone rang. It was Haydn Price. He wondered if they could meet for a drink. Libby dreaded it, but she knew she had to go if only for Pepper's sake.

She met him early in the evening in the lobby of her apartment building. "I've been wanting to try the club downstairs here since I've moved in," she said. "It's this way."

They walked into the building's tiny grocery store, where the clerk recognized Libby and allowed them behind the counter so they could go downstairs.

The club had just opened for the evening, and they were setting up chairs. It was not a large space, but it was elegantly furnished with a small stage, piano, and a black lacquered bar. Several lighted glass shelves were behind the bar lined with rows of bottles and barware.

Haydn checked his hat and ushered Libby to a table in the corner. He looked tan and wealthy in his expensive three piece suit. Even though he was polite, Libby was not comfortable with him. She found him oily and over-solicitous.

After he had ordered them drinks, he said, "Thank you for seeing me. I know how busy you are. Pepper said the launch is going well."

Libby nodded and opened her cigarette case. "I've just finished hiring several people locally to handle things here. That should help a bit."

"Just be careful," he said, lighting her cigarette. The flame reflected in his round glasses.

Libby wanted to reply, "Oh really, daddy?" but instead she said, "Yes, I will."

"How is your grandmother doing?"

"I just saw her a few days ago. She's is much better thanks to you and Pepper."

"I plan on looking her up on my way back from the North Shore."

"I hear you are opening some clubs up there."

"Yes, two resorts and a lodge."

When their drinks came, Haydn said, "I asked you here because I have a very lucrative business venture that might interest you."

Libby clenched her jaw.

"Forgive me if I am being presumptuous but, have you ever considered offering your own line of perfume?"

Libby drew her eyebrows together. "I've considered it."

He lowered his voice. "You know what my business is on the North Shore, do you not?"

"Yes," and she gasped. "Ah ha, there's alcohol in perfume."

He smiled. "And your company could import vast quantities of it from Canada, all quite legally."

She stared at him. Well, the impudent bastard. He wanted to use her company as a cover for his rum-running business.

"I would make it worth your while."

Putting her cigarette out, she said, "No thank you. I have more than I can handle right now. Thanks for the drink, but I'm late for a date."

When she stood up, he grabbed her wrist. His grip was like iron. "I helped your grandmother out, Elizabeth," he snarled. "And I think it's only good manners to consider my proposal. Please have an answer for me by tomorrow."

A chill went up her spine, and she mumbled, "I—I will."

*   *   *

That night Libby sat at her dressing table, hairbrush in hand, looking at her bottles of perfume. She was stunned. Suddenly Elizabeth Durant Cosmetics was no longer her company. Haydn Price now owned it. He was not *asking* to use it as a cover to smuggle his liquor into the country, he was *telling* her. All her years of hard work and dreams were gone in an instant, hijacked by this tyrant who married Pepper. He now would call the shots.

She jumped up and started to pace. Certainly, she could say no to him but what would the repercussions be? He could ruin her business, and with the stroke of a pen, put Grandmother Brennan back into financial ruin. Who knew what sort of legal loopholes his attorneys had woven into the Brennan bailout? What violence could he unleash on them all?

She rubbed her temples as she paced. Her first inclination was to go to Uncle Owen. But that was not an option. His money was at stake here too, and she knew he would try to meet Price head on. Doing combat with that man was dangerous. She may even be endangering her Uncle's life. The same applied to Grandmother Brennan, and Pepper was out, of course.

All night she paced, and the next day she tried to work, but it was fruitless. She was too preoccupied. At last, she picked up the phone and called Haydn.

"I've considered what you've said, and I believe it may be lucrative for us both," she said. "But as you can imagine I need details and research needs to be done. Fragrance is new to me."

"Very well, I understand completely," he said. "Come up to the North Shore, stay at our lodge, make yourself at home and we'll get started."

"I'll make arrangements immediately."

"Good." He gave her a phone number to call when she arrived and hung up.

For now, Libby was satisfied. She had bought a bit of time until she could find a way out of this mess. She reminded herself that she had had a lifetime of practice navigating through the house of mirrors that was madness, so staying one step ahead of a calculating thug like Haydn Price may just be possible.

Chapter 18

Griff wanted to see Libby. He told himself that he had come to Minnesota to see Dash, but she was the real reason. Before he left for Chicago to visit Claire, he had heard she was in the Twin Cities launching her cosmetic line, so he took a detour to Minnesota under the pretense of visiting Dash on the North Shore. Do not look her up, he said to himself but she was in his thoughts constantly, and he was losing the battle.

His visit with Claire exceeded all his expectations. The little girl was delighted to see him, and they spent several days together, just the two of them, going to the zoo, out for ice cream, and to the movies. It helped that his relationship with her mother was genial as well. Although Griff gave Giselle regular financial support, she never tried to exploit him. She had a regular job and made it quite clear that she wanted her independence. A mutual love for Claire was all they had in common, their weekend fling only a dim memory.

Claire was adjusting well to her new American home. Having her mother back meant everything, and now she had a father as well. She adored him, and Griff was a committed parent.

Years earlier, when he was fifteen, he had had a sexual encounter with a girl at school, as did most of his friends, but when the experimentation resulted in pregnancy, no one stood by her. She was sent away to an institution, and he never saw her again. The guilt of abandoning her still haunted him. And from then on, he swore he would never shirk his responsibility again. So when he looked at Claire, he knew it was the best decision he had ever made.

When he stepped off the train in the Great Northern Depot in Minneapolis, he picked up his bags and went right to the ticket booth. "What time is the next train to Duluth?"

"Not until four tomorrow afternoon from The Milwaukee Road Depot."

Griff frowned. He had hoped there had been a train right away. He knew if he stayed in the Twin Cities for even a day, he would be tempted to look up Libby. "Thank you. I'll take a ticket please."

Griff crossed the loud, busy atrium of the train station. It was a massive building with stone columns, a restaurant, and newsstand. By a shoe shine stand, he put his bags down and looked up at the art overhead.

"Shoeshine, sir?" the attendant asked.

"No thank you," he replied.

He went back to staring at the huge paintings overhead depicting scenes from Minnesota history. It was the work of his parents. He would know it anywhere. It was the first time he had seen these paintings. He had been an adult when they created these. Seeing their work once more was bittersweet. They had been gone from him many years now.

Griff took a room at the Nicollet Hotel, and after bathing, he returned to the lobby and sent Dash a telegram to let him know what time he would be arriving up north. Standing in his room looking down at the street below, he thought once more about Libby. It felt strangely intimate to be in her city. He was so close to her now, but he must not call her. She may not even be here. She may be in New York or heading back to California. He decided instead to do a little spying. She mentioned that she had grown up in a house in a park. He still recalled the name--Loring Park. He was amazed at remembering it, but then he shouldn't have been, he had memorized everything about her.

He hailed a cab and rode down Hennepin Avenue to the park. When he stepped out, his jaw dropped. The houses here were massive. Surely she didn't grow up in one of these American palaces. Libby had said her father had hardware stores. They could never have afforded such opulence.

He paid the cabbie and started to wander. It was a warm summer day, and the park was filled with people having picnics, riding bicycles and feeding the ducks. Griff walked along the path admiring the homes. After buying some peanuts at a stand, he sat down on a bench across from The Plaza Hotel to watch people.

Suddenly he stopped chewing. "The Durant Center for the Arts," it said on the museum next door.

"Impossible," he mumbled.

He walked up the steps and went inside. There was a woman behind a desk. She looked up and smiled. "May I help you?"

"I was wondering if you can tell me, do the patrons of this museum, The Durants live in one of these homes on the park?"

"At one time yes they did, but it is now a home for foundlings."

"Which house is it?"

"It's at the very end of this block."

"Thank you."

Griff immediately walked down and stood before the house at the end of the block. Can it be? This house looked like a miniature castle. Maybe these were rich relations. Suddenly the front door opened and an older woman stepped out with several children. "Come, come now," she said in an accent. "Everyone hold hands," and they started down the stairs.

Griff seized the moment, ran up and asked, "Excuse me, but I'm looking for Elizabeth Durant—Libby Durant?"

The woman smiled. "She lives here no longer, young man," she replied. "This is a home for children now. She has been living in Los Angeles for many years."

Griff stared at the woman, flabbergasted. This had been Libby's home! Why had she lied to him?

"May I tell her who called?" the woman asked.

"No—no thank you."

"Very well, come children."

Griff turned away and walked back toward Hennepin Avenue. So who was the real Elizabeth Durant? He had always suspected she was hiding something, but her money? No, it had something to do with those scars. Determined to find out more, he hailed a cab. "The main library, please," he said.

After requesting a stack of old newspapers, Griff rolled up his sleeves, sat down at a table and started reading. It didn't take long for him to find the name Durant, and yes indeed they had been in hardware but on a much grander scale than Libby had ever admitted and lumber too. For hours he combed through papers. Most of the articles were about business ventures, but then, in a 1917 paper, he came across an article that astonished him. It was about the suicide of a woman by the name of Lillian Durant survived by her two daughters Elizabeth and Jennifer.

Griff dropped back in his chair and gasped. Libby's mother had thrown herself out of a window at the home on Grove Avenue. Libby had talked about her sister's death too, but she had said it was the flu. Had she committed suicide too?

"I'm sorry, sir. We're closing," a librarian said.

"What time do you open tomorrow?"

"Eight."

"Thank you," and he grabbed his jacket.

That evening at supper, when Griff reached into his pocket, he pulled out the phone number of a woman he'd met on the train. She was a native of Minneapolis, and she may be able to tell him more about the Durants. Even if she knew nothing, he needed a drink, and she looked like the kind of girl who would know where to find bootleg.

"Sure, honey," she said on the phone. "I know a great place. I'll pick you up at nine."

Olive Anker honked as she pulled up in front of the hotel in her 1925 Tin Lizzy. She was a skinny brunette with short hair and bright red lips painted into a cupid's bow. It was obvious she was emulating Clara Bow.

Griff threw his cigarette and walked down the steps, jumping in the motorcar.

"We're goin' over to St. Paul," she said. "Alright?"

"Alright."

She ran her eyes over him as she snapped her gum. "You're kind of classy guy. I think you'll like this joint."

"Let's go."

They drove through downtown and then out along the Mississippi River until the landscape started to look rural. Griff spotted an old wooden building with a sign that said, "Hotel Fort Snelling."

"I hope that's not it."

"Nah, that's just an old hotel."

"Way out here?"

"You can't see it because it's dark, but there's a fort out on the river."

They came around a curve and pulled into the driveway of a private residence. It was a large, three-story Colonial Style home. There were automobiles parked everywhere on the grass, and the house was flooded with light. They could hear loud music and see people dining on the main floor.

"Not very discreet," Griff said as they walked to the door.

"No raids in St Paul," Olive explained. "The police have a hands-off policy here, honey."

An attendant in a tuxedo met them at the door. "How's tricks, Bobby?" she said.

"Just fine, Miss Anker," he replied and stepped aside, allowing them to climb the main staircase to the speakeasy above. The room was hot and crowded with elegantly dressed patrons. A three piece band was performing on a small stage, and there was gambling room in the back.

Olive saw a couple leaving and darted over to the table as Griff purchased drinks.

"You have to know someone to get in here?" he asked, sitting down.

"Sure thing. I know a lot of people. But the real trick is to grow up in Minneapolis and know people in St. Paul."

"Why is that?"

"Eh," she said, shrugging. "They don't mix."

"You've lived in Minneapolis all your life?"

"Been in the Twin Farms my whole life," she replied, rolling her eyes. Taking a pull of her drink, she said, "Let's dance."

She took Griff's hand and dragged him through the crowd to a small dance floor. She stepped in close and pressed her breasts against him. "Hold me close, baby," she murmured.

After one dance, Griff had had enough and took her back to the table. He was more interested in gathering information than rubbing against Olive Anker.

He decided to get right to the point. Since it was loud, he leaned close to her ear and asked, "You heard of the

Durants?"

"Who?"

"The Durants, a wealthy Minneapolis family."

"The ones that own that lumber company?"

"Yes."

"Ya, I know of 'em. When we was kids we used to walk by their house on our way downtown. We always crossed to the other side of the street though."

"Why?"

She made a circular motion at her head and said, "You know, crazy."

"What makes you say that?"

"I dunno. My mother said to stay away from the house, or they would hack us to bits. I think one of 'em jumped out of a window years back," and she shuddered. "Money sure can't buy everything."

"Can you remember any more about them?"

Pushing her lip out, she whined, "What the hell? Are you here for fun or a history lesson?"

Griff wasn't listening. *No wonder Libby had hidden her past from everyone. She had probably been ostracized and ridiculed her whole life. That's why she moved to Los Angeles. It was the perfect escape. Everyone was starting fresh. But what happened when she was growing up? Why was everyone afraid of the family?*

Olive ran her hand up Griff's thigh, and he jumped.

"What's wrong with you?" she asked.

"Oh, sorry, let's go. I just remembered that I have a meeting in the morning."

*   *   *

The next morning Griff was the first one in the library. All morning long he pored over newspapers, this time methodically, starting with recent editions and working backward. He had to narrow the search, so he looked at only front page news.

The first thing he found were headlines about Jennifer Durant and her suicide in the Anoka Asylum. His hunch had been right. Next, he found more about Lillian Durant jumping from the window and drowning in the garden pond. Her maiden name was identified as Brennan, so he added that to his search.

By late morning he was getting bleary-eyed and hungry. Nothing seemed to be happening from 1917 all the way back to 1911, so he decided to take a break. He went across the street to a diner, had a Coney Island and a cup of coffee and came right back.

He continued to comb through newspapers until he pulled out an edition dated 1910. When he read the headlines, his eyes grew wide.

"Prominent Citizen Stabs Daughter"

He read the article twice, slumped back in his chair and gasped. *So there it is. That's how Libby sustained those scars.* He had been right. There had been no motorcar accident. She had been stabbed, and not just by anyone; it had been her mother. He thought back to that day on the set of *Jack the Ripper.* She said she was vomiting because of a hangover, but it was memories torturing her.

Now Griff was curious about Lillian Durant. Who was Libby's mother?

He paged through earlier papers, looking at the front pages and the society columns. He found several pictures of her at various functions and saw her name in articles. *So she was sane some of the time.* He hesitated on one page, Lillian was standing with someone that looked familiar, but dismissing it as a mistake, he moved on. He found more articles about her attending this event or that event, but beyond that, there was nothing unusual.

Suddenly he saw the time. It was almost three. He had

to catch his train. He dashed back to the hotel, stuffed everything into his grip, paid his hotel bill and rushed to the depot. He had just enough time to grab a something to eat in the station. He sat down at the lunch counter and ordered a fried egg sandwich.

Griff wished he hadn't wired Dash about arriving today. Now, after everything, he wanted to see Libby again. He wanted to tell her he was sorry, and that he understood, but then he reconsidered. What good would it do? It would probably anger her, and she would resent him for digging into her personal life. No, it was better he was leaving town. He would distance himself and take the time to think things through.

He finished his sandwich and walked out into the atrium. As he passed through the depot, he thought about the pictures he'd seen of Libby's mother. She had been a beautiful woman. It was a shame she had to suffer, but surely there had been some good times. In fact, he'd seen pictures of her with friends.

Griff stopped and blinked, trying to bring something into focus. "Impossible," he muttered.

Walking out to the tracks, he stopped again and barked, "Damn it!" Turning, he dashed through the depot doors, jumped into a cab and said, "To the main library."

Once inside, he asked the startled librarian for all the April 1910 editions of the *Minneapolis Sentinel*. Like a madman, he paged through the papers until he found the picture again.

He was a much younger man, but the gentleman in the photograph with Lillian Durant was none other than Haydn Price.

Chapter 19

Libby had to admit, Haydn Price picked an excellent lodge to renovate. Otter Bay Hideaway was rustic elegance at its finest. After a long journey from the Twin Cities, the warmth and luxury were a welcome sight. The lobby was open to the second story with jack pine rafters and rough-cut log walls. A massive fieldstone fireplace dominated the room with large leather easy chairs surrounding it, and colorful Indian print rugs were on the hardwood floors.

Stepping up to the front desk, she requested her room. As she picked up her keys, a gentleman came out from the back to greet her. "Miss Durant, welcome," he said, extending his hand. "My name is Gil Chambers, the owner of Otter Bay Hideaway."

He was a tall man around thirty years of age with light brown hair fashionably slicked back. He was wearing a well-tailored, three-piece suit and had a broad smile. Libby noticed his thick eyelashes.

"I understand you are a guest of Mr. Price?" he stated.

"I am," she replied.

Libby could see the interest in his eyes. "I sincerely hope your stay is enjoyable. If there is anything, you need, please don't hesitate to contact me."

"Do you always come out and greet the guests so warmly?" she asked, flirting with him.

"Only the guests who require a special sort of attention," he countered.

Libby smiled and turned away with the bell hop who was carrying her bags. She could feel Chambers' eyes on her all the way up the stairs.

Haydn had reserved a large suite for her. The front room had two overstuffed chairs, a log table, and bearskin rug, with windows that looked out over the rocky shoreline of Otter Bay on Lake Superior. The bedroom was equally cozy with a colorful quilt, dressing table, and massive pine wardrobe.

After Libby had bathed, a note came from Haydn saying he would not be arriving until tomorrow night. The thought of seeing him twisted her stomach. All the way up she had tried to formulate a plan to keep him away from Durant Cosmetics, but nothing seemed credible. She was trying very hard not to panic.

She wondered if Dash was around. It would be good to see a friendly face, but this time of year he was probably flying constantly, the demand for liquor at the resorts keeping him busy around the clock.

"I'll think of something," she mumbled and started downstairs.

More than anything she wanted a drink to help dull the pain. And then she remembered Mr. Chambers. He said to contact him if she needed anything, and she needed a drink. She asked him discreetly about liquor.

"We do serve in the dining room," he said quietly. "But I have another idea. Are you alone this evening, Miss Durant?"

"I am. Mr. Price will not be here until late tomorrow."

"May I accompany you to one of our local supper clubs?"

She smiled. It was the diversion she needed, and Gil Chambers was extremely attractive. He could take some of the sting out of being here, she thought. "I would like that.

Will you give me a moment to change, Mr. Chambers?"

"Of course. And please, call me Gil."

It was a warm night, so Libby put on a sleeveless dress, draped a string of pearls down her bare back and arranged a bandeau over her cropped hair. After pulling on her fishnet gloves, she grabbed her bag and returned downstairs.

They drove along the shore of Superior back toward Duluth. "We're going to one of the roadhouses Price renovated," Gil explained. "Now we call them inns."

"And you own Otter Bay Hideaway, correct?" Libby asked.

"That's right. It has been in my family for years, but it was in poor repair. Haydn Price brought it back to life."

"Does Haydn own these inns?"

"No, they are still owned by the original families. Before he came along, they had been abandoned. He is the 'silent partner' for us all."

Libby detected a note of disdain in Gil Chamber's voice. So they were all strong-armed by Haydn. Price and Izzy Bronstein owned everything and everyone up here, just like they would soon own her.

"You must understand, this is not talked about openly," Gil said. "But everyone up here knows it."

"I understand more than you realize, Mr. Chambers—Gil."

They turned down a steep driveway and at the bottom of the hill was a beautiful lakeside lodge. The sign said Voyageurs Point Inn. When they walked inside, Libby was stunned by the brilliantly colored patterns on the ceilings and walls.

"Cree Indian designs," Gil said.

Although it was crowded, they waited only a short time for a table. Since management knew Gil, they were seated in one of the best spots, by the fireplace, and received cocktails hidden in coffee cups. Libby looked around at the clientele. She recognized several of them as movie people. One of them was a director she had worked with at one time. The rest of the guests looked like well-heeled socialites from the Twin Cities and possibly Chicago.

Almost as if he was reading her mind, Gil said, "Mr. Price brings everyone up to Otter Bay for a reason. Do you mind if I ask why you're here?"

"To discuss a business venture similar to yours."

"Understood," he said and looked out the window. "Everyone up here has business with Price and Bronstein. In the backwaters of the bay, you'll see men employed for no other reason than to hold lanterns all through the night, waiting for shipments to come through from Canada. During the day floatplanes land out there too."

Libby thought of Dash.

"Price and Bronstein have a whole fleet of them," he mumbled.

"Boats or planes?"

"Both."

"What about the Coast Guard?"

He shook his head. "There's no worry about that. They're spread too thin across the Great Lakes, and local law is on the take, so again, there is nothing to worry about."

"I suppose everything grinds to a halt in winter?" Libby asked, hoping she could stall Haydn until spring.

"No, it's business as usual. They drive right across on the ice in whiskey sixes. They even use sled dogs."

"Oh for the love of God," she muttered.

"No escape. I'm sorry. You realize even tonight has been orchestrated."

"What?"

"Price called me with instructions to entertain you until he arrived. I had no idea it would be this amusing though."

She smiled weakly. "Let's change the subject. I don't want to hear anything more about Haydn Price," she said, emptying her cup.

"Agreed, let's talk about *you*."

*   *   *

It was three days before Haydn arrived at the lodge, so Libby and Gil filled every moment. Libby liked him and had no objections to Gil showing her everything the North Shore had to offer. They took walks along the lake, dined together, swam and went on afternoon fishing excursions. They became intimate quickly helping Libby forget her troubles about Haydn, but that was all it did. Being with Gil seemed to exaggerate her loneliness for Griff. Feeling someone else's hands on her breasts, someone else lips on her mouth didn't feel right. Gil Chambers was fun and experienced, satisfying her carnally but something was missing, something that was present only with only Griff.

When she thought about it, she would rage. *Damn it! Will I never be satisfied with anyone again? Am I sentenced to only half the happiness the rest of my life?*

At last, Haydn appeared at the lodge full of apologies and summoned Libby to dinner at the Voyageur Inn. When she walked into the dining room, she noticed he was with another man. They stood up when she approached, and Haydn kissed her cheek. "You look lovely this evening, Elizabeth. May I introduce you to my friend and associate, Isadore Bronstein?"

Libby greeted the man and sat down. So here he is, she thought, the puppeteer's puppeteer. She was surprised at how innocuous Bronstein looked. She had pictured a burly thug smoking a cigar with a booming voice. Instead, he was a soft-spoken, middle-aged man with a broad face, dark hair and, of course, an expensive suit.

Libby smiled to herself. *They always think money can buy breeding.*

"I understand you have created your own cosmetic empire," Bronstein said, lighting her cigarette.

Libby shrugged. "I did, but it appears I am no longer at the helm."

Bronstein raised his eyebrows and looked at Haydn.

Libby swallowed hard. *Already she was acting up. These men were dangerous, and she must govern her tongue.*

Bronstein leaned forward, looked at her firmly and said, "I assure you, Miss Durant, it will remain yours—all yours. We just want to supplement your income."

Haydn cleared his throat and asked, "What would you like to drink?"

"A manhattan please."

He told the waiter. "Have you considered what you would need to start a new line of perfume?" Haydn asked.

"Well, lots of alcohol," she said, and the men chuckled.

Libby brought out a folder. "These are the findings from my chemists, as well as the cost involved in hiring a perfumer. Sales and marketing are also additional considerations."

Bronstein looked at the size of the folder and then up at Libby. "Very thorough."

"Not quite. I have no idea on how to approach the government."

"We'll take care of that," Haydn said.

Bronstein put on his glasses and took a closer look her information while Haydn and Libby talked about quantities. At last, Bronstein sat back and sighed. "Enough business for tonight. Let's relax now and enjoy dinner. You are a most exceptional woman, Miss Durant. Welcome to the family."

*   *   *

Libby did not see Bronstein again but met with Haydn several times after that at the lodge. It was under the guise of a relaxing holiday, but every bit of it was about making deals and manipulating money. Everywhere Libby looked, she felt trapped. If she refused to import alcohol from Canada, she would be endangering her life or the lives of her loved ones. If she cooperated, she would be committing a federal offense.

She spent most nights pacing in her room. Although she ended her evenings in Gil's bed, she refused to sleep through the night next to him. Griff was the only one she trusted enough to sleep alongside. Even if she had wanted to stay with Chambers, she would only keep him awake. She was in and out of bed all night, staring out the window, smoking, or pacing. She simply had to think of a way out.

At last, it was the final meeting with Haydn. Libby was anxious to get back to her apartment in St. Paul, kick off her shoes and sleep in her own bed. She purchased her train ticket immediately and met Haydn one last time in the lobby for a drink in the evening. They sat in big leather chairs in front of the fire, finalized some details and were done.

When they stood up, a heavy set man in a cheap suit dashed up to Haydn. He was bald and sweating profusely. He mopped perspiration from his brow and said breathlessly, "Mr. Price if you please. I must speak with you. There's been a misunderstanding."

"George," Haydn said, quietly. "I'm so glad you're here. Let me buy you a drink. We'll take care of this." He took the man's arm and ushered him into the dining room.

Such a big, important man Haydn is, Libby thought sarcastically. She shook her head and went out to the porch to meet Gil for a walk.

"I'll be on the train with you tomorrow morning," Gil announced when she walked up.

"What?"

"I have business in the city. Stay with me for a few days in Duluth before you go back."

"Oh, Gil, I shouldn't."

"Just the two of us in a hotel room doing what we do best? Come on."

Libby was weary and wanted to go home. "I can't. I've been away from work too long."

"Away from work? That's all you've been doing up here!"

He was right, her stay on the North Shore hadn't exactly been a holiday. She hesitated. Duluth might be a welcome diversion. "Alright, I'll stay one night because I can't resist you."

"How about two?"

"Don't push, Gil Chambers," she said, laughing.

*   *   *

That night, Libby slept for only a few hours until worry and anxiety yanked her awake again. She tried to get back to sleep, but it was no use. She threw back the covers and dressed for a walk, hoping it may help her unwind.

Greeting the night clerk, she walked through the lobby and stepped outside. The full moon was up, and there was a profusion of stars overhead. She walked down a path toward Superior. The lake was a vast expanse of black punctuated by a cluster of lights in the distance from a freighter. Following the rocky shoreline, Libby followed the path into the woods. She could see a lantern in the distance and wondered if someone was waiting on the point for a boatload of whiskey.

Suddenly there was the crunch of tires behind her. She jumped not realizing she was near a road. The headlights went down a hill and stopped. Libby heard doors slam and men's voices. She walked to the top of the hill and looked down. She was only a few feet away. There were three men, and they stood in the headlights.

Libby's heart thumped in her throat. One of them was bound and gagged. It was the very man who had approached Haydn in the lobby earlier that evening. He was trembling, and she could hear his muffled cries.

"Jesus Christ, he pissed all over himself," one of the men said. They were both in suits and wearing fedoras.

"Do it. We need to get back."

The man squirmed and cried even louder.

Without hesitation one of the thugs put a gun to his head and shot. The sound echoed through the trees. The victim dropped to the ground.

Libby stood there, too terrified to move. She knew if they saw her, she would be next. They rolled the body in oilcloth, lifted it back into the motorcar and drove off.

She had just seen a man murdered before her very eyes. She was shaking so violently, she could barely walk. Hugging herself, she stumbled back to the lodge.

Knowing she could not go through the lobby. She entered through a rear door, went up the stairs and ducked into her room. After locking the door, she leaned on it for a long time, panting.

When she could at last move, she walked to the closet and pulled out a bottle of whiskey Gil had given her. Grabbing a water glass, she sat down on the edge of the bed in the dark and started to drink, glass after glass.

*　　　　*　　　　*

Libby had guzzled enough whiskey to render herself unconscious for several hours, so when she stumbled out of bed at sunrise, she was still intoxicated. She bathed, stuffed her clothing into her grip and went downstairs to meet Gil.

He was in his office finishing up some work. He came out and declared, "What happened to you?"

"I am feeling a bit rough today," she mumbled, rubbing her head. Libby couldn't look him in the eye. She didn't trust him. She didn't trust anyone here.

Libby slept all the way down to Duluth, and when Gil woke her to say they were pulling into the station, she went to the restroom and retched. She was shaken to the core. She had hoped last night was a nightmare, but when she sobered up, she realized it was all true, and she was scared. There was no question now that Haydn Price was capable of anything. Suspecting he was dangerous was one thing, witnessing it first-hand was quite another.

Libby was glad to be away from Otter Bay, but it wasn't far enough. As long as Haydn Price was married to Pepper, he would be too close to her.

After checking them into adjoining rooms at the Hotel Duluth, Gil said, "Wait here, Libby."

He dashed away from the front desk and returned moments later, putting his wallet back in his pocket. "I just paid for an appointment for you at the hotel salon. While I work this afternoon, you go have your hair done and your nails or whatever it is you girls do at those places. Try to enjoy yourself."

Libby smiled. "You're very good to me."

He kissed her and left.

Libby couldn't wait to get up to the room. More than anything she needed to hear a friendly voice, so she picked up the phone and placed a call to Clay.

When he answered, she choked up.

"Hello?" he said, anxiously. "Hello?"

"Clay?" she said, thickly.

"Libby, is that you? What is it, darlin'? You sound funny. What's wrong?"

Libby stifled a sob and said, "It's-it's not something I can talk about on the phone. I just needed to hear your voice."

"Are you in some sort of trouble, little girl? Are you in danger?"

She snuffed. "No, no. Please don't worry. It's nothing like that," but she was lying.

"Where are you now?"

"At a hotel in Minnesota."

"Can you tell me anything?"

"No."

"Well, you get your little ass on the next train back here. You need to get back to your ol' friend, Clay. He'll take care of you."

"Alright. I'm feeling better already."

"Good, just know that someone loves you, little darlin'."

"Love you too."

Libby hung up and sat for a long time with her head in her hands. At last, she dropped back onto the bed and slept for several hours. When she awoke, she decided she had better put on a happy face for Gil, or she would have to endure a battery of questions. She freshened her makeup and went down to look for the salon.

The Hotel Duluth was state of the art. Only a few years old, it was built on a grand scale with Renaissance Revival details of wrought iron, bronze, and glass chandeliers. It had fourteen floors, a large ballroom, and three restaurants. What Libby really liked was the arcade with a fountain, florist, small grocer, barber, and jewelry store. She thought that having everything handy and under one roof was a good idea with the long Minnesota winters. She noticed the words Harper's Salon under a striped awning and crossed over to it.

By the time she had her hair and nails done, she was feeling better, and Gil was back in the room. He pulled her close and asked, "Are you feeling better?"

"A little."

He unbuttoned her top button, slid the shoulders down on her blouse and started kissing her neck.

Libby's back stiffened. She was not feeling amorous. "I could use a drink to loosen up, Gil."

He laughed. "Don't you still have some left over in you from last night?"

She stepped away and buttoned up. "I need to blur the edges again."

"What happened last night?"

She shrugged. "Nothing really. When I get homesick, I drink."

Gil looked at her doubtfully but did not press her. He sighed and said, "Alright. I know a speakeasy around the corner, and I would be willing to bet the restaurant here may serve too. They don't want to lose all their clientele to those of us up north."

Libby pulled out her black evening gown with silver trim and undressed to her slip. She laughed and slapped Gil's hands as she tried to dress. "Waiting for it will make it all the more exciting," she said.

Their evening together was pleasant, and for a time Libby was distracted. They had drinks then dined in The Spanish Room at the hotel, an elegant restaurant with Moorish design and rich food. They lingered over dessert and coffee listening to the band until Gil said, "Let's go back to the room. I want to rip that gown off you."

They walked through the arcade which was filled with guests shopping and visiting. Suddenly, Gil exclaimed, "Dashby!"

Dash was standing near the smoke shop, watching the

crowd. His face lit up when he saw them. He shook Gil's hand and kissed Libby on the cheek. "Well I'll be damned," he said to her. "I didn't know you were up here."

"I'd hope to see you," she said. "But I assumed you were flying. You and Gil know one another?"

"We do," Gil said. "From deliveries."

There was a man purchasing cigarettes at the stand, and when he turned around, Libby was stunned. It was Griff. She gasped.

Just as surprised, Griff stared. She looked beautiful standing in the dim light in her graceful black gown. "What are you doing here?"

"I could ask you the same thing," she said.

"So *just* about all of us know each other!" Gil exclaimed. He leaned forward and shook Griff's hand. "I'm Gil Chambers."

"Griffin Gardner," he mumbled. He could see Gil was Libby's date, and his greeting was icy.

They made small talk for a few minutes, and then Dash suggested they go to the speakeasy around the corner. Griff didn't speak with Libby the entire time, and she didn't encourage him. She heard him say he took a detour up from Chicago, and she clenched her fists. *So, he had been visiting Claire and that French woman. Nothing has changed.* She longed to smash him in the face.

When he wasn't looking, she ran her eyes over him. She wished he didn't look so good. Griffin Gardner had that natural appeal. He didn't try to slick back his curly, auburn hair or overdressed. His charm came from his mischievous smile, his athletic build, and that overinflated confidence. Nevertheless, she detested him.

He has a nerve being cool to me. While he has that French woman, should I be home waiting? No!

They had only one drink and said goodnight. Gil

wanted to get back to the room, and Libby wanted to escape the frigid atmosphere.

The moment they stepped into their rooms, Gil was all over Libby, and she returned his kisses with a passion she did not have to pretend. She had been smothering her lust for Griff all night. It bubbled to the surface the moment Gil kissed her. Delighted with her enthusiasm, Gil was thoroughly satisfied and fell into a deep sleep immediately afterward.

Sleep did not come that easily for Libby. She slid out of bed and went to her own room sitting down at the vanity. There was too much bothering her, and now she had to add Griff to the mix. When she turned on one of the vanity lamps, she noticed a note on the floor by the door. It was from Griff, and he said to meet him downstairs in the arcade. It was urgent.

Libby looked at Gil. He was still sound asleep. He would never miss her. Tiptoeing over, she slipped her gown and shoes back on and stepped out the door. *What could possibly be so important?* Something told her it was not about reconciliation. Griff was far too proud. It must be something else.

When she walked into the arcade, he was standing by a pillar smoking. He looked at her, and immediately his eyes softened. Libby saw the expression, and she felt her heart melt. "Hello, Griff," she murmured.

When he looked down at her, she thought he was going to kiss her.

"Hello, Libby." He ran his eyes over her face as if he was memorizing every feature. "I'm sorry I've disturbed you, but this just cannot wait."

Taking her elbow, they sat down by the fountain. There were still guests in the arcade, but it was late, and the crowd had thinned.

He looked down at his hands.

"What is it, Griff? You're scaring me."

"I had a layover in Minneapolis earlier this week and I--" He hesitated. "Well, I was bored and thought I'd go and see where you grew up."

Libby looked surprised. "You went to Loring Park?"

He nodded. "I saw the Durant Center for the Arts, and I went inside to see if it was the same family. They told me where the Durant house was and I met a woman there who said you had lived there at one time. Why didn't you tell me the truth about your upbringing?"

Libby bit her lip and looked away. "I didn't want anyone to know. I wanted to make it on my own without the name or the money."

"Or the gossip."

"What?"

"I'm sorry, but I did some more checking."

Libby's back stiffened. "You did, did you?"

"I went through old newspapers and found out about the family illness--"

"You pried into my personal life!" she exclaimed, jumping up.

"Wait, Libby," he said, grabbing her arms. "I'm sorry, but there's something more important. Something you don't know."

"No! I've heard enough. There's nothing more you could possibly tell me. I was there. I lived it, and it was *my* secret to keep."

She turned and ran through the lobby, jumping into the elevator. Just as she was pulling the gate shut, Griff grabbed it. "Wait, Libby!"

"Let go!" she barked, struggling against him.

He pushed into the elevator and shut the door. "You're not going anywhere until I finish."

When Libby pressed the button, Griff stopped the car. Pushing her against the wall, he snapped, "Goddammit, this is for your own good!"

"How could you, Griff?" she said, tears filling her eyes.

Searching her face, he relaxed his grip. "Please listen to me."

She wiped her eyes and nodded.

"I came across a picture of your mother. She was about your age, and she was with a man. It was Haydn Price."

"What?" Libby stared at him, dumbfounded.

He nodded and stepped back, letting her go.

"Haydn Price? You're mistaken," she said. "What would he be doing with my mother?"

"*That* is a good question."

"Well, that's impossible."

"I thought you'd say that," he replied. Reaching into his breast pocket, he unfolded the clipping and handed it to her. "So I took this from the library to show you."

Libby looked at it, and her lips parted. She blinked and mumbled, "Oh my God." Stepping into the light, she exclaimed, "Oh, my God. Is that him?"

"It is."

She looked at the caption. "But this man's name is Frank Collins."

Griff raised his eyebrows. "People change their names."

Libby looked back at the picture and sank back against the elevator wall. "It *is* him. There's no question. But why? What did he want with *my* mother?"

"Money? Maybe he thought she was an easy mark because of her illness."

"Oh Griff," she exclaimed, grabbing his wrist. "Let's go back downstairs. I have so much to tell you."

Chapter 20

They talked in the arcade until sunup. Libby told Griff everything that had happened with Haydn, from Pepper's bruises to his interference in her business, to the murder of the man in the woods.

"We need to learn more about this monster," Griff said. "Starting with his relationship with your mother. We have to get back to Minneapolis."

"And talk to my grandmother." Suddenly Libby gasped. "I just realized, Grandmother has never met Haydn Price."

"Ha! That is no accident. I'm guessing she knows Frank Collins though."

"I always thought it was curious he refused photographs," she said. "He had to be the only one in all of Hollywood."

"When do you leave?"

"The eight o'clock train this morning."

"I'll be on it too," he replied.

Gil Chambers graciously offered to take Libby to the station, but she declined. Her relationship with him was over. He was far too immersed in Haydn's business ventures to trust. The thought crossed her mind that maybe he had been assigned, not only to entertain her but to keep an eye on her as well. Whatever his motives, the affair was over.

Libby and Griff booked a compartment to discuss things in private, but the train was barely out of the station before she fell asleep. She thought she would be on edge with Griff, but instead, for the first time in weeks, she felt safe. She knew he would take care of her, and at last, she could rest.

Griff chuckled, watching her sleep. She always played the hard-boiled act with him, but he knew how vulnerable she really was. Poor kid, he thought. She's been through the wringer. He eased her down onto the seat, putting a pillow under her head and covered her with a blanket. Haydn Price had swept in like a hurricane and ruined her life, and her cousin's as well.

He looked out the window as they raced through the countryside, but his eyes always returned to her face, a face he could never forget. The high cheekbones, the perfectly arched brows and the full lips were burned into his memory forever. He longed to run his hands over her. He didn't need to see her body to remember that it was supple and slender as a willow. She looked defenseless sleeping so peacefully, but he knew she was dangerous. She had a power over him that was occult.

He lit a cigarette and sat back. How would they ever get through this mess? Price and Bronstein would stop at nothing to win. They were ruthless crime bosses capable of anything.

At all costs, I must protect Libby, Griff thought. Whether I like it or not, she is my main concern. "You're in over your head, Gardner," he muttered, and then he looked back at her. "Just where you wanna be."

*   *   *

The first thing Libby did when she returned to her apartment was to place a call to Clay and tell him that she was safe and feeling better. She would not be returning to Hollywood yet. She was with family, and they were helping her. She left out the part about Griff Gardner. She didn't want to hear Clay's lecture.

Late that afternoon, Libby picked up Griff at his hotel,

260

and they called on Grandmother Brennan. When they pulled up under the *porte-cochère* and parked, Griff made a face. "This house is so damn big."

"Well, you just had to go nosing around, didn't you?" she said. "Now you have to see the life of the *real* Elizabeth Durant."

"Alright, I'm ready."

"Now Griff, there can't be any slip-ups. Grandmother is smart and will pick up on any mistakes. Knowing everything could be dangerous for her."

"How to make a guy relax. You know I'm no actor. I'm only a cameraman."

"You'll be fine. Now, get out of the motorcar, Gardner."

The housekeeper took them to a small conservatory upstairs overlooking the lawn where Oliva was reading. The room was all windows with a domed glass ceiling and filled with plants. Olivia was sitting at a white wrought iron table, reading. There were seed catalogs strewn everywhere.

She jumped up and kissed Libby. "This is a wonderful surprise."

"Grandmother this is Mr. Griffin Gardner."

He shook her hand and said, "A pleasure to meet you. This is a beautiful room."

"Well, it's pretty when you can use the thing. It can get so damned hot here." She looked at Libby and then back at Griff. With a twinkle in her eye, she said, "Sit down, young man. I want to know everything about you."

"Grandmother, it's not what you think. Mr. Gardner and I are--" and she swallowed hard. "Mr. Gardner is a private detective."

Olivia's eyebrows shot up. "A private detective!"

Griff cleared his throat. "I apologize for the intrusion, Mrs. Brennan."

"Are you investigating me?"

"No," he said with a chuckle. "I found an old clipping of your daughter, Lillian taken many years ago. The man I'm investigating is with her in the photograph." He handed it to her. "Do you know him?"

Libby watched the blood drain from her grandmother's face.

"I know him, yes. His name is Collins."

Libby's heart skipped a beat.

"My client is very interested in his past."

Olivia took a jagged breath. "Does your client have a good deal of money?"

"Well, yes, I believe so," Griff said.

"Then they may be in grave danger."

Libby's stomach twisted.

"Why didn't you come to me directly with this, Mr. Gardner?" Olivia asked.

"You were out of town, Grandmother," Libby said, quickly. "It was a few weeks back when you were in Asheville. How did mother know this man?"

"They met at a fundraiser. You had just gone away to school, Elizabeth. They kept company for almost a year."

"Did he know about mother's illness?"

"Oh, he knew. He was *so* solicitous," she sneered.

"Who was he?" Griff asked.

"Believe me, I tried to find out, but I hit a dead end. I believe he may have created his identity. How he obtained the money to live the lifestyle he did was a mystery to us all."

"And you think he wanted more money?"

"Without a doubt. That's why he married Lillian."

"Grandmother!" Libby gasped. "They were married?"

"Indeed they were, but I had it annulled after a few months, on the grounds that she was incompetent."

Griff and Libby stared at her, stunned. So Haydn Price was more to Lillian Durant than a just few dates. They were married.

"Why didn't you tell me any of this?" Libby asked.

"There was no need for you to know. I wanted to put it all behind me. I was foolish to think that I could."

Olivia stood up and looked out the window, twisting a handkerchief in her hands. "Your mother was furious with me."

"Where did Collins go after the annulment?" Griff asked.

"Not far. He married Mary Freely, a young woman from an old Minnesota family. She too had money but *her* vulnerability was not schizophrenia, she was unattractive and lonely. Shortly after they wed, she was walking her dog with Collins, and she slipped and fell to her death off the St. Paul bluffs."

Libby put her hands over her face. "My God, murder."

"Was there an investigation?" Griff asked.

"Yes, poor woman. I worked with her father to further the inquiry, but nothing was proven."

"Did Collins know of your involvement in this?"

"He did."

Griff darted a look at Libby and then back again at Olivia. "What happened to him after that?"

"He disappeared. Mr. Freely and I made sure he was not welcome in the Twin Cities anymore."

Libby could see how distressing this was for her grandmother and announced that they had heard enough.

"You have been a great help, Mrs. Brennan," Griff said.

"I'll check in on you tomorrow," Libby said and kissed her goodbye.

Libby and Griff drove down Summit Avenue into downtown St. Paul too stunned to speak.

At last, Griff said, "You look pale, Libby. You need to eat something."

"I'm not hungry."

"I'm not either, but we should try. I don't want you fainting on me."

Libby nodded and drove them to The St. Paul Auteria, an automat on Wabasha Street. After buying nickels from the cashier, they grabbed trays and made their way around, depositing coins and opening the little compartments, each grabbing a sandwich and side dish.

They ate in silence. When Griff finished his sandwiches, he said, "Libby, Haydn Price is out to destroy your family."

She pressed her eyes shut and nodded.

He continued. "I believe it was for money at the beginning. But then your grandmother won the annulment and drove him out of town. His greed turned to revenge."

"I thought the same thing, Griff. But what I can't figure out is why he would he bail my grandmother out financially?"

Griff frowned and rubbed his chin. "What do you know about that accountant that ran off with her money?"

"Just that he had been a trusted friend of the family for years."

"Suddenly a good man changes. Don't you find that curious? I'm guessing Price threatened him if he didn't cooperate."

"Good lord," Libby said. "It is all beginning to make sense. There were other financial losses in the family at the same time. Pepper's father too. In fact, Haydn tried to put me under his thumb, trying to get me to join Mirador Studios." Her jaw dropped. "And before Uncle Owen invested in Durant Cosmetics, I almost signed with someone else. This investor seemed to come out of nowhere. Do you suppose Haydn was behind that too?"

"Uh, huh," Griff said, lighting a cigarette. "He wanted to make sure everyone was too crippled and in too much debt to bail her out."

"So Haydn Price to the rescue. Now, he not only has Grandmother's first fortune, but she is repaying a second fortune to him as well."

"He has his revenge and all the money to boot."

"Do you think he came all the way out to Hollywood to find us and ruin us too?"

Griff frowned and rubbed his chin. "Probably not. He was after those failing studios, but low and behold, there were Olivia's granddaughters. How very convenient."

"He met Pepper at a moving picture convention in the Twin Cities though."

Griff shrugged. "That could be when he hatched the whole plan. Being back in Minneapolis may have triggered old hatreds, so while he was here, I suppose he thought he'd try to meet one of the heiresses. Just like he met your mother, years earlier."

The clerk started sweeping the automat floor. It was closing time. Libby sighed and slumped back into her chair. "So what now?"

"I honestly don't know, but we certainly can't meet Price head on."

"Griff, I can't thank you enough for all you've done. I need your help, but this really isn't your problem."

He shrugged it off and said, "You helped me with Claire. Consider it debt repayment."

"Debt repayment with slightly higher stakes."

*   *   *

It was difficult turning their attention back to their careers, but with no plan in sight, Libby and Griff decided to return to their daily lives until an idea presented itself. Griff returned to Hollywood first, and Libby returned a week later.

One of the first people she tried to contact was Pepper, but she would not return Libby's phone calls. When she stopped by the set of her latest movie, Pepper told her she couldn't talk.

"You can't or won't?" Libby asked.

"I'm just so busy, and filming is not going well," she replied. She darted a look at Libby and then dropped her eyes. "Haydn returns tonight."

"I thought so," Libby said. "Just so you know, he is having me start to import alcohol for a new line of perfume."

Pepper looked up, her eyes wide. She opened her mouth to speak but then reconsidered. When Libby started to walk away, she ran after her with tears in her eyes. Grabbing her arm, she said, "I've done this to you, Libby! I'm sorry!"

"What? How is this your fault?"

"I brought him into our lives. Please stay away from me, Libby. You must believe me when I say I know what's best."

Libby grabbed her wrist. "Pepper, are you in danger?"

"No, I'm fine," she replied, darting back into her dressing room and shutting the door.

*   *   *

Days turned to weeks, and Libby held her breath, knowing that one day the phone would ring, and it would be Haydn, telling her that the government paperwork was ready. It was then she would have to put her signature on legal documents swearing that the alcohol being imported from Canada would be used solely for the manufacture of Elizabeth Durant perfume. She would be committing a federal offense.

She had no idea how she was going to get out of this,

and time was running out, but knowing Griff Gardner was by her side, gave her hope. He assured her he would stand by her and help her find a way to escape Haydn's grip, and she trusted him. She had unshakeable confidence in his ability to keep both of them safe.

Since his birthday was approaching, Libby wanted to do something special. He had never followed through on his promise to teach her to bake a cake, so she decided to make one herself. If it turned out poorly, she could always blame him for not teaching her, and she giggled. So one afternoon, she cleared her schedule and headed home to bake.

Determined to do it without help, Libby made sure Mrs. Lockhart had the day off. She rushed home, put on an apron and pulled out a cookbook. Bending over the counter, she paged through the book until she found a recipe for a chocolate layer cake.

She had to read it three times before she felt ready. It took her almost two hours to find all the ingredients, get the batter mixed, poured into pans and put in the oven. When she was done, she sighed. *Well, that wasn't too bad.* She felt good about herself. She had tried something new and succeeded without anyone's help. In fact, it was invigorating. She jumped up and did the dishes, humming a tune.

All seemed to be going well until she took the cake from the oven. She had forgotten to grease the pans, and the rounds clung tenaciously to the edges and bottom. "Son of a bitch," she muttered, digging the cake out.

Nevertheless, she would not give up. She couldn't have been the first person to have made this mistake, so arranging the pieces, she patched it together with mounds of frosting. Stepping back, she looked at it. Although the cake was lopsided and the frosting was messy, she had done it herself, and she was proud.

She took her apron off and went upstairs to change. She was going to take it over to Griff's house immediately. If he wasn't home, she would leave it on the back porch.

Libby was beyond excited. She hoped he would be there. She wanted to see the look on his face. He would be so proud of her.

When she pulled up to his house, she was delighted. His motorcar was there. She wanted to surprise him, so with cake in hand, she tiptoed up the steps onto the front porch. Just as she was about to knock, she heard voices inside, and they were not speaking English. When she listened more closely, she realized they were speaking German, and one of them was Griff. To be sure, she bent down and looked through the porch window. Griff was leaning forward with his hands on his knees, speaking urgently in German to a man with his back to her.

Libby straightened up, blinking. She didn't understand. When she asked Griff how many languages he spoke, he had said, "Just French." Why had he lied to her?

Chairs were scraping, and she realized the conversation was ending. She flew down the steps and dashed to her automobile. Putting the cake on the floor, she started up the motorcar and slammed it into gear, roaring down the block and out of sight. But she had to know who Griff was talking to. Turning around, she came back and parked down the block.

After a few minutes, a tall, well-dressed gentleman came out and got into an expensive automobile. Libby recognized him, and she was stunned. It was Ernst Baumann. What was he doing there and why was he speaking German with Griff?

It scared her. What sort of clandestine activity was this and was it dangerous? Yet another riddle for her to unravel about the enigmatic Griff Gardner. And Ernst Baumann? What was the connection?

Now I know how my mother felt. "Trust no one, Elizabeth," she used to whisper with her eyes wide and her hair in tangles. "They will always fail you."

Libby drove home at top speed, ran into her house and threw the cake in the trash. She rushed into the living room, opened a decanter of whiskey and filled a water glass. "What the hell," she said out loud. "I'm a Durant. We drink ourselves to death."

Chapter 21

The next day, Libby received a note from Griff saying he had been called away to Chicago and would be back as soon as possible. Libby did not allow herself to feel anything. She could not afford to. She must remain vigilant and strong. As difficult as it was, she must try to trust Griff.

The next day, a phone call came from Haydn. "This is just an update, Elizabeth," he said. "More delays. This is to be expected when dealing with the government. And when it involves alcohol, there is even more red tape. I am confident though we will have it wrapped up soon."

"Very well," Libby said, quietly breathing a sigh of relief. This news bought her more time.

"Why don't you join us for dinner tonight at the country club?" he continued. "Pepper misses you."

"Thank you, but I have another commitment. Give my love to her though," she said and hung up. Libby had no commitment, but seeing Haydn socially was not going to happen.

Over six weeks passed, with no word from Haydn or Griff, and it was as Libby would have it. She was working long hours, trying to channel her anxiety into some sort of productivity. The expansion of Elizabeth Durant Cosmetics was a huge success. Her company was fast becoming the largest cosmetic firm in the country, rivaling Max Factor. There were interviews to do for magazines, she had to pose for promotional shots, hire more staff and meet with designers to approve the new luxurious packaging. It was enough work for ten women.

"Darlin' you're exhausting yourself. Come out with us tonight. You need to have some fun," Clay said, late one afternoon in her office.

"I'm going home to bed," Libby said, stuffing papers into her briefcase. "I'll relax that way."

"If you're going to bed then why are all those papers going home with you?"

She didn't answer.

"We'll pick you up at 8," he said, standing up.

"Who's we?"

"Betty Boyd. You told me once you liked her."

"I did?"

"Yes, ma'am. See you at 8," he said putting on his cowboy hat.

That night when Libby sat down at her dressing table, she was disturbed. She looked rough. After some careful makeup application and styling her hair, she opened her closet and looked at her evening wear. She pulled out her most flattering dress, a sleeveless, copper-colored Schiaparelli gown. It had a dropped waist, gathered to one side and pinned with a brooch. The gown was covered in beads. *My gown better be good. The rest of me looks like hell.*

She slipped it over her head and looked in the mirror. She was satisfied. She always liked the drape of it on her body and how it accentuated the copper highlights in her hair.

The doorbell rang, and she picked up her gloves. Knowing Mrs. Lockhart would answer, she took one last look in the mirror and started down the stairs. Halfway down she stopped, stunned. Griff was standing in the entry.

"I apologize," he said, looking up. "You must have a

date."

"I thought you were Clay. We're on our way to Divona's."

"I'm sorry to interrupt. I have news—important news."

Libby stared at him. Pulling on her gloves, she said, "Griff, I can't tell you how much I appreciate your help, but I will find my own way from now on."

"What?"

She walked down the stairs and opened the door for him. "Thank you, but I'm expecting Clay."

"What the hell is it this time, Libby? *Now,* what did I do wrong? Dammit, what do I have to do to prove to you that I--" and he stopped. "Worry about you?"

Libby felt a surge of anger twist her stomach. She threw her evening bag down and barked, "Well I don't need your concern! What I want is the truth, Griffin Gardner, and this time I want it all. I want to know your past, your present and your future. Who are you really? Where is it you go for long periods of time and why? And above all, I want to know why the hell you were talking to Ernst Baumann in German several weeks back at your house. If I don't get answers tonight, and I want all of them, believe me, I will *never, ever* let you into my life again."

Griff's jaw dropped, and he stared at her. The only sound was the ticking of the clock in the entry. He swallowed hard. "You heard us?"

"Yes, at the house on your birthday. I brought you a cake."

Libby could see the wheels turning as Griff reviewed the day. He said slowly, "That was dangerous. We were indiscreet and lucky it was only you." He rubbed his chin and sighed. "I was planning on telling you everything tonight anyway. The news I have has forced my hand."

"Hello, darlin'," someone said behind Libby. Clay was

standing in the door, and he looked from Libby to Griff and back again. "Evenin', Griff," he said with a nod.

"Hello, Clay."

"Something serious has come up," Libby said. "I won't be going out tonight. I apologize, Clay."

"I see you two have bigger fish to fry," he drawled. Kissing Libby on the cheek, he put his hat back on and left.

Without a word, she picked up her bag and walked out to Griff's automobile. They drove in silence until they arrived at the Hollywood Bowl. A concert was going on, and there were motorcars parked everywhere. Libby had not yet seen the new stage. It resembled a pyramid with a stair-step design along the sides.

Griff said, "What I have to say cannot be said in any establishment. Let's stop up here. At least we can hear a bit of the music."

They drove past the Bowl and parked. The stars were out, and Libby slid onto the hood of the Marmon as Griff lit a cigarette. He looked tense and started pacing. The Los Angeles Philharmonic was playing in the distance, but they didn't hear the music or notice the beautiful September evening. There were both too anxious.

"None of this is to be talked about with anyone. Do you understand?" he said.

She nodded.

"During the war, I flew reconnaissance doing aerial photography."

"You already told me."

"Well, what I didn't tell you is that I still do it."

"You do?" she said with surprise. "Why? The war's over."

"The war never ended, Libby. This is just intermission. The Germans aren't done yet."

"With war?"

273

"That's right. We believe they will build another war machine and try again."

Her jaw dropped. "Do you think it's possible?"

Griff took another puff and nodded. "I *know* it's possible."

Libby gasped. "This is frightening."

"Yes, it is," and he started to pace again. "So with another aviator, I fly over Germany taking footage, looking for things that may point to a military build-up. Sometimes I go directly into the country too."

"On foot?"

"That's right. I do surveillance in the towns and cities, mingle with the people, watch, listen and take photographs."

Libby stared at him wide-eyed. "So you're a spy?"

Griff laughed. "You must work in Hollywood. Let's just say I'm a reconnaissance specialist."

"So you weren't in Chicago this time, were you?"

"No, I was in Nuremberg."

"And you can do this because you speak fluent German."

He nodded. "It was the only language we spoke at home when I was growing up. My parents were from Germany. The language is as natural to me as speaking English."

"I had no idea. You never told me about your parents."

"Well, I don't advertise it. Germans aren't very popular nowadays. It was incredibly hard on them, especially during the war. When Americans heard their accents, they shunned them."

Libby bit her lip. At last, she was starting to understand. Strains of Puccini floated up through the canyon on a breeze.

"So how is Ernst Baumann involved?"

"He gathers information too on his trips back to Germany. But his assignment is different from mine. We each have different radical groups we are watching over there."

"So who do you watch?"

"I'm assigned to observe a group called, The National Socialist Party. It is hard to tell right now whether they will succeed or not, but one thing is certain, they are gaining momentum."

Relief washed over Libby. It was all making sense now; the sudden departures, the long unexplained absences, and Griff's reluctance to be close. At last, she had the truth.

"Which brings me to the reason I came tonight. A man by the name of Adolf Hitler has emerged as the leader of this group along with another rising star in the organization--a young man by the name of Hartmann Price."

"A relation of Haydn's?"

"I thought it was unlikely. The name is common, but something told me to check into it. It turns out, Hartmann and Haydn are brothers. Haydn's parents were German immigrants too, but unlike my parents, they went back to Germany shortly before the war broke out. Haydn did not go with them, but he didn't forget them either. To this day he supports his brother's involvement in this National Socialist Party. He is on a list of regular contributors."

Libby frowned. "So how does this help us?"

Griff lit another cigarette. "They run on a platform of hatred against Communists and Jews, promoting violence against both groups. They blame them for every weakness and evil in Germany today." He stopped and looked at Libby. "Izzy Bronstein, Haydn's partner, is a Jew."

Libby's jaw dropped, and then a smile spread slowly across her face.

Griff continued. "Haydn's parents and two siblings live

in Munich and Haydn has business interests there. If this National Socialist Party goes all the way to the top who knows what could happen. He could become a very rich and powerful man. I'm guessing he knows that."

"Tell me more," Libby said.

"I'm famished," Griff said. "I know I said we shouldn't discuss this in a public place, but I can't wait any longer. I know a quiet little café downtown."

Suddenly Libby felt hungry too, something she hadn't felt in weeks. "Let's go," she said, sliding off the hood.

They drove back into downtown Hollywood to a small café and gas station. An old man and a trucker sat on stools at a lunch counter, and a young couple with their heads together sat at one of the tables. Heading straight to the back, Griff and Libby ordered the blue plate special.

"I'm sorely overdressed," Libby said, laughing.

"You give the joint class," Griff replied in Bronx accent.

After the waitress had brought coffee, Libby took out a cigarette. Her hand was shaking. She blew her smoke, looked around and whispered, "This whole thing is unnerving. What will happen to Haydn if Bronstein finds out?"

"I honestly don't know. At the least, it will ruin the partnership. At the worst—well--"

Libby nodded. "How can we get the information to Bronstein without giving ourselves away?"

"That's where Ernst Baumann comes in," Griff whispered. "He rubs elbows with all the studio heads. They hate Haydn and would take great pleasure in ruining him. They will gladly deliver the information to Bronstein."

"Ah ha!" Libby exclaimed. "That's brilliant. Most of them are Jewish too."

"Right you are," Griff said, tapping the table.

"But do they know Bronstein?"

"That's what Ernst will find out. I'm guessing one or two of them may have investments with him in liquor."

"Why is Ernst doing all this? It's dangerous for him too."

"Not only as a favor to us, but he is Jewish as well."

The waitress brought their fish dinners, and Libby thought she would faint, the food smelled so delicious.

When she finished bolting her meal, Griff declared, "You're done already? What's wrong with you?"

"Nothing now. I feel human again."

Sitting back and watching him eat, Libby tried to sort things out. "Will the studio heads believe Ernst? I mean anyone can put names on a roster."

Griff wiped his mouth and put his napkin on the table. "There will be no question when they see Haydn's canceled checks to the National Socialist Party."

"You have those too?"

"Yes, I have clearance for that sort of thing."

"My, but you're thorough," she said.

He noticed Libby was staring at him. "Are you uncomfortable with what I told you about my work?"

She straightened up. "No! I'm glad. In fact, it makes all the difference in how I see--" and she stopped.

A smile flickered on his lips.

They paid the bill and were driving through downtown when Griff noticed the headlights dimming on the Marmon. "What the hell?" he exclaimed. He pressed on the accelerator, but nothing happened. Turning the wheel, he pulled over to the curb as the auto slowed to a stop. He groaned and got out.

Libby stood beside him as he looked under the hood. "Any idea what's wrong?" she asked.

"I can't see a thing," he replied, looking at the street light a half a block down. He fiddled and fussed with the engine for several minutes while Libby sat on the curb. At last, he said, "I'll have to come back tomorrow. Shall we try to find a cab?"

She stood up, brushing herself off. "Not right away. Let's walk for a while."

"Alright," he said, shutting the hood and putting his fedora back on his head.

She took her shoes off, and they started down the street.

"Downtown is quiet tonight," Griff observed.

They passed under a dark marquee, and Libby said, "Yes, it looks like the movie houses have let out."

An occasional pedestrian would pass by, or a motorcar would rattle down the street as they walked along. It was a warm evening, and the late night cafes had their doors open. The smell of stale beer would drift out, revealing the bootleg sold there. Neon lights hummed over hotels, Chinese restaurants, and smoke shops. A neon cowboy riding a bronco over a furniture store caught Libby's eye, and she smiled. "You know, I feel better than I have in months, Griff. I've been so scared lately."

"I know," he replied. "But I'm here now, and I'll take care of you."

She swallowed hard.

They passed a cafe and music drifted out from a radio. "They're playing our song," Griff said.

Libby smiled. The song was "Someone to Watch Over Me," and the lyrics seemed written for them.

He took her hand and pulled her inside the diner. It was empty except for a waitress filling ketchup bottles and a drunk with his head on the lunch counter.

Griff took her shoes and tossed them into the corner. Pushing his hat back on his head, he pulled her close and started to dance. With her cheek next to his own, he moved her slowly around the floor.

Laughing, Libby said, "You're crazy, you know that?"

Griff ignored her. He was humming.

She felt herself soften into him.

"You love me, don't you, Durant?" he murmured.

She looked up. "Sure of yourself, aren't you?"

"Just the opposite. I'm a coward. I want you to go first."

"And do what?"

"Say that you love me."

"Why do I have to go first?"

"Because you've been dying to say it all night."

She laughed. "Oh, I have, have I?"

"Yes, it's so obvious."

They continued to dance, and at last, he stopped and sighed. "Alright, I'll take the fall for you, like I always do. I love you, Elizabeth Durant," he said. "My God, how I love you."

He pulled her back into his arms, and they danced again.

She murmured, "You see that wasn't so bad. I love you too, Griff Gardner, and I always will."

*   *   *

When the cab dropped them at Libby's front door, she took Griff's hand and led him up the stairs to her room. When she shut the door, he asked, "Why so clandestine? Is your housekeeper here?"

"No, I'm shutting the whole world out tonight."

She clicked on the radio, and soft music filled the room. As she was turning the volume to low, Griff stepped up behind her and wrapped his arms around her, kissing her neck and running his hands over her breasts. She turned around and kissed him deeply, feeling his heart hammering against her chest. Slowly he slid the shoulders down on her gown until it dropped to the floor. He ran his hands over the smooth silk of her slip, feeling her supple flesh beneath it. The sensation was intoxicating.

Holding her waist, he stepped back and looked at her. The amber light from the radio illuminated the soft curves of her body. Easing the straps of her slip down, he kissed one breast and then the other. Libby sighed, running her fingers through his hair.

He moved up to her ear and whispered, "I going to be here for you always. You know that, don't you?"

"It's what I want," she murmured. "Here, alone just the two of us, forever, without the rest of the world."

Griff kissed one hand and then the other. "Should we leave for food now and then?"

"Maybe but we always come right back."

"Agreed," he said tenderly.

*   *   *

For two days, they were true to their vow. They did not allow the world to interfere. They canceled all their commitments, and Libby gave Mrs. Lockhart two days off as they immersed themselves in each other. After taking care of Griff's auto, they had breakfast in bed, swam and had drinks by the pool. The second night, they ordered Chinese takeout and spent hours giving each other pleasure behind the closed door of Libby's bedroom.

"I've never been in love until now," Griff said, running his hand over Libby's hip as they lay in bed.

"It's certain that I haven't," Libby replied. "I would have remembered the excruciating pain and pleasure."

"I knew all along that I loved you, but I couldn't admit it. It seems like you kept me at arm's length."

Libby sighed and rolled onto her back, staring at the ceiling. "I suppose I did. Funny though, I felt the same way about you. You know I dated Dash to get even with you."

He laughed. "I had hoped that was true, but I wasn't sure. The ladies do like him."

"You were always the one for me. And what about you and that Frenchwoman?"

"Giselle? I barely remember the time I spent with her and believe me, I don't care to revisit it. Everything about the war seems surreal to me now, like a bad dream."

Libby rolled over and hugged him. "How is everything going to turn out, Griff?"

"We'll find a way," he said. "Together we'll break Haydn's grip on you."

"I'm scared. I don't want him to unleash his fury on either one of us."

"If we do things properly, he won't ever know." He brushed the hair from her face. "Now look what you've done. You opened the door and let the world in. You vowed not to do it."

She nodded. "You're right. We still have until tomorrow."

*   *   *

They went back to work the next day, and even though Libby was worried, everything seemed to have a brighter sheen to it. Having Griff again, gave her hope. She was madly in love with him. Sometimes it swept her with exhilaration, but she could not allow herself to feel it fully until they were completely safe. If she loved him and lost him, she couldn't endure the pain.

After agonizing over it all, Libby, at last, came to a decision which gave her some measure of peace. She decided not to sign Haydn's contract to bring alcohol in from Canada, if and when, he presented it to her. If it meant giving up her business and going into hiding forever, she would do it, but she would *not* go to prison for the man. She hoped she was getting ahead of herself. If Griff's plan worked, she might be freed from Haydn's grasp forever.

At the end of each day, Griff and Libby met at his bungalow or at her home. It was usually late, but they always made time for each other. Late one night, when he returned from filming a Chaplin movie, he told Libby he had spoken with Ernst Baumann. "He met with several studio heads, and they want to move forward with the information on Price. Sometime this week, Bronstein will be informed of Haydn's affiliation with the National Socialist Party, and the canceled checks will be presented to him."

Libby's stomach jumped. "Oh, Griff. I'm scared. Will there be any way to trace it back to us?"

Griff took a pull of his scotch and shook his head. "The information will have changed hands too many times. Besides, you know the studio heads; intrigue is their specialty."

"What do you predict will happen to Haydn?"

"It won't be good," he warned. "But I don't think it will happen right away. Nevertheless, I want you as far away as possible. I don't want you caught in the crossfire. And I mean that quite literally."

"Where should I go?"

"Back to St. Paul or out to New York, anywhere but here. Haydn is immersed in his big production about Joan of Arc. He won't be going anywhere for a while."

Libby rubbed her forehead and started to pace, considering everything. "It'll be hard to just pick up and go. I'll have to--"

Griff put his arms around her. "Do it for me, Libby. Do it soon, in the next few days."

"But what about you? You're staying here."

"I'll be fine. I am not a part of Haydn's life the way you are."

"My God, I hope Pepper will be safe."

Griff sighed. "I believe her own husband is more of a threat to her than anyone. There's no avoiding that."

Libby nodded. "Alright, first thing in the morning, I'll start making arrangements."

*   *   *

Libby boarded the train for St. Paul late the next night. When she arrived in the Twin Cities, days later, loneliness dogged her every step. She had only just found Griff again, and now they were apart. She called him when she arrived and then threw herself into work to distract herself.

She visited with her sales representatives, introducing them to new products and organized a meeting to update her employees on the expansion of Elizabeth Durant Cosmetics into the South. She had lunch with Grandmother Brennan and went to see Uncle Owen which helped with her loneliness too.

One morning when she was at her office, she received a telegram from Pepper. She told Libby that she was on her way to Minneapolis, and her train was arriving that afternoon. Libby was shocked and confused. She thought she was shooting a new comedy. Why was she suddenly coming here?

Libby met Pepper at the St Paul depot. She barely recognized her when she stepped off the train. She had on a black wig with bangs and dark eye makeup. Laughing, Libby hugged her and exclaimed, "That's some disguise. I thought you were Colleen Moore when you walked up."

"So did everyone else, Libs. They kept coming up and asking for her autograph. My bid for privacy backfired."

"Here, put these on until we get to my house," Libby said, handing Pepper her sunglasses. "I hope you're staying with me."

"No, I had my bags sent to the Women's Club."

"You're not staying with me *or* your parents?" Libby

asked, with surprise.

"They're out East, and you know me, I'm too scared to stay alone."

Libby picked up Pepper's hatbox and started for the automobile. "I have a spare bedroom. Are you sure?"

"I'm sure."

Libby knew she wasn't getting the whole story, but she didn't press her.

Their first stop was Dayton's Department Store where the staff fussed with wigs, hats, and eyewear so Pepper could go unnoticed in the Twin Cities. Next Libby's driver took her to the Women's Club in Minneapolis so she could settle in and get changed for their night out.

At nine o'clock that evening Libby pulled up to the club on Loring Park. She had stopped at the Grove house and had dinner with Tante and Zabby, and then drove over to pick up Pepper. Libby stepped out of her motorcar and looked up. The Women's Club was a brand new building which reminded her of an Italian palazzo with arched terraces on the upper and lower floors. She adjusted her hat and walked inside to the reception area where she waited while an employee informed Pepper that she had a guest.

Libby looked around the lobby taking mental notes for Grandmother who had not been there yet. The room had large a fireplace, a winding stone staircase with a decorative wrought iron railing, plush patterned sofas as well as chandeliers overhead. A row of floor to ceiling windows with French doors overlooked Loring Park. Libby stepped outside and ran her eyes over the green expanse. It was indeed a beautiful setting.

"There you are," Pepper said coming out onto the terrace. She had on a light brown, shingled wig and round eyeglasses with clear lenses.

Libby started to laugh, "Now you look like Phyllis Wesley."

"Are you serious? That studious kid we used to make fun of?" and Pepper punched her in the arm. "It was *your* staff who made me up like this."

Libby smirked and shrugged. They went downstairs and jumped into the automobile. It was a warm evening, so they rode with the top down.

"Where do you want to go?" Libby asked Pepper.

"Can we go over to St. Paul? I have to drop something off for Haydn."

"Where?"

"It's a speakeasy on Wabasha Street."

"Not the caves. That's a rough place."

"Yes, the caves. I know it's questionable," Pepper said, wrapping a scarf around her head. "We'll have one drink and leave."

Libby bit her lip, feeling uncomfortable. "Alright."

They drove along in silence. Their relationship had become strained. In the past, they would have been chattering nonstop. Fearing the worst, Libby asked, "Will Haydn be joining you soon?"

"No, he's married to Joan of Arc these days, and that's just fine with me."

Libby looked at her. That was the first time she had ever expressed discontent with Haydn. But Pepper looked away, making it clear she would say nothing more.

"I thought you were working on a comedy."

"For a while, but there were some issues with filming, so we are taking a break. Haydn said if I wanted to get away for a little while, now was the time."

They rode down University Ave, crossed the University of Minnesota campus and passed into St. Paul. On the other side of downtown, just off the Mississippi river were the caves. They ran along the river with bluffs rising high above. The caverns had been used for many things over the years, and now one of them housed a speakeasy.

Libby was unsure how they would find the entrance as they drove down the dark street, but at last, she spotted a cluster of motorcars. They parked and walked toward a large man smoking a cigarette by the entrance. As they drew closer, Libby guessed his bulk was from the firearms he carried inside his topcoat.

"Good evening, ladies," he said and opened the door, admitting them into the speakeasy. It was jammed with mostly men, smoking, drinking and playing cards. The ceiling was carved out of stone and arched overhead. An old mahogany bar ran along one wall and behind it were stacks of crates and barrels filled with bootleg. Someone was banging out a honky-tonk version of "The Sheik of Araby" on an old piano as ladies of the evening solicited to customers.

Pepper and Libby crossed to the bar. Pepper opened her handbag, took out a fat envelope and handed it to the bartender. He put it quickly under the bar and made them drinks, telling them they were on the house.

Libby needed to settle her nerves and guzzled her drink quickly.

"Bottoms up," Pepper mumbled. "This place gives me the creeps."

"You don't have to tell me twice."

Everyone in the caves looked dangerous. They were all dressed in flashy clothes, with slicked back hair, gaudy rings and judging from the bulges in their suitcoats, they were all carrying handguns.

Afraid one of them would approach, Libby hurried her drink along. But after a few moments, she started to notice none of them even looked at her or at Pepper. In fact, if any eye contact was made, they looked away quickly.

Aha, somehow they know who we are, and there is a hands off policy courtesy of Haydn Price.

"I've seen enough. Let's go," Pepper said, draining her glass.

They edged their way through the crowd and out the door again. Opening her motorcar door, Libby took a deep breath and announced, "Well, that was an adventure I never want to revisit."

"Ditto," Pepper replied, jumping in. "Now how about we go to a decent joint where we can run wild."

"I know just the place. We passed it on the way here."

They drove back down to The Coliseum Pavilion on Lexington Avenue. When they turned into the jammed parking lot, Pepper exclaimed, "Hey, Libs wasn't this a roller rink when we were kids?"

"Right, but now it's a ballroom."

When they walked inside, the club was jammed with couples dancing to the sounds of Wally Ericson's Coliseum Orchestra. Soft drinks were available at the bar, and if you didn't have a flask, a man stood in the back room with a pitcher pig full of bootleg. If there was a raid, which was highly unlikely in St. Paul, it could be dumped quickly.

Immediately they were asked to dance, and after several turns on the floor, Libby stepped into the back and paid the attendant to freshen her drink. When she walked back out into the club, someone murmured in her ear, "So you're back in town."

She turned around. It was Gil Chambers. "Hello, Gil," she said with surprise. He looked debonair in his three-piece blue suit and silk tie.

"This is a treat seeing you. How have you been?" he said with a smile.

"Fine."

"You're back in the state, and you haven't looked me up?"

"Well, I've been busy with work."

He looked Libby up and down. "You look absolutely wonderful." Lighting her cigarette, he asked, "Will we be seeing you on the North Shore again?"

"That remains to be seen," she said with a shrug. "How about you? How is it you're down here?"

"Business."

Pepper stepped up and said, "Hello, Gil."

"Pepper! Both of you standing right here? Well, this is a sailor's dream," he said with a grin.

"Still so charming," Pepper commented flatly.

The smile faded from Gil's face.

Turning to Libby, she said, "I'm feeling sick. Can we go home now?"

Libby looked from Pepper to Gil and back again. "Sure, Pepper we can go."

"I'll look you up," Gil called to Libby as they walked away.

"How the hell do you know him?" Pepper asked as they wound through the crowd.

"When I was on the North Shore I stayed at his lodge. We had a fling for several days."

Pepper stopped and stared at Libby, dumbfounded. "Is that what he told you?"

"Well, yes."

"Stay away from him, Libs," Pepper stated, pushing the door open and stepping outside. She walked quickly to the auto, looking one way and the other. "Gil Chambers doesn't own any resort up north," she said, getting in and slamming the motorcar door.

"What?"

"He's Izzy Bronstein's number one hit man."

Libby's jaw dropped, and she stared at Pepper. "But, but--" she stammered.

Pepper's eyes filled with tears. "I'm in trouble, Libs. Big trouble and so are you. Can we go to your apartment and talk?"

Chapter 22

They said nothing all the way back to the apartment. Once upstairs, Libby poured them each a stiff drink, and they sat down.

Pepper stared out the window at the city lights, gathering her thoughts. "Haydn was wonderful at first," she said with a melancholy smile. "What you saw was true. He treated me like a queen. But after we were married, things started to change. More and more he dictated my choices and the first time I argued with him, he grabbed me and punched me in the chest. He was all apologies at first, saying the stress of being a studio head was overwhelming, but it continued."

Libby didn't pretend to be shocked. She had known all along. "He hit you in places that wouldn't show, didn't he?"

Pepper nodded. "Heaven forbid he damage his investment. He had to keep his star working. But that wasn't the worst of it," she continued, taking a gulp of her drink. "Unusual people, rough looking people, started visiting the house and had meetings with Haydn behind closed doors. I turned a blind eye at first. I didn't want to know. Eventually, though, he dragged me into his schemes having me sink everything I had into his rum-running operation. He launders his money regularly through my bank accounts. That's another reason I'm here. Some of those banks are in Minneapolis. And I suspect he had ulterior motives lending money to Grandmother, although

I'm still not sure what that was."

Libby swallowed hard. She couldn't tell Pepper the truth, not yet. Haydn still had too tight a grip on Pepper.

Pepper grabbed Libby's wrist. "You opposed loaning Grandmother the money from the start, Libs. You knew something was wrong. I should have listened to you. I am so sorry. I treated you poorly."

"Don't apologize, Pepper. You were being loyal to someone you loved."

"But I loved you too," and she put her head in her hands. "And now he wants to involve you in everything as well."

"What was that packet you delivered tonight?"

"It was money, a great deal of it. Beyond that, I don't know what it was for."

"Was that the reason he sent you to St. Paul?"

"That and I have transactions to make for him at my banks."

"Was he the one that called off the filming of the comedy?"

"Yes, but it truly wasn't going well. He's pouring all of his money and time into this Joan of Arc movie."

"And what of Gil Chambers? My God, Pepper, a hit man?"

Pepper nodded. "He does all kinds of work for Bronstein, killing happens to be his specialty. The man is dangerous."

"And I had an affair with him!" Libby exclaimed. "He just seemed like a nice, regular guy from the North Shore."

"He's a smooth operator, that one," Pepper said, throwing some ice cubes into her glass and pouring another drink. "I'm sure Bronstein hired him to keep an eye on you and getting you in bed was an added bonus."

Libby suddenly felt a chill. Had he been awake that

night in the Hotel Duluth when she went downstairs to meet Griff? The nightmare seemed to be getting worse and worse.

They talked for another hour until Pepper asked to be taken back to the Women's Club. Libby offered her a room at her apartment, but she refused.

Even though it was the middle of the night, when Libby returned home, she called Griff and told him everything. "I don't like it, Libby," he said. "I'm getting on the next train."

*   *   *

In the morning, Libby called and checked on Pepper. She was up, and about to leave for lunch with school chums. This was just what she wanted to hear, so she carried on with her day.

Later that afternoon, a call came in from Uncle Owen. "Elizabeth, there is something of great importance I would like to discuss with you. Would you stop by the house today?"

"Of course. Would six o'clock be all right?"

"Just fine. See you then."

When Libby arrived that evening, she was shown into the library. Uncle Owen was seated in an easy chair, and Grandmother Brennan was sitting across from him.

"Grandmother!" Libby gasped.

"Hello, Elizabeth."

"Why are the two of you together?"

Grandmother Brennan replied, "That's what we're about to tell you. Will you pull the pocket doors closed please?"

Libby pulled them shut and slid onto the edge of a chair, her eyes wide.

"Darling, I'll get right to it," Uncle Owen said. "You know I love the movies."

"Yes."

"Well, being the star struck fool that I am, the first thing I did was check to see what Pepper's new husband looked like."

Libby held her breath.

"Believe me, it took me a while to find a picture. The man is successful at staying out of the limelight. When I did see a photograph of him, he looked familiar, but I thought nothing of it. Yet off and on, his face would spring to mind, until at last, I was able to place him."

Grandmother narrowed her eyes. "That's when Owen came to me."

Biting her lip, Libby looked down.

"You and that young man who came to see me this summer knew all along who Haydn Price was, didn't you?" Olivia asked.

She nodded. "I didn't want to involve you. We thought it could get dangerous."

"That was a mistake, Elizabeth," Uncle Owen said.

"You underestimate the Durants *and* the Brennans," Uncle Owen said. "Do you honestly think we haven't encountered bottom-feeders like Price hundreds of times before with our businesses? And are you naïve enough to believe our families came this far without bending a few rules ourselves?"

"I-I've never really thought about it," Libby stammered.

"Foolish girl," Olivia stated.

"We have people of our own, dear girl, and I had them do some checking," Owen said. "It seems this Haydn Price is pressing you to import alcohol for him."

Libby's jaw dropped. "You know about that!"

"Of course, and it's been taken care of. The government will never approve your application."

"Oh, Uncle Owen, this is wonderful news, but won't there be repercussions?"

"Absolutely not."

"Now Pepper's marriage is quite another story," Olivia said. "I have Irish connections in St. Paul, and they are prepared to go head to head with Bronstein and Price."

Libby gasped. "You know people like--"

"Elizabeth please," Grandmother Brennan said, holding her hand up. "Let us not forget, I'm a lady."

*   *   *

Libby was stunned. She drove back to her apartment that night feeling elated. It may just be over. She couldn't wait to tell Griff. She went to bed and slept soundly. In the morning, she woke up feeling refreshed and decided to take the morning off to have her hair and nails done. She wanted to look her best for Griff when he arrived.

Grabbing her clutch bag, she rode down the elevator, chatting with the operator about the beautiful fall weather. Libby crossed the reception area, her high heels clicking loudly on the gold and black checkerboard floor and stopped at the front desk to pick up her mail. The clerk was talking with two policemen.

"Oh, Miss Durant," he said. "I was just about to call upstairs. These officers would like to speak with you."

Libby stared at them, in shock. One officer was tall and thin with sunken cheeks. The other was squarely built with a thick Irish brogue. They had her to sit down in the reception area. Her heart started hammering. "Has there been a train accident?" she gasped, thinking of Griff.

"No, ma'am," the officer with the brogue said. "Are you are relative of Mr. Owen Durant?"

"Yes, he's my uncle," she said, looking from one to the other.

"You are the first relative we have been able to locate. Your uncle died this morning."

Libby jumped to her feet. "No!" she cried, covering her

mouth. "Uncle Owen!" and tears filled her eyes. "I just saw him yesterday. He was fine. My God, what happened?"

"The detective will tell you. He's at the house. Will you kindly come along? We need a family member to identify the body."

Libby nodded and looked around, trying to collect herself. She couldn't think straight. Did she forget something? Where was her purse? The tall officer picked up her clutch and handed it to her. Wiping the tears from her eyes, she followed them out to the police automobile.

By the time they arrived at Uncle Owen's home on Park Avenue, Libby was thoroughly shaken. They took her upstairs to Uncle Owen's bedroom where a man in a suit with a pug nose, stood in the doorway of the bathroom. "Miss Durant, I'm Detective Walsh. Thank you for coming. I'm sure this is difficult. The housekeeper found your uncle early this morning."

He stepped aside and allowed Libby to go into the bathroom. Uncle Owen was in the tub on his back, naked with his eyes staring at the ceiling. The window was open over the tub, and a sheer white curtain was blowing in the breeze. It looked oddly delicate and beautiful, sweeping out over the macabre scene.

Libby stared, dumbfounded. The bathroom floor was wet.

Detective Walsh said, "Water is how the housekeeper was alerted that something was wrong. The faucet was still running after the accident, and it flooded through the ceiling. It appears your uncle was running a bath and as he pulled himself into the tub, he slipped and hit his head. He was knocked unconscious and drowned."

Libby stared at Uncle Owen, dumbfounded. He looked like a department store mannequin, white and bloated laying in the water. And there were marks around his neck.

"But-but he looks like he was already in the tub bathing. I don't understand. Where was his valet? He always had help getting in and out of the tub."

The detective referred to his notepad. "Mr. Johannsen had the day off. May I have a statement from you now, please?"

Libby blinked. He was so abrupt.

"Is this Mr. Owen Durant?" he asked.

Choking back a sob, she mumbled, "It is."

Taking her elbow, he hustled her to the door. Libby jerked her arm away and asked, "Detective, are you quite certain this was an accident?"

"I'm quite certain, Miss Durant. Thank you for coming."

The officers took her downstairs, offering to take her home, but Libby refused, having them call a cab instead. She dropped down onto a wicker chair on the front porch to wait.

My God, Uncle Owen is gone. A sob escaped her and then another. She fumbled with the clasp of her handbag, opened it and took out a handkerchief, wiping her nose. *God, it was so horrible seeing him like that. It was so— grotesque.*

Taking a deep breath, she rubbed her temples. She had to get control of herself and think. There was so much to do. She had to inform the relatives, make funeral arrangements and a million other things to consider. Grandmother Brennan would know what to do. She could help Libby with the arrangements. She was good at that sort of thing.

Suddenly, Libby sat up straight. *Was Grandmother Brennan safe?* She blinked. *Of course, she was. Why even ask such a thing?* She felt a sudden chill, and her heart started to pound. Jumping to her feet, she started inside to call her when the cab pulled up.

Libby ran down the walk, jumped in and said, "410 Summit Avenue, St. Paul and hurry."

The ride seemed to take an eternity. When at last they arrived, she tossed some bills at the driver and dashed in the front door of the house calling, "Grandmother!" She ran to the foot of the stairs, and called, "Grandmother!"

The house seemed empty and quiet. A feeling of dread swept over her as she turned toward the kitchen. The dining room door swung open and Margot, the housekeeper, rushed out. "Miss Durant, what's wrong?"

"Where's Grandmother?"

The young Irishwoman looked startled. "She left last night for Chicago on the spur of the moment. Your aunt is bad again. I was just on the phone with Mrs. Brennan when you arrived."

Libby staggered backward, and dropped down onto a dining room chair. "Thank God."

"What about Uncle Roger and the kids?"

"On holiday. What is it, Miss?"

"There's been a family emergency. Will you ring up my grandmother up again please?"

"Certainly."

*   *   *

Libby kept the phone conversation brief. Olivia also believed that Owen's death seemed suspicious. She was moving to another hotel immediately and no one, except Libby, would know the location. It was all Libby could do to keep her from rushing home. The only thing that kept her in Chicago was the assurance that Griff was coming that evening and that he would take care of her.

The next thing Libby did was contact her Aunt Bertie, Uncle Owen's sister. Overbearing and officious, she immediately took charge of everything to do with the funeral which was a relief.

"Lock the house up, Margot," she said to the housekeeper before she left. "Grandmother said you and the staff are to take a paid holiday until she returns home." Libby and Olivia didn't want any of them in danger.

Margot's eyes grew wide. "With pleasure, Miss Durant."

Libby's heart was pounding. She couldn't wait to get out of this house. It was so massive, anyone could be hiding anywhere.

As she waited for a cab, she paced back and forth under the porte cochère. She knew now after talking with her grandmother that Uncle Owen had indeed been murdered. They both agreed that the position of his body in the tub was suspicious, the fact that his valet was gone and the marks on his neck.

Libby knew the detective was covering something up. She believed he was being paid or threatened by someone to not pursue the investigation.

My God, the horror for my poor uncle during his final moments. The thought made Libby sick to her stomach, and she ran inside to the powder room and wretched. Straightening up, she pushed her hair back and looked in the mirror. Had it been Gil Chambers? Does he work for Bronstein *and* Haydn too? She had kissed that monster and shared intimate moments with him. The thought brought the bile up into her throat, and she wretched again.

She had to see Griff. She would not feel safe until he was at her side. The cab came at last, and she headed back to her apartment. When she checked in at The Commodore, he had sent a telegram. He was arriving that evening.

Libby sighed. She noticed the front desk clerk staring at her. She must have been a sight. "Is everything alright, Miss Durant?" he asked.

"Everything is fine, thank you," she replied, with a

weak smile. He handed her the key to her apartment.

"Was anyone here today, asking for me?"

"No, ma'am."

She swallowed hard and said, "Thank you."

She started for the elevator and stopped. She couldn't go up to her rooms. Someone could be waiting for her there. If Haydn could buy the silence of the police department, getting past the front desk of The Commodore would be a breeze. She must stay in public places until Griff arrived.

Suddenly she thought of Pepper. Was she safe? Libby couldn't tell her about Griff's plan, but without a doubt, it was time she be informed of Haydn's past and his connection to the family.

She walked back inside the lobby, went to the house phone and called The Women's Club. They told her that Pepper had checked out that morning. Confused, she called her parent's home. When, Pepper answered, Libby, swallowed back tears and asked, "Why are you at the house on Park Avenue?"

"Hayden arrived unexpectedly this morning."

A chill ran through Libby. She lowered her voice in case he was nearby. "I need to talk to you right away. Something terrible has happened."

"I need to talk to you too," she whispered. "I've been trying to get ahold of you all day. We must meet in secret. I'm being watched."

Libby's stomach flip-flopped. "Oh, dear God."

"Where can we meet that's private?"

"Let me think," Libby said, rubbing her forehead. Her mind was spinning, and it was hard to focus. "Do you remember the gate to my house that opened onto Loring Park?"

"Of course."

"It's all overgrown now. Pretend like you are taking a walk in the park. Duck through the bushes and in through the gate. I'll meet you in the garden. How soon can you get away?"

"Seven at the earliest," she whispered.

"See you then."

*   *   *

It was twilight when Libby arrived at the park, and the street lights were just coming on. Not wanting to involve Zabby and Tante, she walked around the house, stepped through the bushes and opened the wrought iron gate. The hinges creaked loudly as she stepped inside. Goosebumps crept up her arms as she walked through the green darkness. *Why the hell did I want to meet her here? What was I thinking?*

The wind was blowing, and leaves skittered at her feet. Moss had grown up between the flagstones, and the branches of the trees hung low over the walkway. The flower bed, now just tangled weeds, held a cracked urn that was on its side with dried soil spilling out.

"Pepper?" she called softly, but there was no answer.

Libby looked up at her mother's bedroom window. She could practically see her there on the sill, her hair a mass of black tangles, and her eyes wide with madness. She turned away. *I mustn't think about that.*

She started to pace. "Where the hell is Pepper?" she murmured, looking at her watch.

It was getting dark, and she could barely see. Someone turned a light on in the house, and it threw a golden light over the pond. It was empty and overgrown but the stone nymph, once broken, was standing erect once more holding the shell. She had not realized that Axel had fixed it years ago.

She started pacing again until something caught her

eye. Resting on the bed of the shell was a piece of paper with a rock on it. A note from Pepper, she thought. She pulled it out, stepped into the light and read:

Tell Price if he wants his wife alive, to bring $75,000. No police or she dies. Watch The Sentinel classifieds.

Libby's jaw dropped, and she felt dizzy. The trees and the house whirled around her. She staggered, steadied herself and read the note again. *Is this a prank?* She looked around the garden. *This can't be true! Someone has kidnapped Pepper?*

"Oh dear God!" she cried.

Jerking open the gate, she dashed through the park and ran to her automobile. *Who would do this? Is she tied up in some dark basement? Are they brutalizing her?* Her mind was racing. Tears started rolling down her face as she started the car.

I have to call Haydn. But wait, before I do anything I must be sure Pepper is truly missing.

Libby raced back to the Women's Club. Jumping out, she wiped her eyes and took a deep breath. Steadying herself, she walked to the front desk and asked if Penelope Brennan had taken rooms again. They said no, so she sat down at one of the club member phones in the lobby. Her hands were shaking so badly, she could barely open her purse to find her phone book. Carefully she dialed Pepper's parent's home. The housekeeper said Pepper had gone for a walk in Loring Park. Libby's heart sank. "Then I must speak with Haydn."

"Mr. Price is not here either, Miss Durant."

"Please have him call me immediately. It's an emergency."

Libby looked at her watch. Griff was arriving in less than a half hour. Jumping back into her motorcar, she started for St. Paul.

There was quiet in the depot when she arrived. Every voice, footstep, and door closing echoed loudly, bouncing off the high arched ceiling overhead. When the loudspeaker announced the arrival of Griff's train, it startled Libby.

Steam billowed up as she rushed down the platform, pushing her way past passengers. Searching every face, she found Griff at last. He was wearing a fedora. His coat was draped over his arm, and he was carrying a small grip. When he saw her, he held out his arms, but his smile dropped when he looked at her face. "What's wrong?"

She ran into his arms, shaking with muffled sobs. "Someone's taken, Pepper. They want money," she said.

"What!" he barked.

Although her words were garbled, she managed to tell him what happened. Griff stared at her in disbelief. "Do you have the note?"

She opened her purse and handed it to him. He read it and said, "I'm guessing Bronstein is behind this. Have you called Haydn yet?"

"I left a message. I told the housekeeper it was an emergency."

"Alright. Let's get to your place. We need to be there when Price calls."

Libby handed Griff the keys to her motorcar. "You drive."

On the way to the apartment, she told him about Uncle Owen.

"Good lord," he growled. "Things are heating up, Libby. You stay close to me."

"That won't be a problem."

When they stepped off the elevator at The

Commodore, Griff reached into his suit coat and pulled out a handgun. Libby's eyes grew wide.

Putting his finger to his lips, he nodded for her to unlock the door to her apartment. The moment she opened it, he pushed in front of her and walked inside, clicking on lights and scanning each room.

"Alright," he said. "Lock the door."

Libby slid the bolt and headed to the bar, as Griff collapsed into a chair. Pouring them each a strong drink, she handed him a glass and sat down on the ottoman in front of him, putting her arm over his knees.

She was shaking, and he leaned forward rubbing her arms. "We'll get through this, Libby. I promise."

"I didn't know you carried a gun."

"I never had to in the States, until now."

"I suppose you know how to use it—I mean after--" she stammered.

"Just drink. You need to calm your nerves."

Griff took a pull of his drink, lit them each a cigarette and said, "Kidnapping Pepper is the work of Bronstein. He's trying to clean Price out before he kills him."

"Are you sure it's not someone trying to abduct a movie star?"

"I'm sure, although that's what Bronstein wants it to look like. He'll take the ransom money, kill Price *and* have the monopoly on rum-running here. This all plays well for him."

Libby began to shake again, and she took another drink. "Do you think they're hurting Pepper?"

"Certainly not. She's their leverage."

"Griff, maybe we should call the police."

"That is the worst thing we could do. You saw for yourself when your uncle was killed that Price had them in his pocket."

"But that's just it—maybe they would help Haydn."

"Then let Haydn ask them."

The phone rang, and she jumped. It was Haydn.

"Haydn I--" and she stopped.

"Libby, what is it?"

Swallowing hard, she said in a shaky voice, "Someone has kidnapped Pepper."

"What!"

"I went to meet her this evening at the house where I grew up. Someone must have followed her. They left a note in the garden."

There was a long pause. He said at last, "I'm on my way."

"I'll meet you in the lobby."

A half hour later, Haydn came through the doors of The Commodore where Libby was waiting for him. Griff was in the market attached to the building, watching.

They sat down in the lounge area, and she handed Haydn the note. As he read it, she watched his demeanor harden. The transformation was so drastic, it was surreal. For the first time, Libby saw the real Haydn Price, and it was terrifying. His eyes turned lifeless and icy. It was like a body devoid of a soul.

"I'll take it from here," he said mechanically. "It looks like all communication will be through the classifieds."

"Are you calling the police?" she asked, squeezing the armchair.

"No, we don't want the media getting wind of this, especially in Hollywood."

"Surely you'll pay the ransom," she asked, anxiously.

He looked outside. "I'll teach these small time sons-a-bitches," he muttered.

"Haydn, you're going to give them what they want, aren't you?"

He didn't answer.

"Haydn?" she pleaded.

Again he didn't answer. He stood up and put his hat on.

"Haydn, you'll let me know what's happening, won't you?" she asked in an even louder voice.

There was still no response. When he left, she stared at the door.

"What happened?" Griff asked, rushing up.

"He said he'd take care of it," Libby mumbled. "But I don't know what that means."

Chapter 23

There was no sleep for Libby or Griff that night. Neither of them even undressed. When Libby wasn't pacing, she was smoking. "I'd go right now and pay if I had the money," she said, just before dawn. "You know Grandmother would too, but Haydn has ruined everyone financially in this family."

"Libby, you know it's not about that. This is about Bronstein's revenge on Price."

"Then if that's true, *we* are responsible for Pepper's kidnapping."

"And how's that?" he snapped, slapping his thighs and jumping up. Griff too was edgy. His shirtsleeves were rolled up, his trousers were wrinkled, and he had dark circles were under his eyes.

"Contacting Bronstein with this information about Haydn brought everything down on Pepper," Libby said.

"Oh, and the alternative was acceptable? You going to prison for his rum-running?"

She clenched her teeth and looked out the window.

"Pepper married Haydn Price," Griff argued. "She was in this up to her eyeballs long before we came forward with *any* information."

Tired and angry, he squashed out his cigarette and announced, "I'm going down to see if the morning edition is out yet. Lock the door behind me."

He returned with the paper, and they combed through the classifieds, but nothing seemed remotely significant.

"Oh no!" Libby gasped. "I just realized, it was too late in the day for them to post anything in the morning *Sentinel*. It won't be in until the evening edition." She covered her face with her hands. "Dear God, how are we going to get through the day?"

Griff sighed. "We're going to have to."

Time seemed to crawl all morning. Griff took Libby out for breakfast, but she ate little, her appetite poor. She contacted Haydn around noon, who said he had collected the ransom money and was ready for the hand-off. She told him she would come over the minute the note appeared in the paper.

Libby and Griff dozed off in the afternoon, but after an hour, they were up again pacing. "I'm going down to see if the paper is out yet," Griff said. He dressed, went downstairs but returned empty-handed.

Every fifteen minutes after that Libby badgered him to return to the lobby to check. At last, he came back with *The Sentinel,* and they spread it out on the kitchen table. They found the post right away. The notice read:

Your star appears at midnight at Split Rock Lighthouse. Tonight only.

"The lighthouse north of Duluth!" Libby exclaimed. "Let's go see Haydn."

When they arrived at the home on Park Avenue, the housekeeper looked surprised. "Mr. Price packed his bags and left hours ago, Miss Durant."

"What?"

"Mr. Grayson took him to the train station early this afternoon."

"Did he say where he was going?"

"No, Miss Durant."

Libby looked at Griff, puzzled. "He's started up to the North Shore already?"

Griff frowned and turned to the housekeeper. "May we speak to the chauffeur, please?"

"Certainly, please come in."

Moments later, the elderly chauffeur appeared. "How may I help you?" he said.

"Which depot did you take Mr. Price to this afternoon?" Griff asked.

"The main depot, sir," he replied.

Libby blinked and straightened up. "Not the Milwaukee Road depot?"

"No, ma'am. It was the main station."

She looked at Griff. "Trains for the North Shore leave only from The Milwaukee Road Depot."

He nodded. "That's what I was afraid of. Price isn't ransoming Pepper. He's going to the East Coast to catch a steamer for Germany. He's been tipped off." and they ran to the motorcar.

"We have to get to the lighthouse by midnight," Griff said, starting the engine. "We have some fast driving and some fast talking to do."

*   *   *

It took hours on rough roads to get up to the North Shore, and the weather was much colder than in St. Paul. Libby had protested when Griff insisted on gathering a few things before setting out, but now she was now grateful. They took turns driving and dozing.

Whenever she looked at the black woods surrounding them, it gave her a chill. She remembered, as a child, being terrified when Grandma and Grandpa Durant had taken her and Jennie to their lake home up north. She remembered the headlights flooding the road with white light, throwing the woods into shadows. She always feared being abandoned in those dark expanses, and the trips seemed endless. She realized now that the cars were slower. She had a child's perception of time, so everything took an eternity.

Nevertheless, Libby was glad to be out of the city. Word was out about the kidnapping. When they stopped at a café, it was on the radio, and in the papers. Restaurant patrons and people on the street were talking about the abduction of the beautiful and beloved star, Penny Davis and their sympathies were with her husband.

It made Libby's blood boil. *In a matter of hours, this monster has turned everything to his advantage. He knew it would sell movie tickets, so he had fabricated a story.* Journalists reported that a note was found by one of the staff at the house on Park Avenue and that the police were informed immediately. Haydn said he was devastated when he received a telegram on the ship from authorities. Had he known about his wife's abduction, he never would have boarded a steamer for Europe.

Libby sighed and tried to relax her grip on the steering wheel. She knew she must concentrate on her driving, and just in time. When she rounded a corner, a deer darted across the road. She hit the brakes and swore.

Griff lifted his head from the window. He had been sleeping. "You alright?"

"A deer," she replied.

"Well, be careful."

"Don't worry. I will," she replied looking down at the lake. "It's a long way down."

North of Duluth, the roads became treacherous, weaving and winding along the rock face with Lake Superior far below. During the day it was breathtaking, but at night, it was hair-raising.

"What time is it?" Libby asked.

"Eleven forty-five."

"There it is," she announced, pointing to the lighthouse.

Split Rock was a solitary sentinel standing guard upon a cliff. It was silent tonight, but its light still swung around and around warning sailors of the dangerous shoreline.

An automobile was parked alongside the road near wooden steps leading down to the lake. "There's a motorcar," Griff said. "Pull over." "Do you know where those stairs go?"

"Down to a landing used by the lighthouse," Libby replied.

Griff took his handgun out, checked it and put it back in the shoulder holster. "Stay near me, Libby," he said, opening the car door.

She slid out, buttoned her coat and turned on her flashlight.

As they passed the motorcar, Griff shined a light to see if anyone was hiding inside. It was empty. "You light the steps," he told her. "I'll scan the woods as we walk down."

It was a clear cold night, and the winds were gusty, swinging the trees overhead. Waves breaking on the rocks below sounded like ocean surf. At the bottom of the stairs, a large figure loomed up in front of them, and Libby gasped.

"No flashlights," the man barked in a gruff voice.

A lantern was on the railing of the landing, illuminating a rough-cut platform with a dock. Three men were standing on it, dressed in overcoats and fedoras.

"Where's Price?" one of them asked.

"He's not coming," Griff said. "He left for Germany today."

There was no response. The tension was palpable.

"We do not represent him. We are here for his wife," Griff stated.

"And who the hell are you?"

Griff told them their names and added, "Tell your boss, he can have Price *and* the money if he does things our way."

"Oh ya, big shot?" a short, stocky thug roared, darting up to Griff.

"Shut up and get back here," the first man said.

The hooligan stepped back, bouncing like a boxer.

"I have information for your employer," Griff continued. "But I talk *only* to him, and it has to be tonight."

Again there was a silence as the leader of the group considered the offer. "Alright, follow me."

"What happens now?" Libby asked when they slid back into the motorcar.

Griff shrugged and started the engine. "Let's hope they take us to Bronstein."

They followed the group a few miles and turned down a private road heading to the lake. On the shore was a lodge flooded with lights. The sound of music rolled out from the restaurant. The leader of the group told Libby and Griff to wait by their motorcar. The men searched them and took Griff's gun. After a few minutes, they were escorted to a balcony attached to the lodge.

Bronstein was sitting in an Adirondack chair, smoking a cigar and wearing an overcoat. The light from the night club behind him threw his face into shadows. Two of his minions stood behind him.

"I'll talk with Miss Durant," he ordered.

When Griff moved forward with her, the men grabbed his arms. "Hands off, assholes," he said, struggling.

"It's alright, Griff," Libby interrupted. "I'll talk to him alone. I need to set something straight anyway." Her heart hammering in her chest, Libby walked over and stopped in front of Bronstein.

He smirked. "What does my girl want to tell me? Sit

down. Have a drink."

"No, I prefer standing, but I would like a cigarette," she announced. Libby knew smoking would help settle her down. The people inside the nightclub chattered, laughed, and drank, oblivious to what was happening outside.

Bronstein nodded, and one of his men handed her a cigarette. She blew the smoke and said, "We'll give you the exact location of Price's home in Germany, but you have to let my cousin go."

Bronstein narrowed his eyes. "How the hell do you know where he is?"

"Mr. Gardner has contacts in Germany."

Bronstein looked at Griff. "So you're the one who found the goods on that little bastard?" he called over to Griff.

"I am."

Bronstein looked back at Libby. "What's to prevent me from beating the address out of him right now and killing the princess?"

"You won't get any money. Price has been hiding assets in his wife's bank accounts for over a year. Let her live, and she'll give you every penny. If she dies, Price inherits it all and may even get a hefty life insurance policy to boot."

Bronstein's eyebrows shot up. He puffed on his cigar. "I refuse to let that sneaky son-of-bitch use me."

Libby added, with a quiver in her voice, "And I want you to leave *me* alone forever."

"What the hell does that mean?"

"It means you will not use Elizabeth Durant Cosmetics to bring alcohol down from Canada."

Growling and shifting in his chair, Bronstein considered her proposal. At last, he said, rubbing his forehead, "This whole goddamn mess makes me tired. Alright, come here," he said, waving Griff over. "I want that address, and then I'll tell you where to pick up the princess."

Hearing those words, Libby thought she would collapse. She stepped aside to wait, her knees shaking. Griff and Bronstein exchanged information, and when they finished, Bronstein called to Libby, "I'll be expecting that money before the week is out, Miss Durant."

She nodded.

Once back at the motorcar, Griff took back his firearm, and they drove off.

"So where's Pepper?" she asked anxiously.

Griff didn't answer. He reached over and pulled a blanket up over her knees. "Are you alright?"

"I can't stop shaking," she exclaimed. "Part of it is nerves, part of it is the cold."

"That's why we have to hurry," he said, shifting gears and stepping on the gas. "Pepper's out in this, tied to a tree off a logging road."

*   *   *

"My God, this is taking too long!" Libby exclaimed. "Is this the wrong way?"

"I think it's after this abandoned building," Griff said, leaning over the steering wheel.

"What if Dash is out on a run?"

"Then I drive like a bat out of hell to Sawbill Lake."

They turned and drove down a bumpy path with branches smacking against the windows. At last, they came to a tiny logging shack. There was a motorcar parked out front. "This is it," Griff said.

"Thank God!"

When he turned off the lights, everything went black. Libby grabbed a flashlight, and they walked to the cabin.

"I don't want him to shoot us," Griff muttered. "Dashby?" he called.

"John?" Libby said.

They stepped up to the door and knocked. There was no answer. Griff knocked again and then tried the handle. It was open. He leaned in and called, "Dash! It's Griff."

Libby shined her light around the shack. There were dirty dishes on the table and a jacket thrown over a chair. The room smelled like greasy cooking. When Griff walked into the bedroom, he found Dash on the bed, fully clothed and snoring. An empty bottle was on the floor.

"Oh, that stupid son of a bitch!" Griff exclaimed. He put his foot up and pushed him.

Dash moaned and rolled over onto his back.

"Wake up, you drunken bum!"

There was no response.

Turning to Libby, he asked, "Can you light a lamp?"

When she brought in a kerosene lantern, Griff pulled Dash upright and slapped him. Opening his bloodshot eyes, he mumbled, "Gardner?"

"Wake up, Dashby. We need your help."

"What the hell?" he replied, rubbing his eyes. "Why are you way up here?"

"Pepper's been kidnapped," Griff said. "We have to get to her before she freezes to death.

"Who's kidnapped?"

"My cousin, Pepper," Libby said. "You know, Penny Davis."

"Who the hell would want to do that?" Dash slurred. He stood up unsteadily.

"You have to fly us--" Griff said and stopped. Dash had stumbled into the door frame. "Never mind. I need to borrow your plane."

"What?"

"Your plane. I need your plane."

"I'll take you up."

"No, you're too drunk."

"I'm fine," Dash argued as he stumbled toward Libby. "Hello, toots," he said, grabbing her.

"Back to bed," Griff ordered, taking his arm. "But first, where's the plane?"

"I don't want you to take it."

In a flash, Griff had him by the shirt. "I don't have time to argue, John! Now, where's the goddamn plane?"

"Well hell, you don't have to be such as asshole," he muttered. "It's in a barn down the road. The only farm around here."

Griff put Dash back in bed and said, "Thanks, buddy. Now go back to sleep."

They jumped into the motorcar and drove down to the farm. Griff looked up and nodded. "A perfect night to fly. We need the stars."

"What about the farmer?" Libby asked, looking around nervously.

"Not to worry. He'll think it's Dash."

They flung the barn doors open, and there was the plane.

"It's amphibious," Griff said. Having Libby hold a flashlight, he looked at the engine and made some adjustments. At last, he declared, "All set. Now let's see if I can remember how to fly."

Libby's jaw dropped. "What?"

"It's been years, but it should come back to me," he said, pulling on Dash's leather helmet.

"I thought you flew all the time?" she gasped.

"Where'd you get that idea?"

"You said you flew air reconnaissance in Germany."

"Yes, I film, I don't fly."

Libby stared at him.

"Come on," he said, punching her arm. "You have

nothing to worry about."

She frowned. That had been Peppers attitude when they jerked and lurched down Park Avenue in her parent's motorcar ten years earlier.

She moaned and put her helmet on. "How will you know where to go?"

"I'll use the stars and the moonlight. I'll follow the lakeshore until we see the Beartooth River. It's the first river to the north, Bronstein said, and Sawbill Lake is the first lake in. It should be simple enough. There's a logging road to follow too."

"So we will be flying low?"

"Yes."

Griff climbed into the plane and said, "When I tell you, turn the propeller and get the hell out of the way."

She nodded, her heart pounding.

"Now," he shouted.

She yanked the propeller, the engine started, and she jumped back. A second later it killed.

Griff made some adjustments on the panel and said, "Again!"

This time it ran. When he pulled out of the barn, Libby hoisted herself into the seat. As they rolled down the field, she lowered her goggles. She hunched her shoulders up as they soared up into the night sky, the cold wind biting her skin. Griff banked the craft and headed toward the lake. The black, endless expanse of water was dotted with lights from freighters.

Libby looked up at the stars, and then down at the shoreline below, jagged and rocky. She hoped Griff knew what he was doing. The air was frigid, and she put her gloved hands to her cheeks to shield her skin. Griff glanced back and waved. At least *he* seemed confident.

They followed the shore for a few minutes and then

turned around a point. A black ribbon of the river came into view. Griff banked the plane and followed it inland. Flying just above the treetops, they snaked their way along the waterway until a lake opened up below. It was Sawbill Lake.

They started to descend, and Libby's stomach flip-flopped. Lower and lower they dropped until there was a jolt and the sound of rushing water. Griff slowed the engine and taxied to a long dock. The lake was surrounded by pines, moonlight reflecting on the rippling water.

Thank God we made it, Libby thought, heaving a sigh. "Are we on someone's property?" she asked as Griff helped her onto the dock.

"I don't know. All Bronstein said was on the other side of the road by the lake there's a deer stand. Pepper is tied up beneath the stand."

Libby pulled off her helmet and goggles while Griff checked his gun. They ran through the trees and up a hill. Just as they reached the crest, Griff jerked her back. "Turn off your flashlight," he hissed. "Someone's across the road."

They crouched down to look. Someone was running with a kerosene lantern. A motorcar was parked nearby.

Griff took his gun out, grabbed Libby's hand and ran closer. They crossed the road, and dashed through the brush, jumping over logs, and pushing aside branches. The spotted Pepper. She was lashed to a tree, slumped over, unconscious. The man walked over to her, set his lantern on a stump and took out a gun.

Griff roared. "No!" and pulled Libby to the ground.

The man whirled around and fired.

"Stay here," Griff barked at her and dashed through the trees out of sight.

Libby looked back at the man and gasped. It was Gil Chambers. He was standing right in front of her, about to kill Pepper and maybe even Griff too. She had to do something.

Chambers scanned the woods, and then so they couldn't shoot, he stepped closer to Pepper. Libby watched him with her heart pounding. Where was Griff? What was he going to do? He stood no chance against this professional assassin.

Suddenly he burst from the trees and jumped onto Chambers' back, toppling them both to the ground. When they hit the earth, shots rang out. Chambers drove his elbow into Griff's face, and they rolled over, struggling and punching each other.

Libby dashed up, grabbed Chambers by the hair and yanked his head back, dragging her nails across his face. He roared in pain but never stopped striking Griff. Spotting a gun on the ground, Libby grabbed it and pointed it at Chambers, or was it, Griff? She couldn't be certain in the dim lamplight.

"Oh, my God! Oh, my God," she gasped, as they rolled back and forth. With her feet apart and both hands on the firearm, she tried to follow their movements, but it was too dark, and she couldn't be sure. Frantically she pointed the gun at one and then the other. *There he is! That's Chambers!* She aimed and fired. But at that moment they rolled, and she shot Griff in the arm. Libby shrieked with horror. Griff could no longer hold Chambers back, and he started choking him. Wounded and unable to defend himself, he lost consciousness.

Libby's eyes grew wide. There was no question now who was who, and with the cold indifference of an assassin, she stepped up and shot Gil in the back of the head. All was quiet as the shot echoed through the trees. Chambers slumped on top of Griff, blood pumping from his head.

Holding the gun limply at her side, Libby stared at his body. The shot still ringing in her ears. She had just taken a life, yet she felt oddly detached. She felt calm and relieved, almost vindicated.

When Griff started coughing, she was yanked back to reality and cried, "Griff!"

She pushed Chambers off and helped him sit up, pleading, "Don't die, Griff. Please don't die."

"Oh, for the love of God, Libby," he muttered, irritably. "I'm not going to die," but blood was soaking his sleeve. She put a handkerchief on his arm and tied it off tightly with her scarf.

"That's good enough until we get to the plane," he said. "Now take the knife from my pocket and cut Pepper lose. We have to warm her up."

She grabbed it and dashed over to Pepper. Her skin was like ice, and she was barely breathing. Frantically, Libby sawed through the ropes. When the last cord was cut, Pepper slumped to the ground. The jolt revived her, and she opened her eyes.

"You're safe now, Pepper. We're taking you home," Libby murmured as she scooped her into her arms.

"Libby? Libby?"

"Yes, I'm here."

Sobs wracked Pepper's body.

Libby took off her coat and put it on her. "Can you stand?"

"I-I think so."

"We have a plane here. You won't have to walk far."

They started back toward Griff, who was waiting nearby, clutching his arm. Libby looked one last time at Chambers' body and grabbed the lantern.

They stumbled through the brush, across the road and out onto the dock. Griff told Libby where to find the first aid kit, and when she returned, she bandaged his arm. "Will you be able to fly?"

"I'll have to."

It took every bit of strength she had to help both of them into the plane, but at last, they were ready to go. Fumbling with the controls, Griff said, "Now!" and Libby yanked the propeller. The engine started, and she climbed in the plane onto Pepper's lap. Even though Pepper was small, Libby had to lean onto the body of the plane. There was so little room.

At last, they started moving across the lake. Yet it seemed to Libby as if they were slow to gather speed. She held her breath. *Was it too heavy with three of them now?* The simply skimmed the surface of the water, never rising. Closer and closer they came to the shoreline, and just as they were about to hit, they rose up, narrowly missing the tops of the tall pines. Libby collapsed with relief when they sailed up into the dark sky. She had no idea where Griff was going, but she knew he would try to find a hospital. She clutched a blanket around herself closely, the frigid wind whipping it around her shoulders. Pepper had slid down into the seat to stay warm, her eyes closed.

They followed the river out to Lake Superior and banked to the south following the shoreline back towards Duluth. She watched Griff anxiously. How much blood had he lost? Would he pass out and send them all crashing into the lake? *After everything we've been through, we may all die because of my stupid mistake shooting him. And if we survive, will killing Gil Chambers haunt me forever?* Libby pressed her eyes shut trying to blot it all out, but it was no use. She thought of Griff, Dash, and Rudy during the war. They too had killed, and how did they justify it? She answered her own question. They did it because it was what they had to do, and so did she. Had she not acted, the two most important people in her life would now be dead. No, she was right to have killed Chambers.

As they followed the shoreline, Libby watched for lights from the lodge where they had met with Bronstein. After about ten minutes, she saw them shining through the trees. Gradually they were making progress, but there no escape from the wind. She put her head down, trying to stay warm and control the trembling.

The trip seemed endless, but the next time she raised her head she saw the lights of Duluth. *Thank God!*

Griff turned inland, and Libby knew he was looking for an open field in which to land, like a barnstormer. She ran her eyes over the terrain. There were trees everywhere. Where the hell would they go?

The plane lurched downward, and her heart jumped into her throat. There's nowhere to land, she wanted to shout. Then, like a miracle, a field opened up before them. They hit the ground with a teeth-jarring shock, smashing and rattling through brush and scrub. Gradually they came to a stop, and all was quiet.

There was a roar of laughter from Griff. "Well, I'll be goddamned!" he whooped. "We did it!"

Too stunned to speak, she blinked and looked around. There was a farmhouse nearby where she could go for help.

At last, she shouted, "You did it, Gardner! You did it. I love you. I love you forever!"

Chapter 24

"Gin!" Libby said, putting her cards down on the hospital tray table.

"You're a cheat, Durant."

"You'll not be calling me Durant much longer," she said, kissing him.

"Even as a Gardner, you'll still be a cheat."

Libby stood up, looked around the privacy curtain and said, "I almost forgot. I brought you this," and she pulled a tuna sandwich from her purse.

"Not tuna again!" he exclaimed. "They'll smell it, and then I'll be in trouble."

"Maybe they'll kick you out early. I'm tired of Duluth. I'm ready to go home."

"Tomorrow's the day," he said, taking a bite. "But we have to get right back to California. I have two movies lined up."

"And we have to make wedding plans," she said. She leaned on the tray with her chin in her hand. "I've been thinking about it. Let's go somewhere, just the two of us. Please, no big, white wedding. I'm not traditional."

"Oh, really?" he said, sarcastically.

"Pepper was certainly happy to get on that train for Minneapolis today," she said suddenly.

"I bet she was. How will she get the money to Bronstein?"

"She's taking it to a speakeasy in the caves in St. Paul," Libby replied, taking a bite of his sandwich.

"That doesn't sound safe."

"She's taking Grandmother Brennan with her."

Griff threw his head back and laughed. "Oh, she'll be alright."

Libby laughed too. "They're planning on fabricating some sort of press release after that about the Penny Davis' rescue. I wonder if Price is still alive."

"Not for long," Griff said. "I can't believe how quickly that bastard saw the opportunity to turn Pepper's kidnapping into profit. He had Chambers lose no time getting up there to kill her. That thug must have known something was up when he heard our plane."

Libby looked down and murmured, "I'm sorry I shot you, Griff."

"Not this again! Put it to rest, Libby. I'm fine, and in the end, you saved us all." Changing the subject, he said, "We need at least a least a day when we get back to St. Paul to relax and have some fun. What do you want to do?"

Libby put her fist to her lips, thinking. "Well, you never did teach me how to bake a cake."

"Ha! You want to learn to bake a cake. Alright, you're a cheap date, but what about after that?"

"How about dinner and a movie?"

"What sort of movie?"

Libby thought for a moment, smiled and said, "Well, Griff, I think I'm ready for a love story."

Thank you for reading *The Looking Glass Goddess. Please look for Amanda Hughes' other novels in The Bold Women Series.*

ABOUT THE AUTHOR

Best-selling and award-winning author, Amanda Hughes is a "Walter Mitty", spending more time in heroic daydreams than the real world. At last, she found an outlet writing adventures about bold women through the centuries. Winner of the Gems National Award for Writing, featured in USA Today, and short listed for numerous book awards, Amanda is a graduate of the University of Minnesota. When she isn't off tilting windmills, she lives and writes in Minnesota.

Don't miss her page-turning novels for readers who like historical fiction with a bit of a love story. All of her books are stand-alone and can be read in any order.

Made in the USA
Columbia, SC
26 April 2017